Outstanding Prai

B

"Chilling and sizzling by turns! Lori Handeland has the kind of talent that comes along only once in a blue moon. Her sophisticated, edgy voice sets her apart from the crowd, making her an author to watch, and *Blue Moon* is a novel not to be missed."

—Maggie Shayne, author of *Edge of Twilight*

"Presenting an interesting and modern twist on the werewolf legend, Lori Handeland's *Blue Moon* is an intriguing mixture of suspense, clever humor, and sensual tension that never lets up. Vivid secondary characters in a rural, small-town setting create an effective backdrop for paranormal events. Will Cadotte is a tender and sexy hero who might literally be worth dying for. But the real revelation in the book is Handeland's protagonist, police officer Jessie McQuade, a less-than-perfect heroine who is at once self-deprecating, tough, witty, pragmatic and vulnerable. She draws you into the story and holds you there until the very end."

—Susan Krinard, author of *To Catch a Wolf*

"Fantastic—one of the best books I've read in a long, long time. Anyone who reads paranormal will love this book and anyone who loves suspense should love it as well. It's an edge-of-the-seat read."

—Christine Feehan, author of *Dark Melody* on *Blue Moon*

MORE...

"The action is fast-paced, the plot is gripping, the characters are realistic, and I absolutely positively cannot wait for the next book in this series."

—*Fallen Angel Reviews*

"A dry wit that shines…Everything about this book is wonderful: the sizzling sexiness, the three-dimensional characters, and the sense of danger."

—*Romance Junkies*

"Great intensity, danger, drama, captivation, and stellar writing."
—*The Road to Romance,* Reviewer's Choice Award

"Lori Handeland makes a superlative debut in the world of paranormal romance with *Blue Moon,* first in an enticing new *Moon* trilogy. *Blue Moon* is simply not to be missed."

—*BookLoons Reviews*

"If you enjoy werewolves that are linked to folklore with characters that seem to be in every town, whether it is small or big, then pick up a copy of *Blue Moon.* You will not be disappointed."

—*A Romance Review*

"A captivating novel that draws readers in from the first page…for a story that will entertain, delight, and have you glancing askance at the full moon, run, do not walk, to the nearest bookstore and grab *Blue Moon*…A book guaranteed to please readers of paranormal, suspense, and romance…a winner on all counts!"

—*Romance Reviews Today*

Dark
Moon

Lori Handeland

St. Martin's Paperbacks

DARK MOON

Copyright © 2005 by Lori Handeland.

ISBN: 0-312-99136-3
EAN: 9780312-99136-4

Printed in the United States of America

St. Martin's Paperbacks edition / July 2005

St. Martin's Paperbacks are published by St. Martin's Press, 175 Fifth Avenue, New York, NY 10010.

10 9 8 7 6 5 4 3 2 1

For my editor, Jen Enderlin
Who always knows what's wrong and even how to fix it.
You really are the best there is.

I

I have always loved the dark of the moon, when the night is still and serene, when all that can be seen are the stars.

There are those who term the dark moon a new moon, but there is nothing new about the moon. It has been here from time forgotten and will be here long after we are dead.

I spend my days, and most of my nights, inside a stone fortress in the wilds of Montana. I'm a doctor by trade, though not the kind who gives out lollipops after dispensing vaccines and pills. Instead I mix a little of this and a little of that, over and over again.

My degree reads "virologist." In English, that means I have a Ph.D. in the study of viruses. Don't worry, I won't let the excitement kill me. The boredom might, though, if the loneliness doesn't do it first.

Of course, I'm not *completely* alone. There's a guard at the door and my test subjects, but none of them are great conversationalists. Lately I've started to feel watched, which is pretty funny considering I'm the one in charge of the surveillance cameras.

Paranoia is one of the first signs of dementia; except I don't *feel* crazy. Does anyone? I've come to the conclusion I need to get out more. But where would I go?

Most days I don't mind being locked tight inside the safest place in the West. The world is pretty scary. Scarier than most people realize.

You think the monsters aren't real? That they're merely the figment of childish imaginations or delusional psychosis? You're wrong.

There are things walking the earth worse than anything in *Grimm's Fairy Tales*. *Unsolved Mysteries* would have a stroke if they got a look at my X-files. But since lycanthropy is a virus, werewolves are my specialty. I've devoted my life to finding a cure.

I have a personal interest. You see, I'm one of them.

The powers that be say a life is formed by changes—decisions made, roads not taken, people we've left behind. I'm inclined to agree.

On the day my whole world changed—again—a single decision, that fork in the road and the one I left behind walked into my office without warning.

I was at my desk updating files, when the scuff of a shoe against concrete made me glance up. The man in the doorway made my heart go *ba-boom*. He always had.

"Nic," I murmured, and in my voice I heard more than I wanted to.

The strong nose, full lips, wide forehead were as I remembered. But the lines around his mouth and eyes, the darker shade of his skin, hinted at a life spent exposed to the elements. The flicker of silver in his short hair was as shocking as him being here in first place.

He didn't smile, didn't return my greeting. I couldn't blame him. I'd professed love, then disappeared. I hadn't spoken to him since.

Seven years. How had he found me? And why?

Concern replaced curiosity, and my hand inched toward the drawer where I kept my gun. The guard hadn't called to clear a visitor, so I should shoot first, ask questions later. In my world, an enemy could lurk behind every face. But I'd always had a tough time shooting people. One of the many reasons the boss kept me isolated in the forest.

I'd learned long ago how to gauge a suit for a shoulder holster. Nic had one. A disturbing change in a man who'd once been both studious and dreamy, in love with the law and me, not necessarily in that order. Why was I carrying a gun?

Since he hadn't drawn his, I drew mine, then pointed the weapon at Nic's chest. Loaded with silver, I was ready for anything. Except the punch of his deep blue eyes and the familiar timbre of his voice. "Hey, sweetheart."

In college that endearment had made me all warm and stupid. I'd promised things I had no right to promise. Now the same word, uttered with cool sarcasm, annoyed me.

I'd left for his own good. However, *he* didn't know that.

I got to my feet, stepped around the desk, came a little too close. "What are you doing here?"

"I didn't think you'd be thrilled to see me, but this isn't exactly the welcome I expected."

His gaze lowered to the gun, and I was distracted by the scent of him. Fresh snow, mountain air, my past.

He grabbed the weapon, twisted it away, then tucked me against his body with an elbow across my throat. I was no good with firearms. Never had been.

I choked, and Nic released the stranglehold on my windpipe, though he didn't release me. Out of the corner of my eye I caught a glimpse of metal on the desk. He'd put my gun aside. One less thing to worry about.

"What do you want?" I managed.

Instead of answering, he nuzzled my hair and his breath brushed my ear. My knees quivered; my eyes burned. Having Nic so close was making me remember things I'd spent years trying to forget. And the memories hurt. Hell, I still loved him.

An uncommon rush of emotion caused my muscles to clench, my stomach to roil. I wasn't used to feeling anything. I prided myself on being cool, patrician, in charge: Dr. Elise Hanover, ice queen. When I let my anger loose, bad things happened.

But no one had ever affected me like Nic. No one had ever made me as happy or as sad. No one could make me more furious.

I slammed my spike heel onto his shiny black shoe and ground down with all my weight. Nic flinched, and I jabbed my elbow into his stomach. I forgot to pull my punch, and he flew into the wall. Spinning around, I watched him slide to the floor, eyes closed.

Oops.

I resisted the urge to run to him, touch his face, kiss

his brow. For both our sakes, we couldn't go back to the way things had been.

Nic's eyelids fluttered, and he mumbled something foul. I let out the breath I'd been holding. He'd be all right.

I doubted he was often on the losing end of a fight. Since I'd seen him last he'd bulked up—the combination of age and a few thousand hours with a weight machine.

What else had he been doing in the years we'd been apart? He'd planned to become a lawyer, except he didn't resemble any lawyer I'd ever seen. The suit, yes, but beneath the crisp charcoal material he was something more than a paper-pushing fast talker. Perhaps a soldier decked out in his Sunday best.

My gaze wandered over him, catching on the dark sunglasses hooked into his pocket.

Suit. Muscles. *Men in Black* glasses.

"FBI," I muttered.

Now I was really ticked off.

Nic's eyes snapped open, crossing once before focusing on my face. "You always were smarter than you looked."

I'd been the victim of enough dumb-blonde jokes to last me several lifetimes. The moronic jabs and riddles had bothered me, until I realized I could use the speaker's attitude to my advantage. If people thought I was stupid, they weren't expecting anything else.

So I didn't rise to Nic's bait. He'd been sent here by the big boys, without warning, and that meant trouble.

"I suppose you want me to hand over my gun?" he grumbled.

I shrugged. "Keep it."

A weapon filled with lead was the least of my worries.

He struggled to his feet, and I experienced an instant of concern when he wobbled. I'd hit him way too hard.

"Let me give you some advice," he said. "I've always found that the people we least expect to shoot us usually do."

Funny, I'd found that, too.

"What are you doing here?" I demanded.

His brows lifted. "No hugs, no kisses? You aren't glad to see me? If I remember correctly I should be the one who's angry."

He sat on a chair without being invited.

"Oh, wait." His eyes met mine. "I am."

Nic had every reason to be furious. I'd snuck out in the night as if I had something to hide.

Oh, wait. I did.

Nevertheless, being near him hurt. I couldn't tell Nic why I'd left. I couldn't apologize, because I wasn't really sorry. I couldn't touch him the way I wanted to. I couldn't ever touch anyone that way.

"You didn't come here to talk about our past," I snapped. "What does the FBI want with the *Jäger-Suchers*?"

I wasn't the only one fighting monsters. I was merely the geeky member of a select group—"hunter-searchers" for those a little rusty on their German.

Though financed by the government, the *Jäger-Suchers* were a secret from all but those who needed to know. If it got out that there were monsters running all over the place, people would panic.

Not only that, but heads would roll. Unlimited cash for a Special Forces monster-hunting unit? Someone would definitely lose their job, and we'd lose our funding. So we pretended to be things we weren't.

For instance, I was a research scientist investigating a new form of rabies in the animal population. Most of our field agents carried documentation identifying them as wardens for various natural resource departments.

Until today, the precautions had worked. No one had ever come snooping before.

The question was: Why now?

And why him?

2

"I work in the CID."

Criminal Investigations Division, my mind translated as Nic reached into his suit and withdrew his ID, flipping it open with an ease born of practice.

I didn't bother to look. I knew who he was. I didn't care about his badge. I wanted to hear why he'd stepped out of the past and into my life. I wanted to discover where the boy I'd loved had gone and when this man had taken his place.

Seven years ago Nic had been easygoing and fun. I'd laughed more with him than I'd ever laughed with anyone else.

He'd been a wealth of contrasts. Quick with numbers, clever with words, fast hands, slow smile, a great kiss.

We'd both been alone in the world, searching for something, or maybe someone. We'd found it in each other. My life had forever been divided into before and after Dominic Franklin had come into it.

I still don't know if I believe in love at first sight.

I saw him so many times before I loved him. But a true, deep, forever love? In that, I do believe.

"Why you?"

I didn't realize I'd said the words out loud until he answered them.

"Because I'm the best at what I do."

"Which is?"

"Finding missing persons."

"What does that have to do with us?"

"You tell me. What do you do?"

Could I put him off by telling the lies I'd told a hundred times before? Wouldn't hurt to try.

"I'm studying a new strain of rabies in the wolf population."

"Never heard of it."

"The government doesn't want people to know the virus is becoming resistant to the vaccine."

"It is?"

"No, I made that up."

My teeth clicked together as I snapped my mouth shut. Why couldn't I keep quiet?

His lips twitched, almost a smile. But the expression faded as quickly as the moon did at dawn.

"You always wanted to be a doctor."

"I am."

"A Ph.D. isn't an M.D."

I'd given up my hopes of treating people after I'd turned furry the first time. Kind of hard to build a practice when you never knew if you were going to wake up covered in blood the morning after a full moon.

In truth, I'd always been fascinated by viruses—where they came from, how they were transmitted, how in hell we could cure them. One of the few bright spots in the past seven years had been my work. I'd been given carte blanche to study something no one else even knew about. What scientist wouldn't be tempted?

Nic continued to stare at me, no doubt waiting to hear the reason I wasn't delivering babies or performing brain surgery. He'd be waiting a very long time.

"You were going to be a lawyer," I said.

When in doubt, point the finger elsewhere.

"I am. A majority of our agents have backgrounds in accounting or law."

Huh. I guess we do learn something new every day.

"This facility seems huge," he continued. "How many researchers do you have?"

We'd reached the end of my lies and my patience.

"If you want more information, you'll have to talk to the boss, Edward Mandenauer."

One call from Edward to Washington, D.C., and Nic would be out on his ear.

"Fine. Where is he?"

"Wisconsin. That's east of here, by a lot."

His eyes narrowed. "*Where* in Wisconsin?"

"Classified." I shrugged. "Sorry."

"Elise, you're starting to piss me off."

"Only starting?"

The smile nearly broke through again, and I thought, *There you are,* an instant before he caught himself and frowned.

This new Nic disturbed me. Had he become so serious and sad because of the job or because of me? I didn't like either choice.

Leaning back, he laced his fingers together and rested his head against his palms. "I'll just wait until he calls in."

I opened my mouth, then shut it again, stumped. I couldn't have him hanging around. I was behind schedule. Besides, how was I going to explain that there wasn't anyone in the compound but me, a single guard, and the werewolves in the basement?

I could throw Nic out, or have the guard do it; however, that kind of behavior would only add to the questions, and no doubt insure we enjoyed more visits from the FBI. Better to convince Nic to leave on his own if possible.

"Edward won't be calling for several days," I said. "He's in the field. You may as well tell me what's going on."

Nic stared at me for a few seconds before leaning forward and lowering his arms to the table. "I've been working on a case for years. A lot of people are no longer where they're supposed to be, and they haven't shown up anywhere else."

"Since when do missing persons come under FBI jurisdiction?"

"Since we have good reason to believe we're dealing with more than disappearances."

I heard what he wasn't saying. The FBI thought they had a serial kidnapper, if not a serial killer, on their hands. Hell, they probably did. What they didn't know was that the culprit was most likely less than human.

"A lot more people vanish in this world than anyone knows about," I murmured.

Nic lifted a brow. I guess I didn't have to tell him that. His business was finding the missing. Which made him dangerous to my business.

To keep the populace calm, part of the J-S job description was to invent excuses, smooth over the edges, make sure that those who were murdered by evil entities were not searched for by the authorities or their families.

"I still don't understand how we can help you. Is one of the missing people from this area?"

"No."

"Did you trace someone here?"

"No."

I threw up my hands. "What then?"

"We were sent an anonymous tip."

I resisted the urge to snort and roll my eyes. The bad guys were forever trying to throw the government at us. If we were unwinding red tape we weren't hunting and searching for monsters.

Until today, all such attempts had been quelled higher up. The word in Washington was that Edward Mandenauer stood above reproach. He was not to be bothered, and neither were any of his people. Obviously Nic hadn't gotten the top secret memo.

I glanced at him as another possibility came to mind. The *Jäger-Suchers* might be a clandestine organization, and the location of our compound closely guarded, but recently many of our secrets had gone on the market. We had a traitor in our midst, and we never knew when someone might die.

"What was this tip?"

"E-mail. Said I'd find what I was seeking here."

I frowned. "Not much of a tip."

"Imagine my surprise when I saw your name on the employee roster of the *Jäger-Suchers*."

Which explained how he knew so much about me, how he'd remained so calm upon seeing me, while I'd been paralyzed. He'd already known I was here.

"There was precious little information in those personnel files, considering this is a government installation."

Since quite a few of our agents had been on the wrong side of the law at one time or another—sometimes it took a monster to catch a monster—it wouldn't do for their records to be available to anyone who cared to look. Our personnel files were carefully constructed to reveal the very least necessary—or in some cases nothing at all.

"I thought you were dead," he murmured, "and you were right here."

Strange how one small thing was often all it took to break a mystery wide open. People don't realize how often killers are caught because of an accident, a coincidence, nothing more than a sharp eye skimming an unrelated report and finding a connection.

No, I wasn't dead, but that didn't mean I didn't want to be.

As if realizing he'd skirted too close to an emotional edge neither one of us wanted to cross, Nic withdrew a sheet of paper from his jacket.

"Can you check with your people, with Mandenauer, see if anyone knows any of the names on this list of missing persons?"

His face was set, his eyes gone icy blue—back to business. I was alive; *I* was no longer missing. I could almost see him checking my name off a list in his brain.

Would he ever think of me again once he walked out of this room? Probably not, and that was a good thing.

So why did I feel so bad?

Nic still stood with the list in his hand. I took the paper and tucked it into a pocket without a glance.

"My number's at the top."

He rose and his gaze was captured by something on my desk. My breath caught as he stared at the small stuffed crow he'd once won for me at a local fair.

Actually *won* was too lenient a term. He'd spent five times what the cheesy toy was worth trying to sink a basketball into a hoop. Back then he'd been more bookish than buff.

My eyes touched on the broad shoulders packed into the dark suit. He could probably make a basket now, or ram the ball into the hoop by sheer force of will.

I didn't know what to say. That I'd kept the item all these years was far too sentimental a gesture for the cool, distant woman I wanted to be.

"I like crows."

My voice came out impressively blasé, as if the toy meant nothing, but my eyes stung. I had to look away or embarrass myself.

I blinked a few times, swallowed, turned to see if he'd believed my lie and discovered him halfway out the door. Surprised, I scurried after, then paused in the hall.

He was leaving without pressing me for more answers about the *Jäger-Suchers*. I should be glad. People who annoyed Edward Mandenauer often found themselves on the wrong side of dead.

I'd left Nic once so he wouldn't learn the truth, so he wouldn't be hurt. This time I'd let *him* leave for the same reason.

I continued to the front of the building so I could watch Nic walk out of my life forever. He might come back, but he wasn't getting in. I left explicit instructions to that effect with the guard.

I should contact my boss, tell him about the visit from the FBI, but it was just past noon. Edward would still be sleeping after hunting all night. There was time enough to call him once I checked on my latest experiment.

The only way into the basement laboratory was through the elevator located outside of my office. Disguised as a wall panel, the door slid open at the press of my palm to the security monitor.

"Good afternoon, Dr. Hanover."

The computerized voice never failed to irk me; I'm not sure why. Extreme security was part of my life. Though what I was doing was important, there were nevertheless those who would stop at nothing to keep me from doing it.

As the elevator descended to subterranean level, the same mechanical voice intoned, "Retina scan, please."

I positioned my face in front of the camera. Without the appropriate retinas, anyone who managed to get this far would be trapped inside. Of course, there was always the possibility someone would cut off my hand and dig out my eye in order to access the basement.

Luckily, or perhaps not, most of the beings capable of that level of insanity were already incarcerated on the other side of the door.

The elevator slid open. A bank of rooms fronted with

bulletproof glass lined the walls. All of the chambers—
hell, let's be honest, they were prison cells—were occupied.

I hadn't been kidding about the werewolves in the
basement.

3

Werewolves are nocturnal—just like the wolves they resemble. Even underground, beneath fluorescent lights, they continue to behave like the animals they are. Therefore, at this time of the day, the majority of my guests were sleeping.

I hurried down the corridor. While most rooms held a hint of light, the better to simulate the muted rays of the sun, the last was completely dark.

As dark as Billy Bailey's soul would be, if he had one.

In front of each cell stood a table with equipment appropriate for that subject's experiment.

I checked the slides I'd made with Billy's blood. I wasn't sure what I was looking for; I only hoped that when I saw it something would click. But after years of searching, I wasn't sure I'd ever find the answer.

A body slammed against the wall with enough force to shake the barrier. Calmly I lifted my gaze from the microscope to the naked man plastered against the see-through sector of his prison.

"Billy." I made a notation on his chart.

"She-bitch," he said in a conversational tone.

"Redundant," I murmured, and he slammed his fist into the glass.

He wanted me to shriek, to gasp, at least to jump. But I rarely did. Why give him any more satisfaction than he'd already had in this lifetime?

Out of the corner of my eye I watched Billy slither back into the gloom. Only then did I release the breath I'd been holding.

Billy Bailey scared the living hell out of me. I never should have asked that he be brought here, but I was desperate.

I'd tried everything I could think of to devise an antidote that would put people back the way they'd been before they were bitten. I kept coming up empty.

I *had* invented a serum that eased a werewolf's craving for human blood on the night of a full moon. As well as a counteragent that eradicated the virus if the victim was injected before their first change. Sadly, the remedy didn't work on the already furry.

I glanced into the darkness where Billy hovered, waiting for me to make a mistake.

"You need more blood," he said.

His voice slid out of shadows, and I stifled a shiver. Billy was always watching me. He knew I was something, but he wasn't sure what. Because I was like him, and then again I wasn't.

As in the legends, most werewolves are created by being bitten. There are other ways for humans to become furry, of course. The list is as endless as the monsters.

I was a perfect example. I'd spent the first twenty-plus years of my life blissfully unaware of werewolves. Then one night I had just . . . become.

I was a werewolf, but I didn't have the demon—shorthand in the J-S society for the psychotic joy in murdering anyone who crossed our path.

Killing sickened me. Nevertheless, I was still possessed every month by the lust for blood. Hence my first invention.

Yet even when I took my medicine, I continued to change whenever the moon was full. I had little choice. However, no one but myself and Edward were aware of my secret. Which was why my very existence was driving Billy more insane than he already was.

I glanced up as he materialized again from the darkness. Billy refused to wear clothes. I'm sure he sensed that his nudity disturbed me, though not because of any sexual interest.

His extreme height, incredible breadth, and large . . . feet would disturb anyone, even without the crisscross of scars that peppered his chest and back.

Since any scars received before a person became a werewolf remained, I'd come to the conclusion that in his previous life, Billy had been a very bad boy.

"Your arm, please."

Billy's lips tightened. Despite the bulletproof glass, I felt the fury pulsing from him like a flame. Yet his gray eyes were the coldest I'd ever known. Just looking into them for an instant could make me nauseous for an hour.

"What if I don't want to give you my arm?"

With Billy everything was a struggle.

"You know I can make you."

He ran forward, banging against the clear wall again. Sometimes I thought Billy wasn't the brightest crayon in the box. How many times did he have to test the glass before he believed it was impenetrable?

"It's no use, Billy."

Billy had been a trigger away from oblivion when I'd requested his presence in my compound. After chasing him for decades, Edward hadn't wanted to let Billy live.

He was a very old werewolf. No one knew how old, and Billy wasn't saying.

He'd been very difficult to apprehend since he didn't play well with others. Wolves are social animals, werewolves, too. Very few live their lifetimes alone. They seek out those like themselves and create a pack.

A lone wolf is not only a dangerous animal, but mighty hard to find running loose in the forests and large cities of the world. A needle in a haystack had nothing on Billy.

His size made me think Viking, except he was as swarthy as a Hun. The shape of his face recalled Cro-Magnon man, accented by his shaggy black hair.

No matter when Billy had been born, no matter when he was made, the fact remained, he was ancient, deadly, and he'd had practice being crazy for longer than I'd had practice at anything.

"When I get out of here I'm going to fuck you. First in this form and then the other." He lowered his hand and began to massage himself. "I'm going to screw you until you scream. I'm going to fuck you until you die."

Though my hands were trembling, I lifted my gaze and met his without flinching. "You're never going to get out of here, Billy. Never."

He recited his fantasies of rape, bondage, and torture every time I came near him. They did wonders for my guilt over keeping men and women in cages. They weren't human.

Not really. Not anymore.

I snapped on a pair of gloves, lifted a syringe, and pushed a button on the wall of the cell. A whirring noise preceded the presentation of the contraption for Billy's arm. He was supposed to place his forearm in an indentation. Manacles would clamp down, and I could draw blood without risk of injury.

Instead of following procedure, Billy ripped the device from the wall. Sighing, I tossed the gloves and syringe onto the table, as a steel door slid over the hole in the glass.

I'd wanted Billy for this very reason. He was the oldest living werewolf on record. He couldn't have existed for the centuries I suspected without incredible strength. I was hoping powerful blood would allow me to cure a powerful virus.

I considered my options, which were few. I'd tested the other werewolves throughout the cycle of the moon. None of them had been any help. I needed to test Billy's blood tonight, and every night for the next week. I couldn't drug him; that would throw off the results. I'd have to restrain him, which was as frightening as it was difficult.

Billy smirked. He knew what I was thinking, planning, and he couldn't wait.

A frantic howling erupted from the speaker on the wall. The real wolves, which I kept outside.

Glancing at the clock, I bit my lip. Not even close to their usual feeding time. Perhaps a raccoon had trotted past the outdoor run. Done a little "na, na, na, na, na" dance on the other side of the fence. That always set them off.

The howls turned into yips, then lowered to whimpers. Something wasn't right.

"They sound upset." Billy bared his teeth in a grin that was more of a snarl.

The wolves erupted again, and the hair on my arms tingled.

"You'd better check on them." He tilted his head. "But that isn't your job, is it?"

I frowned. How did he know so damned much about me when he was locked in down here?

"I wonder what you're afraid of. Then I imagine bringing it to you."

Billy sidled close enough to the glass that his everpresent erection thumped against it. He started giving himself another hand job, no doubt excited at the prospect of my fear.

"Big, bad *Jäger-Sucher*." His voice had gone breathy. "Oh, yeah. Be scared, baby."

I turned away. I was going to have to take Edward's advice and get rid of Billy. He was too crazy, even for this place.

The elevator's whir was a soothing sound, as was the click of my heels along the tile floor leading to the back door. I was headed away from Billy, the basement, and the compound. What wasn't to like?

After punching in the code to release the alarm, I stepped through, then lifted my face to the sky. Dusk approached. I'd been downstairs longer than I thought. I always lost track of time when I was working.

A security camera shared wall space with a machine gun that could be operated from the inside. Edward spared no expense to keep the compound impenetrable—except from the FBI.

I slipped off my heels and shoved my feet into the ancient sneakers I kept near the back door. I didn't come out here very often, but when I did I always changed shoes. High heels and a dirt trail went together like spaghetti and tuna fish.

I set off down the path, my feet sliding around inside shoes that were made to be worn with sweat socks.

The fence began about thirty yards from the compound and encircled a living area of several miles. Though much smaller than the typical territory of a wolf pack, the reduced size was necessary in order to keep the animals close enough for observation. Still, a prison was a prison no matter how we pretended otherwise.

Inside, the four adults and two pups had stopped howling, although they crouched at the edge of the trees as if frightened.

I'd done some initial experiments with them, but wolves weren't werewolves. Just as werewolves weren't people. These hadn't been of any help.

As soon as they saw me, the wolves scuttled even farther into the shadows. Like Billy, they knew I wasn't what I appeared and stayed as far from me as they could. Sighing, I turned, and my heart slammed against my chest.

Nic stood a few feet away.

How had he snuck up on me? No one did. Perhaps my senses had become muted from too much easy living.

"They wouldn't let me in," he said.

My mouth moved but nothing came out. Nic didn't seem to notice my sudden inability to speak. He jerked his chin at the wolves. "What's with them?"

"I—I'm not sure." There. I *could* talk. "They were howling. Upset." I frowned. "Have you been lurking around out here?"

That might explain why the wolves were acting strangely, although they were used to humans. The guards took care of their needs, so Nick's presence alone shouldn't have set them off.

I glanced toward the compound, narrowed my eyes on the security camera. However, Nic's presence *should* have alerted the guard—especially since I'd told him Nic wasn't welcome here.

"I left," Nic answered. "When I came back your goon wouldn't let me talk to you."

"There's nothing else to say."

"I disagree." He crossed the few feet separating us and flicked a finger toward the animals. "Are these wolves infected?"

His shoulder brushed against mine, and I nearly blurted "Infected?" as if I had no idea what he was talking about.

That single touch, which wasn't a touch at all but an

accident—cloth against cloth, not skin against skin—made me remember far too many things.

The taste of his mouth in the darkness. The scent of his hair covered with rain. The length of his legs tangled with mine.

We'd never had sex, but we'd done just about everything else. I'd wanted him with all the pent-up passion of a deprived youth. Never having had him only served to make Nic Franklin the subject of every one of my fantasies.

"No," I snapped, clenching my hands until my nails bit into my palms. "These aren't infected."

"But—"

"I need healthy wolves, too. I can't cure a disease if I don't know what its opposite looks like."

Which was true. I was trying to cure lycanthropy, a virus that made men into wolves—or something like them.

Nic stared into the woods along with me. The man I remembered would pick at a problem until he had the answer, an annoying trait, which would have made him a terrific trial lawyer. Probably made him an even better FBI agent. I only hoped he wouldn't pick at the mystery of the J-S society until it unraveled.

My boss would do anything to keep us in business. He knew, as did I, that we saved more lives than we lost. What we did was important, and we had to be allowed to keep doing it.

I rested my palm against the chain-link fence. I should go inside, but out here in the forest, with my back to the stone compound, I could almost forget what life was like in there.

Nic's fingers covered mine. His hand was large and dark, both gentle and rough. Startled, my gaze flicked to his, and he kissed me.

In an instant I was young again; I still had hope and a future. All the love rushed back, filling me up yet leaving me achingly empty. No matter how much I touched him it had never been enough.

He tasted the same—like red wine on a cold winter night. His heat had always melted my ice. With Nic I'd been warm, safe, alive. I hadn't felt that way since.

Which was the only reason I didn't shove him away as I should have. Opening my mouth, I welcomed him in, trailed my tongue along his crooked eye tooth. He moaned and crowded me against the fence, aligning our bodies just right.

I forgot where I was, who I was, and who he was, loosening his jacket and tie, then several buttons of his shirt, so I could slip my fingers inside and trace the soft, curling hair that matted his chest. His muscles shuddered and flexed. Calluses he hadn't had seven years ago caught on my panty hose as he traced his hands up my thighs and beneath my skirt.

We shouldn't have been doing this for more reasons than one. The most important, the security camera through which the guard was probably getting a year's worth of jollies.

The thought made me stiffen, but I couldn't escape. My shoulders to the chain link, my front was plastered to Nic. He tugged on my lip with his teeth, then lifted me just enough to grind us together in the best, or perhaps the worst, possible way.

I forgot all about the camera. Right now, I didn't give a damn who saw me. I needed . . . something. Or maybe someone.

A body slammed between my shoulder blades, and I grunted at the impact. If not for Nic, I would have fallen.

He lifted his head; his eyes widened and he loosened his hold. "What the hell?"

I spun around. The four adult wolves had gone berserk, throwing themselves at the steel fence, growling and snarling. The two pups slunk back and forth at the edge of the tree line. Whining periodically, they waited and they watched, but they didn't come any closer.

"You said they weren't rabid."

Nic's arm was still around me, my right side pressed to his left. I moved away. I couldn't be close to him and think straight.

"They weren't. I mean, they *aren't*."

"That looks like rabid to me." He frowned at the spittle dripping from their muzzles and the rolling whites of their eyes.

I'd tested these wolves inside out. There was nothing wrong with them. Present psychotic outbreak aside.

I studied the animals more closely. They were scared but not of Nic. They were angry but not at me. Instead, they continued to hit the fence, slaver, snarl, and stare at the compound as if it held something they'd enjoy tearing into bloody pieces.

Contrary to popular belief, wolves aren't vicious—

unless starved or rabid. My wolves were neither. I'd bet my life on it. Which meant . . .

I took one step in the direction of the compound, and the building blew sky high.

4

The force of the explosion sent us both to the ground. Through some acrobatic maneuver, Nic managed to cover my body with his.

Debris rained everywhere. My ears rang. I thought I'd gone deaf until I realized the wolves were howling right next to my head.

Nic eased off me. "What was that?"

I sat up, staring at the flaming compound. "My guess is a really big bomb."

"Bomb?" He leaped to his feet. "What makes you think a bomb?"

"You're the hotshot FBI agent. What does that look like to you?"

"Gas explosion?"

"If we had any gas out here. Electricity fired this place. And last time I checked, electricity doesn't cause fiery, explosive death."

He peered at his suddenly dirty shoes for several ticks of the clock, then offered me a hand. "You're right."

Since touching him was a stupid idea and kissing him had been an even worse one, I got up on my own. When I touched people, bad things happened.

I contemplated the heat and the flames. Really bad things.

The building was little more than a flaming crater. The guard was dead. I wasn't sure about the werewolves in the basement.

Burning the bodies after they'd been shot with silver left ashes, but would a firebomb kill a werewolf? I didn't have a clue.

A chill came over me that had nothing to do with the wind. What if Billy were alive?

I swayed and almost fell. What if he were alive and free?

Nic, who'd been creeping closer to the blaze, hurried to my side and clutched my elbow. "Are you dizzy?"

I closed my eyes on another cheery thought. Not only did I have to worry about Billy, but my notes, my serum, the antidote were gone.

"Elise, you'd better sit down again."

I shook Nic off, took a deep breath, let it out slowly, then took another.

"My work," I managed. "Everything was inside."

He blinked, glanced at the compound, then at me. "You must have it backed up off-site."

True. However, I didn't know where that somewhere was. Only Edward did, and he was in Wisconsin.

"You don't?" Nic's voice was incredulous.

"Yes, of course. But there were things in there I'm going to need."

I glanced at the sky, contemplating the lopsided, three-quarter moon.

Soon.

Nic patted his pocket, and a bewildered expression crossed his face, followed almost immediately by a dawning understanding. "Left my cell in the car."

Dazed, I followed him around the crackling building to the front parking lot. He stopped walking, and I ran into his back.

"Uh-oh," he muttered.

Leaning to the side, I saw the problem. The cars were on fire, too.

"I guess that makes sense," Nic said, almost to himself. "This kind of damage, usually a car bomb."

I guess he should know.

"How many vehicles were supposed to be in this lot?" he asked.

I glanced at the piles of fiery metal and counted. "One less than we've got."

His lips tightened. "Doesn't really tell us all that much, but I can get someone here who can. Got a phone?"

"In my office."

"Great."

He scrubbed his fingers through his hair, leaving a few strands standing on end. If he hadn't been six-three and about two-twenty, he would have looked like a little boy with cowlicks. As it was, I found myself charmed far beyond what was good for me.

"This makes no sense," he continued. "Why would anyone want to blow up a medical research facility?"

Since we were a lot more than that, there were quite a few people, and nonpeople, too, who would love to blow J-S headquarters to hell and gone. Not just the building, either, but me, Edward, and any other agents they could take out in the process.

We didn't need the FBI here. Lord knows what else they might uncover when they started sifting through the rubble. If I could get to a phone ahead of Nic, Edward would take care of the cover-up.

A cool wind sifted through the trees, bringing with it the scent of winter. We'd been lucky so far; it was November and we'd only had a dusting of snow. I glanced to the west where dark clouds billowed on the horizon. That was about to change.

Something cracked and fell inside the smouldering crater, the sound echoing through the forest. A wolf yipped, beyond the fence, not one of mine, and I started to get nervous about being in the open without a gun.

"Where's the nearest town?" Nic asked.

"Sixty miles, give or take."

His stare was blank. He couldn't get his mind around the concept. "Where do you live?"

I pointed to the flames.

"You live *and* work here?"

"There isn't anywhere else."

Besides, I worked all the time. Why bother to rent elsewhere, even if it was safe to do so?

Sure, sometimes I left the compound, even the state, on special orders from Edward. But once those orders were completed, I hurried back and disappeared once more behind the locked doors.

"What about groceries, clothes . . . ?" He spread his big hands wide. "Stuff and junk?"

"Supplies arrive twice a month."

He opened his mouth, then shut it again, and his eyes narrowed. "There's more to this place than medical research, isn't there?"

I didn't answer. In the end, I didn't have to.

A shadow scooted behind a tree at the edge of the parking lot. I turned that way, wishing like hell I'd brought my gun. Nic had one, but without silver bullets it wouldn't do much good against most of the things that were after me. Still . . .

I reached for Nic's arm, planning to ask for his weapon, or at least tell him to pull it out, and the shadow shimmered, almost taking form, before blending into the half-darkness once again. Curious, I let my hand drop and took a step toward the trees.

A sound came from the woods, one I'd heard only a few times before. However, when dealing with gunshots, once is more than enough. I yanked Nic with me to the ground.

The bullet whistled through the air where our heads had been, then thunked into something solid on the other side of the parking lot.

I glanced at Nic. He had a Glock in his hand, and I hadn't even seen him move. Impressive.

"Where did that come from?" he asked.

"There."

I pointed to the tree where I could have sworn I saw the shape of a human being—except in my world, they might not be human anymore.

If Billy was alive, he wouldn't bother with a gun. He had so many better weapons in his arsenal. Besides, Billy was the kind of guy who liked to get his hands, as well as his fangs, dirty.

Nic made a move to get up, and I pulled him down. "I don't think so."

"I'm not going to be a sitting duck. I've got a gun, too."

Which wouldn't do him a bit of good when shooting at a werewolf.

The conundrum made me hesitate long enough for Nic to slip out of my reach. Instead of running into the woods, he stared at me with narrowed eyes. "Who did you piss off, Elise?"

"Me? Who says they weren't trying to kill you?"

His eyes widened. Guess he hadn't thought of that.

Nic lifted the leg of his slacks and handed me a .38 from the ankle holster. "I'll be right back."

He headed into the forest. When no shots were fired, I concluded that whoever had been there was gone.

I inched across the parking lot, avoiding the burning piles of metal that had once been cars. Gauging the trajectory from the tree where I'd seen the shadowy figure, to the area where we'd been standing, then beyond, I was able to find the bullet embedded in a smoldering signpost.

The spent ammo looked like any other. However, my fingers burned the instant I brought them close to the bullet. The reaction could have been from the continuing heat of the fire, except it wasn't.

The bullet was silver.

"Huh," I murmured as I drew back my hand. "Guess they were after me."

5

No one knew I was a werewolf. My true nature was definitely not in my personnel file. So I couldn't explain how my secret had been sold, but right now I had other things to worry about.

Especially when another gunshot sounded. The wolves howled again, their mournful serenade causing my skin to tingle.

I wanted to shout Nic's name. Instead, I tightened my fingers around his weapon and moved toward the trees.

I'd gone only a few steps when I heard someone coming. From the sound of the voice muttering a litany of curses, that someone was Nic.

"I take it you missed," I said in lieu of a greeting.

He glanced up, his expression curious. "I could have sworn I didn't. He fell—"

My ears perked at the pronoun. "He?"

"Hard to tell. He, or she, got up, then they were just

gone." He snapped his fingers. "Your guess is as good as mine."

Mine was probably better. If Nic had shot someone, and they'd gotten up and disappeared at the speed of the wind, my bet was werewolf.

But if that was the case, why bother to run? Hell, why use a gun in the first place? I didn't want to stick around long enough to find out.

"Can't believe I didn't hit him," Nic murmured.

"It happens."

I considered returning Nic's gun, then decided something was better than nothing even if I had no silver bullets, and shoved the weapon into the pocket of my skirt.

"Not to me."

I didn't comment. Regardless of who had fired the shot, of who, or what, Nic had chased, he would be ill-equipped to catch them. He could be the best FBI agent in the business, but when faced with a traitorous *Jäger-Sucher,* a rogue agent, a werewolf, or something else, he'd be chasing shadows until they decided he was a nuisance. Then he'd just be dead.

What was I going to do with him?

"We need to get to a phone." Nic holstered his gun.

"Good luck."

"There has to be one somewhere."

"Yeah. Sixty miles from here in the next town." I glanced at the thick trees, the steadily darkening sky, then I thought of the shadows, the silver, of Billy, and I shivered. "We should start walking."

Really, really fast.

"Walking?" Nic frowned as if he'd never done such a thing before.

"You have a better idea?" I spread my hands, indicating the parking lot where every car was on fire.

"Sooner or later someone will turn up. Won't they?"

"Sure. In two weeks, when we're due for supplies."

"No one else comes to this facility? No one will call and wonder why you aren't answering?"

Edward would. Then he'd hop the next flight west to discover what had happened. I didn't want him to. Whoever had done this knew far too much about us. Hence the silver bullet. If they knew that, they knew Edward would show eventually, which might be just what they'd been after all along.

I needed to get in touch with my boss without being overheard. Failing that, I needed to get to him without being followed.

I slid a glance in Nic's direction. Either one was going to be tricky.

"I'm on my own," I said.

"There's not a single person in the vicinity? No groundskeeper? No friendly neighborhood hermits? What about those Montana militants we're always investigating?"

"Sorry. The isolation was a big selling point."

However, his comment did make me remember that we weren't completely without wheels.

"There's an outbuilding past the wolf enclosure." I gazed into the trees. "We keep an ATV there."

"How far can we go on that?"

"Farther and faster than we can make it on foot."

I wanted to put as much distance as I could between myself, the compound, any undead monsters, and that silver-bullet-shooting gun before dark. Even though I sensed the shooter was gone, I wasn't going to bet my life, or Nic's, on that feeling.

"You have any idea who might want to shoot you?" Nic asked, as he followed me through the woods.

"The list is endless."

I kept my voice dry. The better to seem sarcastic, even though I wasn't.

"Elise, this is serious."

"I got that when the building blew up."

How was I going to keep him from asking questions all the way to a telephone? How would I keep him, and me, alive until we got there? I didn't have a clue.

I'd reach town a lot easier on my own, but I couldn't leave Nic behind. He had no idea what we were facing.

Figuring the wolf enclosure, at least, should be free of a gun-wielding killer, I skirted the fence line. When one of my wolves slammed into the chain link, I let out a small shriek and slammed into Nic.

He tried to steady me, but I pulled away to move closer. The alpha male—José—stood on the other side of the barricade. He was frightened, and that wasn't like him.

"I need to set them free," I murmured.

"Are you nuts?"

Nic snagged my elbow, but I tugged myself loose and headed for the gate. "I can't leave them locked up with no one to take care of them."

"Wolves can take care of themselves."

Maybe. But they'd do better outside than in.

"Stay back."

I punched in the code that would open the door. A minute later I watched as all six melted into the trees.

Heavy clouds obscured the three-quarter moon. Even though that should make it a lot harder to shoot me, the encroaching shadows made me nervous. The moon might be hidden, but it was still there, and so were the monsters.

Nic kept pace as I made my way double-time down the path. "Any idea who might have planted that bomb?" he asked.

The cardinal rule of Law Enforcement 101 must be to ask the same question a thousand different ways.

"No visitors but you."

I had a sudden flash. Nic had been outside for hours while I was in the basement. Had he been reading a book, or instructing an accomplice where to deliver a bomb?

Then again, why would he blow up J-S headquarters when he didn't even know what we were doing there? Unless he understood more than he was saying. Unless he was more than he appeared—like me.

I stopped and so did Nic. He tilted his head. "I swear I didn't torch the place."

"So swears every mad bomber."

His lips twitched, but when he spoke his voice held steady. "If I blew up the compound, then who shot at us?"

"Your co-conspirator?"

"Paranoid much?"

"Every damn day."

Nic moved closer, and his breath brushed my hair. "You never used to be so tense."

"I never used to be a lot of things."

His hand cupped my elbow, and I nearly jumped out of my skin. "Relax. I'm not going to hurt you."

His thumb slid across a long, black mark that shone starkly against the winter-white material of my favorite suit. Crap now, along with everything else I owned. With Nic touching me, even through the fabric, I couldn't work up the energy to care.

"When we finally have sex," he whispered, "it'll be on silk sheets, in a real bed, where I can show you what I've been fantasizing about for seven years."

The air smelled of heat, fire, of him. My body went tight and wet. If he touched me, I just might forget that we had places to go, monsters to avoid.

"We aren't going to have sex." I removed my arm from his grasp. *"Ever."*

"Right." He made a disgusted sound—but whether that was for me or himself, I had no idea—and turned his back. "You keep on believing that."

I wasn't sure what to say, what to do. One minute Nic seemed to hate me. The next, what I saw in his eyes was far from hate, though the expression wasn't love.

I'd seen love in his eyes before.

The only man I'd ever wanted was Nic. Now he was here, and I couldn't have him. If I did, I risked so much more than myself.

Without another word, I tromped down the trail. The scent of blood reached me long before I found the source.

A flayed rabbit lay in the middle of the path. My gaze wandered over the trees, but I saw no one, heard nothing.

Did they think the blood would make me foolish? If so, they had no idea whom they were dealing with, no clue what I had done so that something like this was little more than a prank—although I doubted the bunny had found it funny. Perhaps whoever was after us didn't know as much as they thought.

"What the hell?" Nic bent to study the blood and the fur.

"Never mind. Let's just get out of here."

"What's this?"

He plucked something from the ground, then offered his hand, palm up, in my direction. I leaned closer and my breath caught.

A tiny wolf—a talisman, a totem, a charm. I'd seen one before, been studying it, too, trying to figure out how and why the thing was magic.

But the icon should have blown up along with the building. Even if it had been thrown this far into the woods, that particular talisman had been fashioned from black stone.

This one was white plastic, with sparkling blue eyes. The thing would have been tacky, if it wasn't so creepy. Even without the bloody kill nearby.

"Elise?"

I blinked and looked into Nic's face. I must have been staring at the wolf for quite a while, because his expression was troubled. "Do you know what this is?"

"Totem."

"Like totem pole?"

"No. The Ojibwe clan system uses totems or *dodiams*. Tiny icons that hold spiritual power—the essence of a clan animal."

"You don't actually believe an icon can hold power? That an animal has an essence?"

"What I believe doesn't matter. They believe it."

And a lot more.

I considered Nic. "You don't put any store in power? Magic? The supernatural?"

His blue eyes met mine. "No."

It would be interesting to prove him wrong, but I didn't have the time.

"Do the Ojibwe live around here?" he asked.

I resisted the urge to sneer. Why would a stuffed-shirt FBI agent know which Indian tribes were common to the area, even though he should?

"In Montana there are Sioux, Crow, Blackfoot, to name a few. The Ojibwe live in Minnesota, Canada, and Wisconsin."

"Wisconsin?" His head went up. "Where Mandenauer is."

Since he wasn't asking a question, I didn't bother to answer.

"Strange," he murmured.

I had to agree. Discovering an Ojibwe icon in Montana, while Edward resided in the land from whence it came, was too much of a coincidence for comfort. However, I didn't know what it meant.

I took the talisman from Nic's palm, then glanced at the rabbit. More arrows than one were pointing me to the land of milk and cheese.

"Come on," I told Nic. "We're almost to the shed."

I pocketed the tiny white wolf and stepped over the dead brown bunny. As I did, I heard a muffled growl.

"Hungry?" Nic asked.

I glanced at the fur and blood. "No."

The muffled growl hadn't come from me but from the totem in my pocket.

6

I couldn't tell Nic. He didn't believe in magic. He'd take me to the nearest hospital, lock me up and throw away the key. Then we'd have real trouble, since my medication had blown up with the compound.

Me, locked inside, with the full moon less than a week away. Yeah, trouble. However, that was the least of my worries at the moment.

We reached the shed; Nic inspected the place with typical FBI precision. No one was inside. No one had tampered with the ATV.

"I'll drive," I said.

"I don't think so."

"You don't get to think. I know where we're going."

"I could figure it out," he grumbled, but he climbed on behind me.

I could tell by the tenseness of Nic's thighs against mine, and the tiny starts he was unable to stop every time the ATV tipped a little too far to one side, that he wasn't used to riding them, and he didn't care for anyone else to be in control.

We reached the highway, a loose term for any paved road in the vicinity, and I took off at the fastest clip the ATV would allow—about thirty miles per hour. Driving at top speed without a helmet wasn't my idea of fun, even though I had nothing to fear from a head injury. Nic, however, did.

"It's going to take us two hours or more to get to town," he shouted.

"Got a better idea?"

His silence was answer enough.

We traveled at a pace slower than the average wolf, which could run forty miles per hour on a bad day. Super-wolves, in other words, lycanthropes, could top that speed with ease.

As I drove I considered the icon in my pocket. Was the totem a clue? A threat? An accident? I needed to show the talisman to Will Cadotte, our expert on Native American mysticism. Conveniently, he had gone to Wisconsin with Edward.

Had the thing truly growled? I would have said no, except Nic had heard it, too.

I'd never observed any supernatural behavior from the black totem, but that didn't mean there hadn't been any.

Jessie McQuade, a J-S agent and former police officer, swore she'd seen the totem move on its own. Who was I to say she was nuts?

We continued in silence for close to an hour. Talking was pointless with the roar of the motor and the thunder of the wind. But I didn't need words to hear Nic loud and clear. The press of his thighs wasn't the only thing I felt.

He'd missed me, in more ways than one.

His palms rode my waist; his thumbs slid under my suit coat and toyed with the skin just above my panty hose. His breath teased the hair that had fallen loose from my customary French twist.

I had to be honest with him. What had been between us once could never be again, despite the treacherous response of my body to his. I had too many secrets I couldn't share. Too much work that had to be done. Too many monsters that wanted me dead.

I tensed, half-expecting him to cup my breasts, then latch his mouth onto my neck and suckle. Legs wide as I straddled the seat, the wind shot up my skirt, stirring me where I needed no help being stirred. His fingertips grazed the swell of my rear.

"Nic," I said. Protest, plea—I wasn't sure. Didn't matter. The wind flung the word into the night.

Snow began to fall—thick, fluffy flakes that would soon obscure the road. I had to concentrate. We needed to reach a town before the storm hit, or worse. I was already half-frozen and I was certain Nic was, too.

But it was impossible to think as Nic's hand slid across my skin, palm warm, hard, flat against my belly.

I glanced down. My skirt was hiked to my hips, and the sight of my stocking-clad legs, my white cotton briefs, his sun-browned hand and callused fingers, excited me so much that I did nothing when his middle finger slid lower and stroked me just once. Lucky no one was on the highway except us.

Or so I thought.

I lifted my gaze, then swerved to avoid the huge black wolf in the middle of the road. The right wheel slipped off the pavement, and we were airborne.

Providence was on our side, and we were thrown clear. Most ATV injuries are the result of the machine falling on top of the riders. As it was, I landed on my shoulder and something crunched.

Ignoring the pain, I scrambled to my feet, searching frantically for Nic. I found him at the edge of the tree line. He wasn't moving.

The wolf swung his head toward me. Light gray, human eyes shone in a feral face. "Billy," I murmured.

I should have known he hadn't died. Guys like him never did. It would take something worse than a firebomb to put an end to Billy Bailey.

But where had he been? Had it taken him some time to heal his injuries, then dig his way out of the rubble?

What about the others? Had they survived, as well?

I strained my ears but heard only the wind, sniffed the air and caught nothing but the scent of snow and crazy Billy.

Either the rest of my basement wolves had found freedom, then scattered, or they were ashes and Billy was a lot more powerful than I'd thought. And wasn't that just special?

Billy's head cocked; his tongue lolled, almost as if he were laughing. Hell, he probably was.

I fingered the gun in my pocket. I could put every bullet into Billy, and it wouldn't slow him down. If I stayed in this form, he'd kill me—if I was lucky—then move on to Nic.

I was going to have to shift.

However, such things took time, and at mid-shift I'd be defenseless. Billy had no scruples. He'd wait until the worst possible moment, then attack. Nevertheless, I had to take the risk, hope my changing at all would confuse him long enough for me to assume another form.

I managed to kick off my shoes—I hated it when my paws burst through them—but I didn't have the chance to remove anything else. Not that I'd strip in front of Billy even if I had a week.

As I lifted my face, snowflakes brushed my cheeks, stuck to my eyelashes, prickled my nose. I pushed aside the sensory distractions and thought of the moon.

If it had been full I wouldn't have had to try. Without the round silver disc that pulled like the ebb and flow of the tide, the transformation was a bit harder, especially for those with stunted imaginations.

I bet Billy had had one helluva time getting furry tonight.

He growled, low in his throat. I was up to something, but he didn't know what. Pretty soon he'd get sick of wondering, come over here and kick my ass. With me still a woman, and him already a beast, he'd have no trouble at all.

Staring at the black velvet sky, I envisioned the cool metallic white of the moon spilling across my face. I smelled the wind, the trees, the earth. *Night.* The totem in my pocket shimmied, and my favorite suit split at the seams.

The shifting of bones, the curving of spine, usually produced agony. Going from bipedal to quadrapedal wasn't supposed to feel good. My skin would burn when the fur came. My fingers and toes always ached as they sprouted claws. My face hurt as my nose and my mouth melded into a snout.

I loathed getting furry—always had, maybe I always would if I never discovered a cure—but pain was the least of it. I hated being covered with hair, sprouting a tail. The drooling, the panting, the howling, and I never could get the dirt out from under my fingernails. Becoming a werewolf was hell on a manicure.

But tonight, the transformation was painless. Tonight I thought about being a wolf, and suddenly I was.

Billy yelped. I was the fastest changer in the West. A damned werewolf savant. Something peculiar was going on, but I didn't have time to figure out what.

Werewolves not only have human eyes, they possess human intelligence. I knew what I had to do and why, so without giving Billy time to think, I charged. This wasn't fun and games but a fight to the death. Billy would come after me, and he'd keep on coming until he had what he wanted.

Me.

I'd rather be dead than Billy Bailey's sex slave. That knowledge gave me an edge. I hit him hard, and he tumbled onto his back.

Either confusion had slowed his reactions, or I'd suddenly become faster than the average werewolf. Maybe both. My teeth grazed Billy's throat before he sent me flying.

I landed on the same shoulder that had hit the ground when I'd flown off the ATV, and I whimpered. Without human blood, I wouldn't heal completely tonight, though just becoming a wolf would improve any injury faster than it was possible to explain.

Billy struck me broadside before I could roll onto all fours. I slammed into the dirt hard enough to make my ears ring. My head ached, and I had a difficult time focusing.

He could have killed me then, if he hadn't been an insane sadomasochist. Instead of going for my jugular, he drew blood from my belly, and then licked it away.

Disgust flowed through me, followed closely by anger. Using my legs, my claws, I threw him free, then I did what he hadn't. Jumping on top, I latched onto Billy's throat and pulled.

Though I tried to get out of the way, blood sprayed my face and chest. I scuttled backward, not even waiting to see Billy's human eyes go wolf as he died.

I shifted into a woman more quickly than I ever had before. My clothes a torn tangle, I still managed to cover myself adequately. Scooping a handful of snow, I let it melt in my palm so I could scrub away some of the blood and the dirt.

Remembering the slash to my stomach, I lifted my suit. Nothing. Frowning, I rolled my shoulder. Not a twinge.

Had the talisman granted fast healing powers along with swift changing ability? Seemed so.

I could get used to this.

I hurried to Nic, kneeling next to him as his eyes opened, crossed, then focused on my face. "I saw a wolf."

"I know. I almost hit him."

"No." He reached up and tugged my hair, loose now

and swirling around my shoulders. "With fur like this and . . ." He frowned. "Your eyes."

I kept my face neutral, even as my heart threatened to choke me. Nevertheless, when I spoke, my voice was as cool as the breeze.

"You must have bumped your head a lot harder than I thought."

7

Nic sat up, groaned, fell back.

I caught him before he cracked his head against the ground again. "Maybe we should get you to a doctor."

"You're a doctor."

"Not that kind."

"I'm all—" His voice faded, and his eyes closed as he slumped in my arms.

Concerned, I leaned close. He was out cold, so I gave in to the urge that had been haunting me since I'd first seen him in the doorway. Pressing my lips to his forehead, I breathed in the familiar scent of his hair.

All the feelings rushed back with a force that staggered me. I'd known I still loved him, but I hadn't realized that I always would.

Once we'd dreamed of sharing a life: marriage, careers, family. Together, we would never be alone again.

I longed for that normal life—a normal me. But I'd come to understand that even if I cured myself, there were things I'd done in the interim for which there could be no forgiveness. Nic was as lost to me now as he'd been the first night I changed.

The wind slapped snow against my face. The drop in temperature had turned the fluffy flakes into icy needles.

I smelled death—probably just Billy's. Nevertheless, we had to keep moving. With the clouds covering the moon, the road was dark. Though there wasn't much of a chance a car would come along and run over us . . . then again, one might.

Taking advantage of Nic's momentary lapse of consciousness, I lowered him gently to the ground and hurried to the ATV. After a quick glance to make sure he was still out, I picked up the machine and set it back on the road.

There was a dent in one side, a bit of dirt on the other, but when I started the engine, it worked.

Nic began to come around. I tugged on his arm, grunting as if he were "oh, so heavy," though I could have lifted him with one hand. "Wanna help me out a little?"

"Sorry, I'm—"

"Hurt," I supplied when he seemed to lose his thought again.

Thankfully, he was too spacey to notice how much I helped him as he got to his feet, too woozy to see that my clothes were torn and I had flecks of blood in my hair.

I hoisted Nic onto the ATV, crawled behind, then adjusted his body so that I could see, drive, and hold on to him. If I hadn't had superpowers, I wouldn't have been able to manage, making this one of the first times I was glad to be what I was.

Nic drifted in and out of consciousness. I'd wondered how to make him stop asking questions. I'd have preferred another method.

The wind shifted, or we were able to get ahead of the storm, because the highway outside of Clear Lake was dry, the forest surrounding it devoid of white. Most of the businesses on the main drag were closed, probably had been for a while. The town was small, innocent, clueless.

I'd been toying with the idea of dumping Nic with a doctor—they had to have one—then disappearing again. But an hour on the ATV with little to do beyond think had nixed that idea.

Billy might be dead, but Billy hadn't blown up the compound. Whoever had, could be right behind us.

I let my gaze wander over Nic's still face. He'd say he was a highly trained FBI agent; he could take care of himself. But I knew better. To werewolves he'd be an easy lunch.

No matter how dangerous it was for us both, I was going to have to take him along to Wisconsin.

I pulled into the only gas station in Clear Lake. The attendant stepped outside. His gaze wandered over my torn suit, the spatters of blood and the leaves in my hair, then flicked to Nic's lolling head. With the typical understatement that characterized inhabitants west of the Mississippi, he murmured, "Trouble?"

"Nearly hit a . . . deer. We flipped."

The story, close enough to the truth to be believable, explained Nic's injuries and my appearance.

"Need a doctor?" he asked.

"No." Nic struggled to sit up. "I'm okay."

The attendant's brows drew together. "If you say so."

Nic tried to prove it by climbing off the ATV. He wobbled, but he didn't fall down.

"You know where I can buy some clothes?"

As the word *buy* left my mouth, I realized I had no money. I glanced at Nic; he was already extracting his wallet.

"And a car," he added, pulling out an obscene amount of cash.

"Got some T-shirts and sweatpants for sale inside." The man scratched his head as he contemplated the money. "Car we'll have to talk about."

I hesitated, prepared to deal, but Nic waved me away. "I'll handle the car."

I let him. The less time we hung around, the better. Inside I snagged a pair of gray sweatpants and an equally cheery gray T-shirt.

Making use of the restroom, I stripped off my torn and dirty suit. After extracting the wolf totem, I tossed the clothes into the nearly full garbage can. Holding the tiny bit of plastic between two fingers, I stared into the sparkly blue eyes.

The idea that something this small, this tacky, could carry enough power to make me superduper wolf was laughable. But standing in a dirty women's restroom in the middle of nowhere, I didn't feel like laughing.

I shoved the talisman into the pocket of my new sweatpants just as I remembered the little wolf wasn't the only thing that had been in my skirt.

Both the list of names Nic had given me and his .38 were missing. I must have dropped them somewhere along the road. I didn't care about the list, but the gun might have been good for a bluff or two.

Since I couldn't go back for the weapon now, I shoved my bare feet into my tennies and picked one last flake of blood from my hair. My nails looked as if I'd been burying dead bodies in the woods, which was close enough to the truth to make me worry. I could only hope that the people we met between here and Wisconsin were less concerned with personal hygiene than I was.

When I exited the bathroom, I found the attendant behind the register. I peered around the station, which was packed ceiling to floor with chips, soda, candy, and borderline pornography. But no Nic.

"I sold your friend a car."

From the man's grin, the deal had been sweet. Of course, we couldn't exactly be choosy. We had to get out of here, and we couldn't do that on an ATV.

"He went across the street to pick it up."

Though I didn't like Nic being out of my sight for more than a minute, his absence did give me time to do something I should have done before now.

"Do you have a phone?"

He pointed to the wall behind me.

I considered the risks. I doubted anyone would have thought to put a bug on this particular phone, and Edward always had his own lines meticulously swept for listening devices. By the time someone traced the call, Nic and I should be long gone.

I punched in the numbers as the clerk moved off to refill a potato chip display. Edward answered on the second ring. "Elise?"

How did he *do* that? The caller ID should have read "Joe's Gas Station," not "Elise Hanover." Sometimes the old man was spookier than everything he hunted.

My response—"Yes, sir!"—was rewarded with a vicious stream of German curse words.

"I know you aren't often glad to hear from me," I muttered, "but is that necessary?"

"I have been calling the compound every half an hour, and the line is dead. If we are having a malfunction, Elise, it is your job to inform me."

"It's a little bit more than a malfunction."

"Be specific."

I'd known Edward all of my life. He'd practically raised me—although paying various nannies, shipping me off to the best schools, then recruiting me to be his right-hand woman was hardly raising someone. There was little warmth between us, no matter how much I might want there to be.

"Specifically . . ." I glanced around. No one was in the gas station but me and the attendant, who was more interested in straightening the *Hustler* supply than listening to me. Nevertheless, I lowered my voice. "There's a crater where the compound should be."

Silence greeted my statement.

"Sir?"

"Sabotage?"

I thought of the shadow, the shot, the silver. "Definitely."

"The guard?"

"Dead."

"Subjects?"

"Could be alive." Edward's grunt told me he understood the ramifications of that as much as I did. "Except for Billy."

"And Billy is not alive because . . . ?"

"He pissed me off."

Though his sigh traveled hundreds of miles before reaching me, the sound lost none of its power to belittle.

"Your temper is, as always, a problem."

Only Edward would think that I had a temper. Everyone else considered my personality one step removed from ice bitch of the universe. Except Nic, but then, he didn't really know me as well as he thought.

"I will send someone to Montana," Edward said. "Someone who can take care of things."

Taking care of things being a J-S euphemism for *cover-up*. Even if Nic managed to send some of his pals into the woods, by the time they got there, there'd be nothing left to see.

"Who is responsible for this travesty?" Edward continued.

"Bad guys?"

The line went silent again, and I waited for the inevitable set-down. But instead of a lecture, I was rewarded with a dry chuckle, which made my heart stutter.

"Who is this?" I demanded.

He had the heavy German accent down to a T, but there was no humor in Edward—never had been. Which was understandable. His life had not exactly been one laugh riot after another.

"What have you done with my boss?"

"It is me, Elise. I have just lightened up in my old age."

Lightened up?

Okay, the world had stopped turning, and I had been too busy to notice.

"So much time with Jessie and Leigh . . ." I could almost see him shrug in that way he had that implied both nonchalance and Old World European manners. "They are amusing."

My teeth ground together at the reminder of Edward's favorite *Jäger-Suchers*. I had known him the longest, had helped him the most, yet when Edward had chosen pets, I was not one of them.

Jessie McQuade and Leigh Tyler-Fitzgerald were Edward's darlings as well as bosom buddies. Not that they hadn't tried to kill each other on occasion—when you released hunters into the same field you got explosions more often than tea parties—but they were two of a kind, and I didn't fit in.

I wasn't the type to banter and snipe. I didn't dare participate in the physical scuffles they relished. Sarcasm wasn't my venue. Nevertheless, having them take the place that I'd always wanted in Edward's affections made me a lot less enamored of them than he was.

"If this is Edward," I continued, "then tell me something only we would know."

Another long swell of silence drifted over the line. For a minute I thought I was right, maybe someone was impersonating my boss. I should have known that no one got the better of the old man, including me.

"By that," he said in a hard, cool voice that made me straighten even though he wasn't there to see, "I suspect you're referring to the fact that I killed your mother."

8

Okay, so it *was* him.

"I could have done without that particular trip down memory lane," I murmured.

"You asked me to tell you a secret, which only we would know."

I'd meant something more along these lines: On my sixteenth birthday he'd taken me to Paris. He'd dumped me on a colleague—who'd shown me the city, the museums, the sights—then gone off to kill someone. But he *had* taken me there.

However, Edward was right. Anyone could discover that information if they took the trouble to look. No one could know that the man who had "raised" me was also the man who had made me an orphan.

I couldn't blame him; my mother had been a werewolf at the time.

"Elise!"

How long had Edward been calling my name? I

wasn't sure. I'd drifted too far down the unpleasant road to my past.

"Sir?"

"You must come to Wisconsin. There is trouble in a place called Fairhaven."

That much I knew. Edward wouldn't be there, along with several other agents, if there wasn't. I assumed the issue was werewolves, since those were Jessie's specialty. I also assumed some type of Native American mysticism since Will was there, too. Although you couldn't have Jessie without Will and vice versa. They'd been inseparable since they met.

"The usual kind?" I asked, which was shorthand for any mysterious increase in the wolf population, wild animal attacks, or sudden, random, and inexplicable bloody death.

"Perhaps. Join me, Elise, and we will sort everything out."

I found it odd, sad, and just a bit rude that horrible things were happening in a town by the name of Fairhaven.

But I had more important concerns on my mind. How was I going to tell Edward there was someone after me? Someone who knew they needed a silver bullet to do any kind of damage.

"There's a slight problem—"

I broke off as Nic stepped through the door. My time had run out.

"Do you have my research with you?" I asked instead.

That question was innocent enough.

"Not *with* me. But it is safe." Edward sighed. "*Everything* is gone?"

"Yes."

"Your serum?"

"Dust."

"Then you'd do well to hurry."

The line went dead without a good-bye. Why should tonight be different than any one of a thousand others?

He hadn't asked if I was all right. Of course, I was as hard to kill as most of the things he hunted. Another of the reasons Edward kept me around. Still, it would have been nice, just once, if he'd asked.

"Everything okay?"

Nic seemed better. Less pale, and he no longer wobbled. I still wasn't going to let him drive.

"Everything's fine."

Or as fine as it was going to get.

I bought some snacks—beef jerky, my favorite, sodas, juice, coffee—and gave Nic the bill. After thanking the attendant, we went outside and contemplated Nic's brand-new car.

Or new to him anyway. The vehicle had to be at least thirty years old and resembled a tank. The Plymouth Grand Fury, once the car of police forces everywhere, had been retired in favor of the Crown Victoria and various SUVs. When that happened, the fleet of Furys had been sold at auctions across the country. We'd obviously been gifted with the results.

I climbed behind the wheel and Nic let me, which telegraphed his thundering headache more clearly than the three aspirin he doused with a cola chaser as soon as his butt hit the passenger seat. I started the car and headed east.

One minute Nic was staring at the dark expanse of highway that seemed to appear magically in front of our headlights, the next he was asleep. Though I'd have to wake him periodically in case of a concussion, still I uttered a sigh of relief. I was too tired to field any more questions right now.

I kept my eyes on both the tree line and the road. Every movement, every shadow made me start. Who knew what was out there? Maybe nothing, maybe everything.

Although I felt as if I were navigating the Starship *Enterprise* from behind the long, shiny, navy blue hood that seemed to stretch forward into infinity, the engine in a Fury could outrun even a werewolf. The knowledge soothed me somewhat, though not as much as having a few thousand silver bullets would have.

In the close confines of the car I could smell Nic's skin, feel his heat, hear him breathing. My body responded in a predictable manner. I insisted I was better than the animal that lived inside of me, but tonight I had my doubts.

In most cases, the lycanthropy virus destroys a person's humanity. They might appear normal in the daylight, but inside there was a demon panting to get out. And with that demon whispering, a lot of bad things happened.

A werewolf in human form is the most selfish being in existence. In the modern world, the behavior has been been written off as aggression, drive, ambition, which makes a werewolf pretty hard to spot in the sun.

Sadly, there isn't a tail or fangs or pointy ears to mark them as one of the bitten.

Sure they're evil, but so are a lot of people. I've always been of the opinion that there are a helluva lot more werewolf lawyers than werewolf pediatricians, but I've never had the time to prove it.

One way to know for certain: Shoot a person with silver. If they explode, werewolf. If not . . . oops.

All I can say is, don't try this at home. You can get in a whole lot of trouble if you're wrong. Homicide detectives don't often swallow the excuse "I thought he was a werewolf."

Such technicalities have never stopped Edward. Lucky for him he's a law unto himself.

A howl rose in the distance, long and mournful. The sound called to me, and I wasn't sure why. I'd never been pulled by the moon, tempted by the pack.

Once a month, I shifted beneath the silver sheen. Though I loathed becoming what I was, I had little choice when the moon was at its apex. But I never enjoyed that night. I merely endured.

Tonight had been different. I recalled the painless change, the rush of energy, the power. To experience that again was more tempting than it should be.

What if I stopped the car, got out, got furry and ran with the others? We'd hunt as one, together we'd kill. I'd no longer be a lone wolf, scorned by both humans and lycanthropes. I'd have friends. A family. Maybe even a lover.

Absently I fingered the talisman in my pocket. My fingers warmed; my skin hummed. I heard whispering, but I couldn't make out the words. I didn't recognize the voice. Male or female? Real or imagined?

Heat radiated from my fingers to my wrist. Curious, I glanced down and choked. My hand had sprouted fur, my nails become claws, and I hadn't felt anything but warm.

I stopped touching the talisman and recited the table of elements in my head. When I looked again, my hand was just a hand.

Had the change actually happened? I'd never heard of such an occurrence. We became wolves, completely, when we shifted. We were not able to pick and choose what part of us turned furry. I should try again, but I was afraid.

If I was turning into something other than what I'd always been, my days were numbered. Edward would have no qualms about killing me and neither would any of the others. Though there'd been times when death was more appealing than life, now wasn't one of them.

I let my gaze drift over the still-sleeping man at my side. Foolish as the idea was, I wanted to be with Nic for as long as I could.

I drove on, tense and alert, slurping coffee as if it were water and waiting for the sun to explode over the horizon—or a werewolf army to explode from the trees. Thankfully, I didn't have long to wait before the first one happened. The sun was as reliable as the moon.

With daylight came a sense of security. At dawn werewolves shifted back into human form. If any had been following us, they'd find themselves a long way from home without clothes or a car.

Nic mumbled and stretched. I'd woken him every few hours during the night, asked his name, his age, my name. Each time he'd answered correctly, then gone back to sleep. He didn't have a concussion as far as I could tell.

His hair was as rumpled as a set of tangled sheets, his eyes were heavy. I imagined touching his taut chest, tasting his smooth back, rubbing my cheek against his, then wrapping my legs around his waist and—

The talisman shimmied and muttered. I slapped a hand over my pocket. "Quit that!"

Nic, who'd been staring at my chest, no doubt outlined in pornographic detail by the thin T-shirt I'd purchased at the gas station, jerked his eyes to mine.

"Sorry," he muttered. "I can't seem to stop myself."

My fingers began to tingle, and I glanced at them, still resting on top of the talisman. Were my nails growing longer even as I watched?

Impossible. The sun was up.

Nevertheless, I jerked my hand from the icon, and wrapped it around the steering wheel. I was "oh, so tempted" to throw the white wolf totem over the nearest bridge, but I didn't dare. I might need it.

I had to get to Edward, to Will Cadotte, to someone who could help me—and quick. I glanced at Nic.

"You ready to drive?" I asked.

He rubbed a hand over his face. "Sure."

We continued throughout the day in alternating four-hour shifts behind the wheel. Drive-thru and Gas 'n' Go were our friends. Bad roads, winding detours, and shitty weather were our enemies.

As we neared the Wisconsin border, darkness threatened. Trees lined the road, so thick I could barely see beyond them, so numerous they seemed to stretch into infinity—or at least to Canada.

Shadows lurked behind every trunk. One minute taking the form of a wolf, the next a human, then something in between.

"Where to?" Nic asked.

I'd been working out the directions as we went, poring over an interstate map since I hadn't had the opportunity, or the hardware, to MapQuest the best route to Fairhaven.

The closer we got to my boss, the more nervous I became. In my head I knew I couldn't have left Nic behind, but in my heart I was worried.

Dominic Franklin had *government agent* written all over him. Edward might have been one himself, once upon a time, but he no longer had any use for them. And what he didn't have any use for, he often got rid of.

"There's something I should tell you," I began. "My boss can be . . ."

"Eccentric?"

"More like dangerous."

Nic's eyes shifted to mine, then back to the road. "From what I've been able to uncover, Edward Mandenauer is eighty-something years old."

"He can still point a gun." Better than anyone I knew, and he was never afraid to use it.

"He's going to shoot me if I ask a few questions?"

"It's happened before."

A second glance was filled with both disbelief and a certain wariness. Nic didn't believe what I was saying, but he was having a hard time disbelieving the conviction in my voice.

"Why are you so afraid of him?" Nic murmured.

"Because I'm smarter than I look?"

I threw his words back at him and was rewarded with a grimace. "I shouldn't have said that."

"You were angry."

"I still am."

The car stopped. We were at the end of the road—literally. A sign pointed left to Fairhaven, right to Wausau. Nic lifted his brows and waited. With a sigh, I jerked my thumb to the left.

We rolled into town well after midnight. The place was silent and still. Not a light flared, even on the street.

I hadn't been in too many small towns. Boarding schools were usually located near large cities, making it easier for parents to fly in for a visit, then out just as quickly.

The few vacations I'd had were to the previously noted Paris, another to Berlin, then London and Moscow. Edward always mixed business with pleasure, and for the most part, werewolves gravitated to large metropolitan areas where it was easier to hide the amount of killing they did.

Only in the past few years had they started hanging around scarcely populated areas, becoming bolder through sheer numbers and the use of magic.

My experience with small towns had been restricted to two: Clear Lake, Montana, and Crow Valley, Wisconsin, where I'd been called about a month ago to test my new antidote on a just-bitten *Jäger-Sucher*.

Fairhaven was enough like Crow Valley to be a clone: a single main street, a few side roads, dark alleys, no streetlights, the woods coming to within a hundred yards of the town.

Werewolf heaven.

Nic parked in front of what appeared to be a bar. But what kind of bar was closed at midnight in a state where the largest town was nicknamed Brew City? Perhaps one that was scared to death of things that went bump, or woof, in the night?

The headlights threw garish yellow streams across the sign on the front of the building.

MURPHY'S. OPEN EVERY DAY UNTIL TOMORROW.

Sounded like a bar to me.

"Where's Mandenauer?" Nic asked.

"No idea."

"You have to trust me sometime," he said quietly.

"I do?"

Nic's fingers curled around the steering wheel, as his lips thinned. Why did I insist on baiting him?

Because if he was angry at me, he wasn't kissing me. I was afraid of what I might do, or say, or admit, if he touched me again.

"I really don't know where Edward is," I blurted. "He neglected to share a forwarding address beyond Fairhaven—unincorporated."

"Oh." Nic took a deep breath and let it out. "Now what?"

"I'm not sure." My eyes wandered over the seemingly deserted town, the chilly, shadowed forest. "But if I know Edward, he won't be hard to find."

9

We hadn't been in Fairhaven ten minutes, when gunshots broke the silence.

"Bingo," I whispered, and climbed out of the car.

"Elise." Nic climbed out, too. "Maybe you should stay inside."

I shook my head and headed for the edge of town. Despite the darkness, I could see pretty well. Enhanced nocturnal vision and superior sense of smell and hearing while in human form were a few bonuses of being a werewolf. No clouds and a three-quarter moon didn't hurt either.

I listened and heard nothing. Drew in a deep breath and caught . . . something. Too faint to tell, almost as if the scent were a memory or a ghost.

Lack of sleep, too much Nic, and the damned talisman had made me edgier than I'd ever been before. I blew the strange smell from my nostrils, inhaled through my mouth for several ticks of the clock, and tried again.

This time when I tested the wind, I detected humans. I heard their voices, even though they were whispering.

Shadows emerged from the trees. Five of them.

Nic joined me. At first hovering behind, then pushing in front, as the shadows became people and drew near.

"It is about time you arrived, Elise."

We'd driven almost nonstop, yet it wasn't fast enough. Which was as typical of Edward as his outfit—dark pants and dark shirt accented by a bandolier of bullets across his chest. He carried a rifle in one hand and a pistol on his hip. A black skullcap covered his fading blond hair.

When the others had teased him about his Rambo complex, Edward had no idea what they were talking about. Once I'd explained, he'd thought the reference a compliment. Go figure.

Edward took in my attire with obvious confusion. Sweats, a T-shirt, and tennis shoes were not my style. His gaze became stuck on my hair, which hung loose to my waist. From his scowl, he didn't like the new me any better than the old one.

"Who is this?"

Edward had turned his faded blue eyes, as well as his rifle, toward our visitor. I tried to inch in front of Nic, but he shouldered me back. I was tempted to force the issue but settled for introductions.

"Nic Franklin." I pointed to the tall, lanky woman on Edward's left. "Meet Jessie McQuade."

With short brown hair and eyes nearly the same color, Jessie was attractive in an athletic sort of way.

She was a law enforcement officer by training, an award-winning deer hunter by hobby, and one of the newest and best agents in our werewolf division.

My gaze shifted to the man on Jessie's left. His high cheekbones and smooth cinnamon skin revealed his ethnicity, even without the golden feather swinging from one ear. With eyes that nearly matched the shade of his black hair, William Cadotte was a professor by trade, an Ojibwe by birth, and an expert in Native American totems and mysticism by choice.

I touched the plastic in my pocket as I introduced Will, making a mental note to show him the totem ASAP.

Both Will and Jessie nodded to Nic, then frowned at me. I was in big trouble for bringing a stranger here, and they knew it. In an attempt to stave off the inevitable, I continued to introduce people.

My arm swung to Edward's right. "Leigh Tyler-Fitzgerald and her husband, Damien."

Leigh was as short as Jessie was tall. Petite, with an almost blond crew cut, her pale skin and blue eyes gave her a doll-like appearance, which had fooled the enemy on countless occasions.

Her family and fiancé having been murdered by werewolves, Leigh had taken to hunting them with a ferocity only Edward could love. She'd fallen hard for Damien Fitzgerald—the hunky, Irish-American drifter at her side—before she'd discovered he was a werewolf.

Nic greeted Leigh and Damien the same way he'd acknowledged Jessie and Will: a quick nod before returning his gaze to my boss. I had little choice but to introduce them.

"This is Edward Mandenauer."

"Sir." Nic stepped forward, hand outstretched.

Edward didn't retract the gun, and the barrel tapped Nic in the chest. The older man continued to stare at the younger one without expression.

"I repeat, 'Who is he?' "

Nic's eyes narrowed, but I gave him credit, he managed to hold his temper and ignore the gun.

"I'm with the FBI, Mr. Mandenauer. I have some questions about the *Jäger-Sucher* agency."

"Uh-oh," Jessie muttered.

"Nice meeting you," Leigh quipped. "Hope you've enjoyed your life so far."

The four of them moved back, away from Edward and Nic, away from me.

"Elise, have you lost your mind?" Edward murmured. "He could be anyone. He could be—"

"He isn't," I blurted before Edward said too much.

In Edward's mind, everyone was a werewolf until proven otherwise.

"Ah, well, it is easy enough to find out."

I threw myself at Nic, propelling him to the ground before Edward could shoot him with silver and see if he erupted into a ball of fire or merely bled.

The others hit the deck, too, just as the rifle discharged above our heads.

"Stay down." I shoved Nic into the grass. He was shaking, which was understandable. Edward scared the crap out of everyone.

I leaped to my feet. "Old man, you're pushing the boundaries of sanity."

He shrugged and aimed his gun at Nic again. I was

tempted to yank it out of his hand, but I refrained. "Leave him alone."

Interest lit Edward's eyes. "Who is he?" he repeated.

He was asking for more than a name, rank, and serial number. He was asking who Nic Franklin was to me, and why I was so concerned for his life. I wasn't going to tell him.

"He's FBI. You can't just shoot him because he annoys you. As much fun as that might be."

Edward's lips twitched. "You are sure he is who he says he is?"

I was sure he was Nic. Pretty sure he was FBI. Certain he wasn't a werewolf—or as certain as I could be with the damned lycanthropes changing the rules every chance they got.

Because there is *one* other way to distinguish a werewolf in human form. If we touch, skin to skin, we know.

I'd touched Nic in anger, in lust, even love. I'd felt emotions I hadn't thought to feel again, but I hadn't felt werewolf.

"Hold on a second." Damien crawled the few feet separating them and brushed his fingers against Nic's.

Frowning, Nic snatched his hand away. Damien's hazel eyes met mine. He shook his head. He hadn't felt anything, cither.

Edward saw the exchange and put up his gun. Nic stood scowling at Damien, who had moved off to join Leigh.

She brushed his shoulder-length, auburn hair back from his face. Just under six feet, Damien towered over his tiny wife. Not only handsome, he had a body that would make a Chippendale jealous. Being turned into a werewolf just after the invasion at Normandy had given Damien a lot of years to work on his pecs.

He pressed his mouth to her knuckles, then rubbed his thumb over his mother's wedding ring, which he'd placed on Leigh's finger less than a month ago.

"Now that that's settled," Edward said. "Go away."

Nic glanced at Damien. "What's settled? Why did he touch me?"

"Damien's . . ." I wasn't sure what to say. Lucky for us, Leigh was a terrific liar.

"Psychic," she supplied. "He can tell all sorts of things just by touching a person."

"Bullshit," Nic snapped.

I couldn't blame him for his disbelief. Nic lived in the world we had created. A world where monsters didn't exist except in fiction. Our job was to keep things that way.

Edward sighed. "Believe what you will. Now come along."

He stalked toward town and Nic hesitated, looking first at me, then at Edward.

I trusted my employer's quick change—*go away, come along*—even less than I trusted myself. I cast my eyes heavenward, then hurried after Edward. "Wait."

Edward turned and stared past me to Nic. "You want to talk? Keep up."

I put my hand on Edward's arm and he flinched. The reaction never lost its power to hurt me. Why I continued to touch the man, I had no idea. Maybe I was hoping that familiarity would end the contempt.

"You can't shoot him, Edward." I kept my voice low, just above a whisper. "Promise."

"I will do no such thing. There is no telling what might necessitate shooting."

He had a point. I leaned forward, ignoring how he tensed as I came closer. "Don't shoot him unless he's furry. Okay?"

"For now."

Nic came up next to me. "Do you have the list I gave you?"

My hand went to my pocket, even as I remembered losing it. The talisman danced beneath my fingers, and I yanked them away. "Must have fallen out while we were on the ATV."

Nic shrugged. "I know it by heart," he said, and followed in Edward's wake.

My boss called back, "Perhaps the five of you should bring one another up to speed on . . . things."

The two men disappeared around the corner of a building. Since I was the seniormost *Jäger-Sucher,* I opened my mouth to begin, and Leigh jumped in.

"Have you found the cure?"

I glanced at Damien, then back at Leigh. "Not yet."

Her exhale of annoyance was accompanied by a few choice curse words.

"I've been experimenting with variations of the antidote I used on you," I began.

Not only had Leigh's family been wiped out by werewolves, but the alpha who had ordered the attack had come after, then bitten, her. His plan had been to make Leigh his mate. Damien had other ideas.

He'd killed Hector Menendez and ended the man's bid for power, but he hadn't been able to save Leigh. Only I could.

"What works on a regular werewolf—"

I took a deep breath. The words *regular werewolf* always stuck to my tongue.

Damien wasn't like the rest, demonic inside, possessed by blood lust and the need to kill beneath the moon, uncaring of who he hurt or who he killed as long as his belly was full. No, Damien was different, too.

"Well, it might not work on him," I continued. "I need to do more tests. Fiddle with the formula. I'm close. Unfortunately, the compound blowing sky-high is going to slow me down."

"Any clue who was behind that?"

Jessie had inched closer as we spoke. Will, too. The four of them stood in a little cluster, with me on the outside, never one of them, even though we fought for the same thing, worked for and admired the same man.

"None," I answered.

"Had to be werewolves," Leigh murmured. "Unless they're like Damien—and no one else that we know of is—they won't want to be cured. They like to kill."

"But how did they find out what Elise is working on?" Jessie asked. "It's supposed to be top secret."

Leigh rolled her eyes. "Sheesh, McQuade, sometimes I wonder how you walk and chew gum at the same time."

Jessie's eyes narrowed. She took one step toward Leigh and Will grabbed her around the waist and hauled her back.

"Behave," he ordered.

Leigh smirked, and that was all Jessie needed to have her struggling against Will's hold. He lifted her clear off her feet, which was quite an accomplishment considering she was only a few inches shorter than he was.

"Leigh," Damien snapped. "We're supposed to be working together."

He glanced at me and shrugged as if to say "Kids will be kids." Sometimes Jessie and Leigh were worse than two-year-olds fighting over a single piece of candy.

I found it hard to fathom how the two of them could be the best of friends when they were constantly arguing and taking swings at each other. Of course, I'd never had a friend, so who was I to judge?

"Let me go, Slick," Jessie ordered. "I won't kick her ass until later."

Leigh snorted. "As if."

Will set Jessie back on her feet and nuzzled her neck. A soft, goofy smile settled over her lips, and I smiled, too. Jessie and Leigh might be annoying, childish, and sarcastic, but they were also totally, adorably in love with Will and Damien. I couldn't help but envy them.

"Promise?" Will pressed.

"What do you want me to do? Write it in blood?"

"Not today." He let her go. She pushed away from him with a well-placed elbow to his stomach.

"Oof." Will doubled over and Jessie's grin grew.

"Quit playing around," Leigh said. "Does anyone remember our traitor troubles? *Jäger-Suchers* getting killed? Monsters getting away?"

I hadn't forgotten; I'd just pushed that issue to the back of my mind as I dealt with more pressing concerns.

"Since our identities are already on the market," she

continued, "someone might have blabbed what Elise is up to."

"If they aren't aware of it already, they could find out soon enough." All eyes turned to me. "The test subjects in the basement . . . I don't know if they're alive, dead, or booking themselves on the next Jerry Springer."

"Edward said you killed Billy Bailey." Jessie's skepticism was evident in the way her gaze flicked over me from head to toe. "How'd you manage that?"

If I told her I'd ripped out Billy's throat, she'd rip out mine.

"It wasn't easy," I said, and left it at that. "But I never saw the others. They *could* be dead."

"Could be." Jessie contemplated my face. "But I have to say, if you'd kept me in the basement, I'd come after you the first chance that I got."

I met her eyes without flinching. "What's your point?"

I had nothing to be ashamed of. They were werewolves, for crying out loud. I wasn't going to feel sorry for Satan in a fur coat.

"My point? If they didn't head straight for you, I think they're ashes."

"Billy wasn't."

"But he is now. Right?"

I blinked. *Hell.*

"You didn't burn him?" Jessie practically shouted.

"I was fresh out of matches."

"Yet you had a silver bullet?"

Not exactly.

"It doesn't matter," Leigh interjected. "The main

reason we burn the bodies is to get rid of the evidence and avoid questions. Where you left him . . . the scavengers will have a field day. Even if they don't, there's a dead wolf in Montana. Happens."

Leigh was right. Still, I felt like a moron for forgetting standard J-S procedure. That I wasn't a standard J-S agent was no excuse. As second in command I should have known better.

And as second in command I should be made aware of what was going on in Fairhaven. My gaze wandered over the trees. What had they been shooting at when we'd arrived?

I took a step toward the forest, and Damien grabbed my arm. "Not a good idea, Elise, we—"

Damien's power slammed into me; I could taste his heartbeat, feel the virus in his blood. I knew what he was, but then, I'd always known, and because of that I'd never let my skin touch his.

Jerking his hand away, Damien stumbled back. The others stared at us as if we'd both lost our minds.

"Damien?" Leigh reached for him, but he stepped out of her grasp.

"Wait. Give me a second."

I sympathized. Touching another werewolf in human form, when you weren't expecting it, was like sticking your wet finger into a buzzing electrical outlet.

Damien licked his lips, ran a trembling hand over his face, then shook his head.

"You're . . . like me."

10

Jessie drew her .44 a millisecond ahead of Leigh's Glock. They leveled the barrels on my face. A gun for each nostril. How poetic.

I wanted to duck, but I knew them too well. They'd shoot first, say *oops* later.

I don't think Damien meant to give me up. He was in shock.

And why wouldn't he be? Who would guess that the most feared werewolf hunter on the planet kept his very own werewolf close at hand?

Not me, if I hadn't been the werewolf in question.

"Everybody calm down," Will murmured.

I'd always liked him.

"Hold on, Leigh." This was Damien. "She isn't—"

"What?" Leigh's blue eyes narrowed. "Human? We got that."

"No. I mean yes. Hell." He sent me an apologetic glance, then tried to inch between me and the guns. I elbowed him back.

"Ah, ah, ah," Leigh warned. "No sudden moves."

Damien stopped pushing me, and I stepped in front of him, putting myself closer to the weapons. Leigh lifted her brows, and her eyes warmed just a little.

"She's not like the others," Damien continued. "When I said she was like me, I meant it. She's different, too."

"Does Mandenauer know?" Jessie blurted.

"Of course," I said.

"As if we'll believe anything you have to say."

"You're the one who asked. Call Edward. Believe him."

Everyone went silent. They knew as well as I did that if Edward didn't know I was a werewolf before, and he found out now, he'd blow my brains out faster than I could say "Have mercy."

"Call him," Jessie ordered.

Amazingly, Leigh did so without argument. Two minutes later, she disconnected her cell call to Edward.

"Well?" Jessie demanded when Leigh just stared at me.

"He says we should leave her alone."

"He understands she turns furry under the moon?"

"Edward agreed with Damien. She's different, too."

After another moment's hesitation, Jessie put away her gun.

I felt no more at ease without the weapons staring me in the face, probably because four pairs of eyes were.

"Is there somewhere we can talk?" I asked.

I still wore only a T-shirt and sweatpants, and the November night wasn't any warmer in Wisconsin than it had been in Montana. Without my fur, I was freezing.

"We've rented a house next to the cop shop," Leigh said. "We can go there."

"Where did Edward take Nic?"

"Mandenauer has a room over the antiques store," Jessie told me. "I'm sure he feels right at home there."

I peered at the buildings lining the street and knew without being told which was his. Windows at the front, so he could watch the town; I'd bet there were also windows at the back, so he could observe whatever came out of the woods. A second-story room is always the best choice for both offense and defense.

As we continued toward the rental property I was struck by the silence. No dogs barked. Not a baby cried. There wasn't a single light in any of the houses or the businesses.

"Too quiet," I murmured.

Leigh cast a quick glance over her shoulder. The expression on her face caused a shiver of premonition to dance down my spine. I imagined an empty town, a very full forest.

"No one's been bitten," Will said.

"Then—"

"What are we doing here?" Jessie interrupted. "We'll get to that."

We reached a large log house at the end of the street. The porch was a bit rickety, but other than that the place seemed sturdy enough. After digging a key from her jeans, Jessie unlocked the front door, snapped on the lights. We blinked in the electric glare.

Jessie motioned me inside. As I inched past her she

plastered her shoulders to the door, insuring we didn't touch, even by accident. I tried not to let that bother me, but it did. I'd always been lonely, but since no one knew of my affliction but Edward, the cringing in my presence had been kept to a minimum.

We took seats in the small living room, and more staring ensued. Jessie, never a patient woman, was the first to speak. "Talk, Doctor, or I'll make you."

She was getting on my nerves. "I'd like to see you try."

Jessie came to her feet and so did I. Though we were the same height, she probably had ten pounds on me. Nevertheless, I knew who would win a physical fight. If only she didn't have that gun filled with silver.

Will grabbed her hand before she could draw the weapon. Leigh put herself between us, and Damien reached out to halt my mad rush. But right before his hand touched me, he snatched it back.

The movement made me pause, remembering why I'd kept my secret all these years. If Damien couldn't handle what I was, how could I expect anyone to? Especially anyone like Nic.

If I told him the truth, he'd think me insane. If I showed him, he'd find me both hideous and terrifying. Better he hated me for a selfish, unloving bitch than that.

Defeated, I collapsed in my chair. "What do you want to know?"

The others sat. At first no one spoke, then they all spoke at once.

"Who?" Jessie asked.

"When?" That was Damien.

"How?" murmured Will.

Leigh merely said, "Why?"

I looked at her. "Why what?"

"Why haven't you been able to cure yourself?"

Since my antidote had cured Leigh, but not Damien, she'd called and harassed me continuously. She'd often been rude, crude, condescending. I'd put up with it because I understood her smart mouth and habitual snarl were rooted in fear.

If I couldn't cure Damien, no one could.

"It's not for lack of trying," I said.

The room went momentarily silent, until Will broke the ice. "Who bit you?" he clarified. "Where? When?"

"I wasn't bitten."

All four of them glanced at one another, then back at me.

"Maybe you should start at the beginning," Will said.

I took a deep breath and a moment to think. I'd never told anyone my story before.

"When werewolves touch in human form we feel each other's power and the demon that sleeps inside of us." I glanced at Damien. "But I don't have a demon, and neither do you."

"I had one," he murmured. "At first."

Damien had been like all the rest, until he'd run afoul of an Ozark Mountain magic woman. He'd been blessed to lose the demon and cursed to remember all that he'd done while having it.

"You're working for the good guys now," Leigh told him. "You're making up for all that you did."

"I can't make up for that. There isn't enough time on this earth."

Leigh lifted her eyes to mine over the top of his head. I could read her thoughts loud and clear.

Fix him, she begged, as she had a hundred times before.

"Get on with the story, Doc," Jessie urged. "We don't have all night."

My story wouldn't take that long, since it was relatively simple.

"I wasn't bitten," I said. "My mother was."

Damien's head came up. "Lycanthropy isn't hereditary. A werewolf can't breed."

"Can they?" Leigh's voice quavered.

Her concern was understandable. I wouldn't want to have puppies, either.

"No," I assured her, and she visibly relaxed.

"As Edward tells it, my mother was bitten while she was pregnant with me. The shock sent her into early labor."

"But—" Jessie frowned. "I thought the virus was passed through saliva."

"Right."

I didn't elaborate. Within a few seconds, the light dawned on them all.

Jessie and Leigh paled. Hell, so did Will. Only Damien had the strength to articulate the truth. "She was bitten in the stomach?"

I nodded.

"And you?"

"The best I can figure is that the virus entered the

amniotic fluid, infecting me, though I wasn't affected the way most humans are."

"You shifted, but you weren't possessed."

"Pretty much."

"What happened to your mother?" Leigh was staring at me with more sympathy than I'd ever seen in her eyes, except when she was gazing at Damien.

"The change killed her."

Which was true. She'd changed, then Edward had killed her.

The room went silent. At least no one said they were sorry. They'd have been lying. My mother, once bitten, had been doomed.

"What about your father?" Leigh asked.

"My entire family was wiped out by the werewolves that bit my mother."

Leigh's eyes softened for an instant. "Sorry. That's rough."

She should know.

"When did you realize you were different?" Damien asked.

"I was twenty-two."

His eyes widened. "You were normal until then?"

I didn't know how normal I'd been—an orphan, raised by the man who'd killed my mother—but I nodded anyway.

"What caused it?"

"At the time I had no idea."

As if the change had happened yesterday instead of seven years ago, the fear came back, along with the pounding panic, the crushing pain.

"I was in college at Stanford—"

"Nice," Jessie muttered.

"Edward spared no expense."

Both she and Leigh frowned. "Mandenauer paid for your schooling?"

"Edward has paid for everything."

As a child I hadn't known why Edward was caring for me, I'd only been glad that he was. I had no one else.

After I learned the truth, I'd figured he felt guilty about making me an orphan. Recently, I'd come to understand his assistance had been based on suspicion.

He'd wondered what I might become and when. The only reason he hadn't killed me when I changed was because I was different, and that difference had been useful to him.

"I always thought there was something going on between the two of you." Jessie's gaze wandered over me again.

For a second I didn't understand what she meant. When I did, my cheeks flushed, and my fists clenched. "He didn't pay for *me,* if that's what you're insinuating."

"If the name slut fits . . ."

"Gutter brain," I muttered, which only made Leigh snicker.

"Stop it," Will snapped. "Let Elise finish."

Jessie and Leigh didn't appear contrite, but they did shut up.

"The first change came under the wolf moon," I began.

"When the hell is that?"

I should have known Jessie wouldn't be able to shut up completely.

"January," Will said, shooting her a quelling look. "When the wolves howl with hunger in the depths of the winter snows."

"Well, not at Stanford," I allowed, "but it was January. As I'm sure you're all aware, full moons are a busy time."

Just ask any ER physician, maternity floor nurse, psychiatric attendant, or waitress at the nearest twenty-four-hour greasy spoon.

My last semester before medical school—new classes, new books, new challenges—I'd been excited, anxious, and in love.

"Why then?" Damien asked. "Wouldn't the changes of puberty initiate . . . other changes?"

I hadn't considered the notion. But now that I thought about it, Edward had.

The years between twelve and fourteen were the only ones I'd spent with him. He'd been possessed by the desire to live in a castle in his native land. To hell and gone, the middle of nowhere, practically on top of a mountain. While there, I'd had a tutor. A huge hulking bear of a man, who was as frightening as he was smart.

When I'd been sent to Austria three days past my fourteenth birthday, I'd thought I'd done something wrong. What I *had* done was gotten my period and neglected to grow fangs. *Good girl.* Funny how things made sense from a distance of years.

"I'd think if you were gonna go furry," Jessie murmured, "you'd have done it right away. Got an explanation for that, Wonder Doc?"

I was used to a certain amount of respect, if not for the Ph.D. behind my name, then for the advances I'd made in lycanthropy research. Trust Jessie not to give a shit about either one.

"I have a theory."

"Which is about as close as we're going to get to an answer, I'm sure." Jessie sighed. "Get on with it."

"I believe the small amount of virus I received *in utero* lay dormant. When it was activated, there was only enough to cause the change, not enough to . . ."

I wasn't sure how to articulate what happened to a human being when the virus turned them into a monster.

"To strangle your soul," Damien whispered.

Silence settled over us all until I broke it with a simple, "Yes."

"So you're the perfect werewolf?" Leigh prodded. "All the superpowers without the pesky demon?"

"I wouldn't say *perfect*. It's not exactly fun to change."

Or at least it hadn't been until yesterday.

"I remember," Leigh murmured.

When a person is bitten, they experience a kind of collective consciousness. As the virus penetrates their blood, they imagine the coming change, remembering things that have happened to others. They feel the pain, the power, both the terror and the temptation.

"What about the blood lust?" Damien asked. "The love of the kill?"

"The killing sickened me. Not that I didn't do it. I couldn't stop myself."

At my words, both Leigh's and Jessie's fingers crept

toward their guns. I doubted they even knew they were moving, so deeply ingrained was their response to a threat.

"But I can stop myself now."

They froze, then frowned at each other.

"I invented a serum. Under a full moon I'll still change, but I'm not compelled to kill."

Their hands left their weapons.

"I wouldn't mind some of that sauce," Damien murmured.

"I'd be happy to share," I said. "If it hadn't blown up with the compound."

II

"Relax," I ordered before Jessie and Leigh could threaten me again. "I'm not going to flip out and start eating the populace."

At least for another few days.

"You can make more," Damien pressed. "Can't you?"

"Sure."

As soon as Edward handed over the formula.

I'd planned to send Damien some of the serum before the next full moon. The item had been on my to-do list. Along with a whole bunch of other things I couldn't quite remember.

I stood and crossed to the window, peering at the second floor of the antiques store. A light was on inside, but no shadows moved beyond the curtains.

"Maybe I should see if they're okay."

"Why wouldn't they be?"

I turned at Jessie's words. "You've never told me why you came to Fairhaven."

The four of them exchanged glances. I was getting really sick of being on the outside looking in. I should have been used to it by now, but I wasn't.

"What?" I demanded.

"We're not exactly sure," Damien said.

Leigh shushed him, and I shot her a glare. "If the compound wasn't toast, you'd be sending me a report. You never had a problem with that before."

"Before, you weren't one of them."

"I was. You just didn't know it."

Leigh's fingers curled into fists. "I can't believe you let your hair down and run naked in the woods once a month."

"It isn't as if I have a choice." I didn't want to talk about my affliction—with her or anyone else. "Can we move on? What's happening here?"

Silence reigned for several ticks of the clock before Will spread his hands. "People are disappearing."

I wanted to say "Same old, same old," but that wouldn't be helpful, would it?

"Who called Edward?" I asked instead.

"The sheriff."

"Bodies in the woods? Mangled? Eaten?"

"Not this time."

"What, then, this time?"

"People go missing," Leigh chimed in. "There's blood but no bodies."

"We thought the victims were shifting more quickly than usual," Will said. "Maybe some new kind of spell."

"Instant werewolf." Jessie made the motions of a drum roll with her hands. "Presto changeo."

My hand went to the talisman in my pocket. *Uh-oh.* I opened my mouth to explain, and Will jumped in.

"But there hasn't been an increase in the wolf population to account for the vanishing citizens. Damien says there aren't any werewolves here at all, except for him."

"No werewolves?" I glanced at Damien.

He shook his head. "No wolves of any kind."

"There are wolves all over this part of the state."

"Except in Fairhaven," he said.

"The only reason for no wolves in a place like this would be werewolves," I murmured. "They don't like one another."

"Exactly," Damien agreed. "So what does it mean if there's neither one?"

I had no idea, but I doubted it meant anything good.

"No one's seen any wolves," Leigh continued, "but the forest is full of crows."

Crows and wolves work together in nature. Wolves tolerated the birds, even let them feed off their kills. In return, many naturalists believe crows fly ahead of the packs, leading them to prey. The behavior transfers to werewolves. Where there's a lot of one, there's a lot of the other.

My own fascination with the large, black scavengers had begun in childhood. While many people used them for target practice, I'd drawn pictures of crows over and over again. When I got older, I began to collect figurines, paintings, stuffed animals—like the one Nic had found on my desk. *Heckle and Jeckle* had been my favorite cartoon.

No wonder Edward had kept such a close eye on me.

"When I'm out in the woods," Damien murmured. "I sense . . . I'm not sure. It's as if something's coming, or maybe just left. I feel watched even when I'm certain nothing's there."

I'd say he was paranoid, except I'd felt something, too.

"What were you shooting at whén I got here?"

"Shadows," Jessie muttered. "We're all spooked."

Which wasn't like them. Werewolf hunters were the least spookable creatures on earth. They had to be.

She saw my expression, must have read my mind. "I can kill anything I see. But what am I supposed to do when I know it's there, but it isn't?"

I had no answer for that.

"Are you sufficiently brought up to speed, Elise?"

Edward's voice from the doorway made me gasp and spin around. "I hate when you sneak up on me."

That he could was amazing in itself. I had the hearing of a wolf.

I glanced past Edward, searching for Nic, my mind already scrambling for a way to explain our discussion of disappearing bodies. But my boss was alone, and that made me more nervous.

"What did you do with him?"

"Who?"

"You know damn well who!"

His eyes narrowed, and I swallowed the rest of the angry words that threatened to spill off my tongue. They'd get me nowhere.

"Where is Agent Franklin, sir?"

"Where do you think?"

My heart skipped, then lunged into my throat. "You didn't."

"That depends on what you think I did."

"You can't go around killing FBI agents."

He frowned. "Why would I do that?"

"Because your answer to every problem is to shoot it?"

"It has always worked well for me."

I couldn't just stand around while Nic might be dead or dying. I started for the door, and Edward yanked me back. "Relax. He is safe."

He dropped my arm immediately, surreptitiously rubbing his fingers against his black pants. Though I'd been expecting it, Edward's typical reaction to being anywhere near me hurt more than usual.

The only man who had ever touched me gently, willingly, was Nic—and he didn't know what I was. Seeing him again made me long for what I didn't, and couldn't, have.

"By safe you mean—"

"Alive," Edward snapped. "I am not completely senile. Yet."

"*Yet* being the operative word," Jessie muttered.

I tensed, anticipating an explosion of German obscenities. Instead, Edward smirked, winked, and the two of them chuckled. I stifled my childish jealousy. He would never care for me the way he cared for Jessie or Leigh, and I'd better get used to it.

Edward glanced at the Fitzgeralds. "I thought I sent you two . . . elsewhere."

"We wanted to hear the story of why your second in command turns furry every month."

The last flicker of humor fled his eyes as he glanced at me. "You told them everything?"

Not *everything*. There were certain secrets only Edward and I could ever know.

"I told them the basics so they wouldn't shoot me."

"They were ordered to leave you alone." He fixed the others with a glare. "Elise is beyond your reach. She answers only to me."

"La-di-dah," Jessie mumbled. "There isn't a scratch on her."

"But not for lack of trying," Will countered, taking her hand when she would have slugged him.

Edward scowled at Jessie, then Leigh. "You are not to play games with Elise. No physical fighting, do you understand?"

A warm glow began in my chest. Edward was worried about me.

"She could kill you without even trying," he continued, and the glow died.

He was worried about *them*. I should have known.

"Can I talk to you?" Damien jerked his head. "Outside?"

I looked at the others, but they were studiously avoiding my gaze. Except for Edward, who merely rolled his eyes and shrugged.

"Sure."

Damien preceded me onto the porch, where he pondered the sky for several moments. I didn't press. I was just glad to get away from everyone else for a while.

"There's more to your story than you told them," he said at last.

"Isn't there always?"

Our eyes met and a flash of understanding, a tug of camaraderie, passed between us.

"What is Mandenauer to you?" he asked.

I was surprised by the question. "My boss."

Edward was the father I didn't have, the mother, too. Even if he didn't love me, more than likely hated me, he was the only constant I'd ever had in my life.

"How close are you, really?" he murmured.

At first I thought he was asking again about me and Edward. Did everyone believe the old man and I were lovers? Hadn't they seen the way he treated me? Worse than a junior agent. Then I studied Damien's face and understood he meant something else entirely.

"To an antidote?"

I didn't wait for his answer. This was why he'd asked me outside. He didn't want Leigh to know if I was further away from a cure than they thought.

"I haven't discovered anything new," I admitted.

Dismay filled his eyes, and I touched him before I thought not to. Power blazed—bright, blinding, painful. I snatched my hand away.

"We're going to have to watch that," I said. "It *hurts*."

I'd never touched any of my test subjects skin to skin. I couldn't afford to have them know what I was. But there'd been other times, other places, where I *had* touched a werewolf in human form. They hadn't lived to see another moon, or blow my cover, but my secret was safe with Damien.

"I will find a cure," I promised. "Count on it."

"I feel better knowing . . ." His voice drifted off.

"That I have a personal interest?"

Damien nodded.

No one could desire a cure more than me—not even Damien. Leigh loved him despite what he was. I didn't have that luxury. No one loved me, and while I was like this, no one would.

"I never doubted you weren't working as hard as you could," Damien said.

"But I did."

Neither one of us jumped at the sound of Leigh's voice. I'd heard her coming, and so had Damien. She wasn't as sneaky as Edward. Not yet.

"Leigh—" Damien began.

"Let me talk." She moved onto the porch and stood between us. "I never trusted you, Doctor, and now I know why. Werewolves murdered my family. I don't like them."

"Yet you're married to one."

Her eyes flashed, and her fingers curled into fists. "We can't help who we love."

"I know."

Leigh cast me a quick glance, and her fingers relaxed. I understood her dilemma. She both loved Damien and hated his curse. She wanted him cured, needed him to be, and she had to depend on someone she distrusted to do it. Whoever said life was fair?

"She saved you, Leigh. Show a little gratitude."

"I thanked her. What do you want?" Leigh tilted her head in my direction. "A hug?"

"I'll pass."

I'd never been big on physical contact. Never knew when a simple touch, like Damien's, could give me a blistering headache.

My gaze was drawn to the throbbing pulse at the base of Leigh's neck—or an intense desire for red meat.

I might be able to control my craving for human blood through medication, but that didn't mean I wasn't blindsided by a longing for it at the oddest moments.

Leigh didn't trust me? Hell, I didn't trust myself.

"Just so we're clear," she continued. "I want you to quit dicking around and fix him. That's what you're paid for."

"Leigh—" Damien sounded exasperated.

"I'd get more done if you weren't bugging me," I interrupted. "Don't you have someone to kill?"

"Always."

"Have a nice trip."

A modicum of respect flickered in her eyes before she took Damien's hand. "We'll be in Washington."

"D.C.?"

Which reminded me of Nic. The Fury remained parked in front of the tavern. Where was he?

"Washington *State*," Leigh answered.

"What's there?"

"Trees. Wolves. Dead people. There's been a significant increase in werewolf activity pretty much everywhere over the past few days. Edward's cell phone's ringing like crazy. Drove him bat shit when he couldn't get hold of you."

"Strange that there's so much action when the moon isn't even full," I murmured.

"They're up to something," Leigh said, "but then, they always are."

With a nod that passed for both agreement and good-bye, Leigh headed for the car, stopping at the bottom of the porch steps when Damien didn't follow.

"I'll be right there," he said.

With one more glare for me, Leigh climbed into the passenger seat.

"I was thinking," Damien continued. "Maybe the werewolves are after more than Mandenauer. If they want you or the information you've gathered, they'll be back as soon as they know blowing up the compound didn't do them any good."

I considered the silver bullet that had nearly hit me in the head. "I think they already know."

"Where's your research now?"

"Edward has it."

Damien shot a quick, concerned glance at the cabin. *Hell.*

What if someone killed Edward before he could tell me where the information was? The thought sent a shiver from my head down to my toes.

I was surprised they hadn't tried already, though Edward wasn't easy to eliminate, and the werewolves, despite their pack nature, weren't exactly organized. Unlike real wolves, they didn't take orders well. There was always a new alpha fighting to be in charge, if not of a certain pack, then the world.

Thus far they'd never joined together with any success. If they did, we might be in serious trouble.

And wouldn't killing my boss, then putting an end to a cure for lycanthropy be a good way for an up-and-coming leader to gain everyone's loyalty?

I didn't like the direction of my thoughts. I had to find Edward and quick.

"Be careful," Damien said.

Instead of shaking his hand—we both knew what a mistake that would be—I murmured, "You, too," before slipping into the house.

12

"I don't care if she is a scientist."

I heard Jessie's voice as if she were speaking in my ear and not whispering in the next room.

"She's also a freaking werewolf," she continued. "Who knows what might tempt her to the dark side? Remember Zee?"

Jessie had once been betrayed by her closest friend, I couldn't expect her to have faith in me.

Still, it stung to realize I held no one's trust. Nobody wanted me here. Except maybe Damien, and he had just left.

I waited for Edward to tell Jessie, again, to leave me alone. He'd be doing so to protect his own interests, but that protection was the only nicety I got from him.

Instead, Will's voice drifted through the house. "Forget about Zee."

"I can't." Jessie's sigh was heavy with regret. "Killing your best friend, even when she is a wolf god, is something you don't put behind you in a few months."

"You can try."

Silence descended, broken only by moist, smacking sounds. They were making out. Which meant . . .

Edward wasn't even here.

I slammed out the front door and sprinted across the street. The antiques shop was locked, no shit. So I hurried to the alley, then around the back, where a wooden staircase led to the second floor.

Seconds later, I knocked. No one answered, though I could have sworn I heard a muffled sound from inside.

My hand tested the brass knob. Locked. Not much of a challenge for me. I turned it, hard, and something went *crunch*. I stepped into an empty apartment.

Edward's space consisted of a living area with a bed, kitchen table, and sink all in one room. Three doors were placed at intervals opposite the entrance. One led to a bathroom, the second held the furnace and an ironing board, the third held Nic.

All tied up and nowhere to go.

He scowled at me from behind a strip of gaff tape. Edward had bound his hands into the prayer position, making it impossible for Nic to open the door and escape the closet, even if he could walk with his feet anchored sole to sole.

"What did you say to him?" I demanded.

Must have been something really annoying to warrant this treatment.

Nic started talking, but with tape over his mouth, he was a little hard to understand. Leaning over, I ripped it free with a single yank.

"Hell. Shit. Damn! That hurt!"

"One quick yank always works best."

"How about we test that theory on *your* mouth?"

"No, thanks. Where's Edward?"

"He was going to call my boss. As if that'll change anything."

I crossed to the window and gazed at the still and silent street. Edward hadn't been at the cabin; he wasn't here; his car remained below.

A figure several buildings away caught my eye. Long and gaunt—that had to be him. He must have gone outside for better cell service. If I wanted to cut Nic loose, I'd better do it quickly.

I found a knife in a drawer next to the sink and sawed at the bindings on Nic's hands. The knife was dull; this could take more time than I had. If I distracted him, I could rip the tape with my bare hands.

"How did he convince you to step into the closet and let him tie you up?" I asked.

"Very funny. He said he wanted to talk to me, then rapped me on the head."

While Nic spoke, I severed the tape with one yank, then paused to peer into his eyes. Two injuries in such a short period couldn't be good. And if you added how I'd knocked him into a wall when I first saw him again—

"You sick to your stomach?" I demanded. "Dizzy?"

"Just finish. There's no telling what he's got planned for me next."

I wanted to argue, to say Edward wouldn't hurt him, but that wasn't true. Edward might do anything.

"Mandenauer's flipped his lid," he muttered.

"This is pretty much his usual lid." Glancing up,

I caught Nic's incredulous expression. "I warned you. He's not a man you want to screw with."

I tugged and the binding around Nic's feet came apart with a sharp split. Before I could get up, he grabbed me by the shoulders and gave me a single, rough shake. "We have to leave right away."

I laughed.

"I'm not kidding, Elise. He's nuts. What's with all the guns and ammo? And the other agents—don't they strike you as a little over the top? I feel like I've stepped into a lost episode of *Buffy the Vampire Slayer.*"

Little did he know how close to the truth he was.

"What were they shooting at when we got here?"

The lies came so damn easy, I didn't even have to think about them anymore before they fell out of my mouth.

"Remember the new strain of rabies I was telling you about?"

"Uh-huh."

"The virus needs to be eradicated before it spreads."

"So there were five agents with guns in the woods blasting infected wolves?"

I stared him straight in the eye. "Yes."

His fingers tightened on my shoulders. "I don't believe you."

I kissed him. Maybe he'd believe that, because it was the only real thing I could give. Not the truth about the *Jäger-Suchers,* Edward, the others, or even myself. But I could touch my lips to his, sweep my tongue inside, murmur, moan, and mean all of it.

He pulled me closer; I dropped the knife. I ended up

in his lap, arms around his neck. So what if we were on the floor of an empty closet, in a rented room, in a town I'd never heard of before yesterday? We were together again, and Nic was making me feel things I hadn't felt since the last time I'd touched him.

I tasted tape on his lips, mint on his tongue. My fingers brushed the back of his neck, missing the longer length of his hair. I'd always loved tangling my hands in the silky strands, but he'd shorn them off and only a dark, short thatch remained. The difference in his hair brought back the difference in me.

Ruthlessly I shoved aside the memory, my fears. I needed this, needed him, as much as I needed Nic to stop asking the questions that could get both of us killed.

He tried to pull away, but I nipped his lip and shifted in his lap, my rear end rolling over his erection. Swallowing his gasp, both pain and arousal, I coaxed his tongue into my mouth and suckled.

His palm lay against my stomach, and when I drew on his tongue, his fingers flexed. The muscles beneath my skin fluttered, and he traced them with his thumb, lower and lower, until his entire hand crept under the waistband of my sweatpants.

I wore no underwear, no bra—neither one had been available for purchase at the gas station. He stroked the underside of my breasts, the swell of my rear, his thumb rode the curve of my hip. I had to get closer, so I swung my leg over his and scooted in.

His zipper bulged, and that couldn't be comfortable. He didn't seem to mind. I considered opening his pants and running my tongue along his length, but I gave up the idea when he arched and hard met soft so perfectly I couldn't put a stop to it even to have his heat in my mouth.

Years had passed since I'd been touched in any way but casual or violent. The only men I'd seen besides Edward were other *Jäger-Suchers* and guards, who'd been threatened with dire consequences should they look at me crosswise.

Oh, and the demonic entities who wanted to fuck me for no other reason than that I was there.

I shuddered at the memory of Billy, and Nic pulled me closer, murmuring nonsensical encouragement. He thought I was coming, and I was close.

His palms slid under my T-shirt, across my back, then up to cup my breasts. The firm, solid length of him ground against me, and I tightened my thighs around his hips.

In an effort to pull me nearer, he grabbed my waist, and his hand closed over the pocket that held the talisman. Trapped between me and him, the thing purred.

"Mmm," Nick answered against my lips.

I didn't have the heart to tell him the murmur of appreciation hadn't been mine.

His skin was warm; he smelled so alive. A vein pulsed and I captured his flesh between my teeth. Blood flowed beneath the surface, calling me.

His palm still covered the talisman, and when his fingers clenched, heat coursed between us like an electric current.

The moon erupted behind my closed eyelids—stark and potent, both agony and ecstasy. Cool silver in the midst of summer, warm and golden in the depths of winter. Power rushed through me. I believed I could do anything, save anyone, become . . .

Nic stiffened, pulsing as he whispered my name. The sound, the sensation brought me around. What the hell had happened?

I opened my eyes. Nic stared back, nothing but curiosity in his. I couldn't have done anything too weird, too wolfy, or he'd be wary.

My gaze was drawn to his pulse. I could still taste his skin, smell it, too. I wanted to bury my face in the curve of his neck and hold on to him forever.

"Did you feel anything move?"

I hadn't meant to voice the question, but when I did, Nic flexed his hips. "Oh, yeah. You were moving."

My face flushed. I dropped my hand to my pocket, but the plastic was just plastic again. No heat. Not a shimmy or a sound.

Had I imagined everything? No. Nic had heard the talisman purr, just as I had. However, I didn't know what that meant. I needed to show the icon to Will and soon.

I tried to stand; Nic tightened his hold. "I don't think so."

He covered my fingers with his and I tensed, but nothing leaped but my heart.

"You can attack me in a closet any day or night." Nic leaned forward and brushed his mouth against mine. "But I'm a big boy now. I'd rather do this naked, in a bed, anywhere but here."

His tongue flicked out. The sensation was a lightning strike, bringing back all we'd just shared, making me long for things we hadn't. I wanted Nic to use his teeth on me, along with several other body parts. Goose bumps raced over my skin and I murmured, "Okay."

Nic lifted his head. "Okay?"

I tried to remember what he'd asked, what I'd agreed to. "I meant . . . sorry."

"Sorry?"

"I can't."

Again, I tried to get off him. Again, he wouldn't let me.

"I think you *can*. You just don't want to."

Oh, I wanted to. More than I should. Which was what disturbed me. Certainly I was attracted to Nic, but I shouldn't have to fight the urge to tear off his clothes every time he touched me. Should I?

Only one way to find out.

"Nic," I breathed and hugged him.

Startled, distracted, still aroused, and, let's face it, a guy, he dropped the questions to hug me back. I tossed the talisman into the corner and kissed him.

He tasted the same, sticky plus mint. His hands roved under my shirt, over my skin. Pressing my body closer, I opened my mind.

13

No moon, no trees, just us. I still wanted to rip off Nic's clothes, but his throat was safe.

I'd kissed him as a test: Was the talisman making me lust after him beyond reason? Since the plastic was in the corner and not on me, I had to conclude the answer was no.

However, it was doing *something* funky.

"Why did you not tell me that he is the man who made you what you are?"

My tongue still inside Nic's mouth, I froze. Slowly, I took it back, lifted my head, shoved my snarled hair out of my face, and sighed. This time when I climbed off Nic's lap, he let me.

I faced Edward. Jessie and Will stood just inside the apartment doorway.

"Hell," I muttered.

Will appeared embarrassed. I know I was. Jessie seemed amused. I didn't find any of this funny.

Nic got to his feet. "What's he talking about?"

Edward lifted a slightly yellowed brow in my direction. I scowled. He'd better not tell the truth.

Since the best defense is always a good offense—I was taught that by the master in front of me—I went on the attack.

"What were you thinking to tie him up and shove him in a closet?"

Jessie's eyes widened; so did Will's.

"He annoyed me."

"Half the known world annoys you."

"Three quarters," he corrected and sniffed.

"Sir," Nic began.

I stomped on his foot. "Let me handle this."

"You were handling him," Edward accused. "What were *you* thinking?"

I'd been thinking I needed someone—Nic—and something—sex—but I couldn't share that with Edward.

His gaze shifted past me to Nic. "You have been recalled to Washington."

"What?"

"Your work here is done. Get out."

"Pardon me if I don't take your word for it."

Edward's eyes flashed. He threw his cell phone at Nic. I ducked before it hit me between the eyes. The contraption bounced off Nic's chest and clattered to the floor.

"Call your superior," Edward sneered. "I did."

Nic retrieved the phone and dialed, then moved to the window so he could hear. Jessie and Will came closer.

"He is the one, isn't he?" Edward demanded.

A chill wind seemed to swirl about the room. My skin, warm with arousal, went tingly with gooseflesh. I knew what he was asking; nevertheless I said, "The one?"

"I am not foolish, Elise. I ran a check on him. He graduated from Stanford—not long after you left."

"Interesting," Jessie said. "You told us you changed, but you never said what set you off." She let her gaze wander over Nic's back. "Sex just might do it."

"I never—" I ended the sentence before it left my mouth, nevertheless everyone knew what I meant.

Will coughed and stared at his feet. Jessie smirked. "Never, huh? No wonder you're so cranky."

"I am not!"

"If sex didn't change you, what did?" she asked.

"Love."

At least her smirk died. She and Will exchanged glances. The one he turned on me was full of pity. I hated that.

When a human being falls in love, variations in body chemistry aren't far behind. I believed those changes were the reason I'd transformed at twenty-two.

However, my case didn't apply to the everyday werewolf, which changed after being bitten. We weren't the same, and therefore what had happened to me hadn't been of much use in my research. All that pain for so little gain.

"Now you know," I whispered furiously, after glancing over my shoulder at Nic, who was speaking with equal fervency into the cell phone. "I fell in love, turned furry, and—"

My voice broke and I couldn't finish. Of course Edward had no such problem. "She came back to Montana where she belonged."

"You couldn't tell him—" Jessie began.

"Right. Would you want to live with a werewolf?"

Jessie's and Will's eyes met again. "Maybe."

There'd been a bit of confusion during the fiasco with the wolf god—who was human, who was not? Jessie had, for a time, believed Will was one of them. It hadn't stopped her from sleeping with him.

Will reached out and touched her cheek.

"Spare us," Edward muttered.

Jessie shot him a glare. "Leigh and Damien are fine."

"If you say so."

I had to agree with Edward. Leigh and Damien were in love, but they were far from fine. Damien lived every day, every night, with the memory of all he had done. Leigh ached for children, and she wouldn't get them from him.

"I left Nic," I continued, "and he never knew why. He hates me."

"Yeah, looked that way from where I was standing," Jessie muttered.

I narrowed my eyes, but she just laughed.

"Elise." Edward beckoned with one long, bony index finger. I joined him near the kitchen table. "Do you know why he is here?"

"Missing persons." I shrugged. "Anonymous tip. Someone's trying to cause trouble, and we know who that someone is."

"This is a little more serious than that. You didn't recognize the names?"

"I didn't get a chance to read them before I lost the list."

Edward's sigh was filled with both disgust and impatience.

"Compound exploding, Billy attacking—I was a little *busy*."

"You should have killed him while you had the chance. Must I do everything myself?"

"I'm not going to let you hurt him."

The two of us stared into each other's eyes until Nic stalked across the room and tossed the cell phone at Edward with more force than necessary.

"Whatever you said, whoever you know, you've got them scared. I've been ordered back to D.C."

"Good-bye," Edward replied.

"But you don't scare me. I'm not leaving."

For the first time I could remember, Edward was surprised into silence.

"I have vacation time. I'm taking it. This town appears . . . relaxing."

"Jessie," Edward snapped. "Get rid of him."

"No!" I shouted, and everyone jumped.

Edward shot a glare in my direction before returning his attention to Jessie. "Make sure he leaves town. Put him on a plane yourself, if you must."

"She can't force me to go," Nic said.

Jessie drew her gun and pointed it at his crotch.

"Okay. She can."

Nic's gaze met mine, and the years fell away. I had

a future, with him. There weren't any monsters. Death didn't wait around every corner.

Then he spoke and the fantasy disappeared. "Come with me. You don't need him."

Except I did. Edward would make certain I got a job nowhere. Without the serum, I'd be eating the populace within a week.

Since my secret no longer appeared safe—Lord knows who or what was hunting me already—alone, out in the world, I'd die, and so would anyone who got too close. Failing that, I'd kill and then I'd be killed. My choices were mighty slim.

I couldn't bring all that down on Nic. He had no idea what was out there—hell, he had no idea what was in here—and I had to keep it that way.

Edward leaned over, whispering so that only I could hear, "He knows the names of the people you've killed, Elise."

My heart seemed to stop. Time slowed. The whole world faded until it was only me and Nic and the elephant in the room.

There was more about me to keep secret than my tendency to howl at the moon. Edward, being Edward, was not a wasteful man. I was the perfect werewolf, danger without the demon. I was useful for a lot more than research. There were monsters out there that even Edward couldn't kill. But I could, and I had.

So why was I hesitating? Did I want Nic to discover that the murderer he was searching for was me? I'd rather be dead.

Still, despite the dangers, the problems, the reality

of my life, I wanted to go with Nic more than I'd wanted anything for a long, long time.

I've heard that first love is imprinted on our hearts. Even if we move on to love others, have children with them, live our lives, our first love is always there. We never forget.

What's felt then, with that one person, carries a gilded sheen—both the best and the worst of times— often never to be repeated with such intensity again. For me this was even more true, because there'd never been anyone else.

But what did Nic feel? He wanted me, certainly. However, he hadn't mentioned love. Even if he did care, could his love survive both my curse and my crimes? I doubted it.

Once we'd whispered of a life together: marriage, careers, children. That dream was as impossible now as it had been then. Even if I found a cure, did I dare bring a child into this world knowing what I did about it? The end of the werewolves wouldn't mean the end of evil. Evil lived everywhere, for always.

A child would be helpless, innocent. What if he or she had to pay for the sins I'd committed? Barring that, what if someday, someone told him or her all about me?

I forced myself to speak past the longing, through the fear. "I can't."

"You heard her, G-man." Jessie motioned toward the door with her gun. "Let's go."

With a sound of disgust that dug into my heart, Nic preceded Jessie out of the apartment.

Nic never looked back.

One glare from Edward, and Will slipped onto the porch, then started fiddling with the door I'd busted.

"He thinks those people are missing," Edward said. "Without the bodies, he'll never be able to prove otherwise."

"Well, that sets my mind at ease."

Edward's lips tightened. "This is not a matter for amusement, Elise."

"Am I laughing? He's the last person on earth I'd ever want to possess a list of my sins. And why does he? You're supposed to cover things up."

"I thought I had," Edward murmured.

"The question remains: Who sent him?"

"We know who sent him."

"The monsters? Most likely. They want us distracted."

"I'm distracted all right."

He flicked me an impatient glance. "You are certain he never knew what happened at Stanford?"

I thought back seven years: the joy of first love, turned to pain, then confusion, the agony of the change. I'd been alone and frightened.

I'd awoken naked and bloody in my own room. I remembered what had happened and whom I'd killed. I had not gone anywhere near Nic. If he'd seen me running wildly across the campus, he wouldn't have recognized me. No one could have.

From my apartment, I'd called Edward, then hidden until he'd arrived and spirited me away, leaving experts behind to clean up my mess.

I'd been quarantined for the next several months. An

army of doctors, psychiatrists, and therapists had poked, prodded, and questioned me.

I was different, but no one knew why, so I'd been given a choice: work for the *Jäger-Suchers* or eat a silver bullet. It was a harder choice than one might think.

Following the loss of Nic and the death of the future we'd planned together, I hadn't wanted to live. Yet I'd also felt a sense of responsibility. I wanted to atone for what I'd done. I could do that by finding a cure for the virus.

"Elise?"

I blinked. Edward still waited for me to answer his question. Will still stood on the porch. And Nic was gone from my life forever all over again.

"No," I said, firmly. "Nic knew nothing then, and he knows nothing now."

"You are certain?"

"Why don't you tell me? Your goons came to Stanford. What did they find?"

For an instant I thought Edward might turn on his booted heel and leave without an answer, but he didn't.

"No one saw a wolf. Or at least no one left alive."

Edward would never let me forget what I'd done. As if I could.

"I still don't understand why you kept me in the dark until you had no choice but to tell the truth," I murmured.

"You wanted to spend your life worrying about what you might or might not become? You wanted to know that whenever I was near you I kept a silver bullet in my pocket with your name on it?"

"No, sir. I could have done without knowing that, even now."

"What *I* do not understand is how those names were connected."

"They're connected by me," I said.

"We know that, but how would anyone else?"

"I suspect if we discover how, we'll discover who—and then we'll have our traitor."

Edward's fingers curled into fists. He had been in charge of the *Jäger-Suchers* for over fifty years, and no one had ever betrayed him before. I wouldn't want to be the one who was betraying him now.

He stalked to the door. "Are they gone?"

Will jumped. "Yes."

"I think it is best if I follow and make certain the FBI agent does as Jessie says."

"She can handle herself."

"She can." Edward glanced at me. "But I need some air."

He clattered down the steps. Seconds later, his beloved black Cadillac roared to life.

"Hey." Will stepped into the apartment. "You okay?"

Not really, but since there was nothing he could do to help, I nodded.

"Mandenauer can be . . ." He seemed to struggle for an appropriate word. "Unpleasant."

"I just thought he was mean."

"He has good reason to be."

I knew that as well as anyone. I should cut Edward some slack; he'd had a rough life.

"He can hardly stand to look at me," I murmured. "He never could, because he always knew."

As a child I hadn't understood why Edward couldn't wait to be rid of me. His neglect had not only hurt but fashioned me into a people pleaser. I'd been teacher's pet, top of my class, everyone's darling. Except his.

"If it's any consolation, Mandenauer never liked me much, either."

I glanced at Will. "What's not to like?"

"Thanks." His smile charmed me. "I take Jessie's attention away from her job. Drives him crazy."

"He's just jealous because he has no one."

Hell, so was I.

"There's never been anyone for him?" Will asked.

"Maybe long ago, before the werewolves."

"There have always been werewolves, Elise."

True enough. My training to become a *Jäger-Sucher,* combined with an intense curiosity about where I'd come from, where I might be going, had caused me to read everything I could find on the subject.

The earliest likeness of a man-wolf was discovered on a cave wall. Many historians believe the first written account of a werewolf can be found in the Book of Daniel, when King Nebuchadnezzar exhibited symptoms of werewolfism for four years.

Tales of lycanthropy abound in Greek and Roman myth, throughout the Middle Ages, and into present times. Sure, most experts insist superstition and psychosis have led to such stories, but we know differently.

The most recent rash of monsters came about because of the Nazis. Who else but Hitler and his pals would be insane enough to manufacture a werewolf army?

Edward had been a spy during World War Two. His mission had been to search out and destroy whatever

Josef Mengele—the doctor who had performed thousands of experiments on the Jews, the Gypsies, and anyone else Hitler disliked—had created in a secret lab in the Black Forest. However, Mengele had released the monsters he'd made into the world before Edward could stop him. My boss had been following his original set of orders ever since.

"You think Mandenauer was married before the war?" Will pressed.

"I don't know. Once, when he was ill . . ." My voice drifted off.

About a month ago, Edward had returned to the compound and secreted himself in his quarters. After a day of silence, I'd pounded on the door. When he didn't answer, I'd yanked it from the hinges.

Edward had been delirious. At first I feared he was bitten, but I couldn't find a single mark.

Turned out he'd had nothing more than a flu virus, hazardous to an old man, but not as hazardous as what he might have had.

I glanced at Will, who was waiting for me to finish, but I discovered I couldn't. When Edward had been sick, I'd taken care of him, and he'd rambled, mostly in German, words I didn't understand, but he'd also said a name.

Maria.

I'd never heard his voice that soft, that tender. I could tell that he had loved her, but who she'd been, where she'd gone, remained a mystery.

One I couldn't share with Will or anyone else. I was Edward's second in command, and though he loathed me with an intensity that made me both sad and furious,

I didn't take my responsibilities lightly. His secrets were as safe with me as mine were with him.

"Never mind," Will said, seeming to understand my hesitation. "You have a suitcase I can bring in from the car?"

"Not anymore."

"Oh, yeah. Sorry."

"An excuse to buy a whole new wardrobe. Although I doubt I'll buy one here."

"Probably not. Fairhaven is a blip on the map. No lake nearby, no tourist trade. Even before the disappearances, the place was dying for years."

"So who lives in a place like this?"

"Folks who want a lot of alone time." Will shrugged. "The highway used to lead to vacation spots on Lake Superior. Fairhaven is a little over halfway between there and Milwaukee, so people stopped for a meal, a stretch, to shop, some even stayed the night. Then they built a brand-new four-lane expressway, which bypassed the town."

"Sudden death."

"Exactly. A lot of people left. Some stayed." He stared at me for a minute. "I bet you could fit into some of Jessie's clothes."

My brain scurried to catch up with the sudden shift in subject. "No, thanks."

Jessie didn't seem like the kind of girl who liked to share.

"You could order some things off the Internet. Have them delivered by express mail."

The idea was more than appealing. Walking around in a thin T-shirt with no bra, not to mention the lack of underwear, was not very comfortable. I could also use a coat that didn't sprout from my pores under the light of the moon.

"You can use my computer." Will started for the door, turning back, curiously, when I ducked into the closet.

At first I didn't see the talisman and I panicked. Could the icon walk off or just plain disappear? Why not, when it moved and mumbled all on its own?

I caught a glint in the far corner and snatched the totem from the floor. "I want you to see this."

I held the tiny wolf between my thumb and forefinger. Will came closer, frowned and pulled his glasses from his pocket. He studied the icon for several ticks of the clock, then lifted his gaze to my face. "Yours?"

I shrugged. "Finders keepers."

"You didn't have it made?"

"No." I tilted my head. "Why?"

His frown deepened, carving lines across his forehead and around his mouth. "Haven't you noticed that this talisman looks an awful lot like you?"

14

When I was a wolf, I wasn't completely white. More golden. Blond with blue eyes in both forms. However, the resemblance was there

"The icon isn't mine," I repeated.

"Odd." Will continued to peer at the plastic and frown. "Talismans are representations of spirit guides. Ojibwe folklore says that those of a particular clan are descended from that clan's animal."

I recalled the information from Jessie's report on the wolf god. According to Native American legend there were several totemic divisions: bear, eagle, moose, wolf, and so on. In the old days, each clan had a specialized task. While one governed, another made war. Members could not marry within their own clan—the ancestral link to the animal or bird made their blood too similar.

"In that case," Will continued, "I'd be descended from a wolf."

"No wonder Edward doesn't like you," I said.

"Didn't go over too well when he heard it, that's for sure."

"What happened?" I asked, though I had a pretty good idea.

Will tilted his head, and his golden earring swung free. "He shot me with silver."

"No ill effects?"

"I didn't explode."

Will rolled up the sleeve of his T-shirt. A bullet-shaped scar marred the smooth cinnamon skin of his upper arm.

"Sorry about that," I said.

"You didn't do it." He let the material fall back into place. "Besides, chicks dig scars, don't they?"

"You better hope not, unless you want a high body count when Jessie gets hold of them."

Will laughed. "She's something else."

"Yeah, but what?"

He considered me for a moment with a bemused expression. "You two are a lot alike."

"Me and Jessie? I don't think so."

I was like no one I'd ever encountered, but that was beside the point. Jessie and I were as different as day and night, new moon and full, human and were-wolf.

I slanted the icon until the light caught the jeweled eyes and sparkled. "What's your opinion?"

"Not sure. Usually, totems are made of stone, bone, something of the earth."

"And this is plastic."

"Which would make me think it's nothing more than a child's toy, sold in tourist shops to folks from away. There isn't an Ojibwe alive who would create a spiritual symbol from plastic."

"Except?"

His gaze lifted from the wolf to my face. "Except this appears to have been made to represent a specific wolf. You."

"Voodoo?"

"Voodoo is an amalgamation of ancient African tribal symbols and the Catholicism the slaves were baptized into upon their arrival. This totem, however weird, is Ojibwe. But the only time I've seen talismans that simulate something more specific than a generic clan animal is when they're shamanic."

"English, please."

"Shamans use talismans to aid them in assuming the form of their spirit animal. To do that, they often construct a totem to resemble themselves in some way: hair color, eyes, distinctive facial feature."

"I'm not a shaman."

"Technically, anyone with the right stuff can transform."

"The right stuff being . . . ?"

"Mystical connection to an animal."

"Got that," I said dryly.

"A shamanic totem."

I jiggled the wolf like a tiny martini shaker. "And?"

"A sacrifice to imbue the totem with power."

My hand froze mid-shake. "What kind of sacrifice?"

"Blood, death."

I thought of the flayed rabbit and muttered, "Hell."

Will's gaze shot to mine. "What?"

Quickly, I told him exactly where I'd found the icon, then I told him the rest. About the totem shifting, spilling silver light into my mind, and the instantaneous change.

"Bam, you're a wolf?" he asked.

"Pretty much. You think that's what's been happening in Fairhaven?"

He blinked, frowned, considered the tiny wolf again, then shook his head. "They'd have to fashion talismans that represent a particular person. Seems like too much hassle. And really, what's the rush?"

Once bitten, the victim would shift within twenty-four hours—rain or shine, sunshine or shadow, full moon or new. Even the dead would rise. They'd heal, then run and kill as a wolf. The first time, the moon didn't matter.

"Besides, we'd have found tiny totems strewn all over the place. Once you're a wolf, no pockets."

My lips curved at the similarity in our thought processes. "So what's going on?"

"With you or with Fairhaven?"

I shrugged. "Pick a mystery."

"There hasn't been a disappearance since we arrived. My theory is that whatever the werewolves were up to in Fairhaven, they're done and they've moved on."

"Or they saw Edward—"

"And they moved on." Will nodded. "I would. According to Jessie, we'll have to leave soon, as well. There are werewolves busting out all over the country."

"What about the mystery of me?"

Will pointed at the icon. "If that was left for you,

and I have to think it was, what did they hope to accomplish?"

"Why do shamans transform?" I asked. "What do they gain from the process?"

"Becoming one with their spirit animal gives them the power to complete a quest."

"What kind of quest?"

"A journey, knowledge. Whatever is most important to them."

"The cure," I murmured.

"Maybe." His forehead creased in thought. "But if they meant to help you, why not just hand you the thing?"

"Yeah, why not?"

"The place blew up," he said slowly, "and then you found the talisman?"

"Right."

"Were they trying to kill you or not? I can't decide."

"Join the club."

He ignored my attempt at humor. Jessie was no doubt a whole lot funnier than I was.

"If they meant for you to die, then the icon being where it was didn't have anything to do with you."

"Okay."

"But—" He broke off, and his dark eyes met mine again. "If they wanted you dead, then why the talisman that resembles you in wolf form? Coincidence?"

"I don't think so."

"Me, neither." Will appeared as stumped as I was.

"How did you manage to be outside when the place went up in flames?"

"The test wolves went ballistic. Howling, snarling,

hiding, then attacking. They were behaving as if—"
My eyes met Will's. "They were trapped by an enemy."

"But which enemy?"

I spread my hands wide. There were so many to choose from.

"I guess if we knew that," Will continued, "we'd know who blew up the compound and maybe even why."

"It's never that easy."

"Never." Will indicated the totem with a flick of one finger. "May I?"

I hesitated. If the totem had turned me into a wolf— *wham*—who knew what it might do to Will? Then again, who better to find out?

In the end, he snatched the thing from my hand and nothing happened. But this icon didn't look like him.

Will studied the tiny wolf with a single-mindedness I admired. "You've told me everything?"

There was one thing I hadn't, one thing that disturbed me more than the rest.

Will's gaze flicked to mine. The seriousness in his dark eyes seemed magnified by the wire-rimmed glasses. "You can trust me."

Edward always preached: *Trust no one. Ever.*

Of course Edward led a life of paranoia. He had good reason to.

I'd lived so long inside a stone compound, I wasn't sure whom to trust. But if I was going to put my faith in anyone, especially with information on the totem, Will would be the one.

"My hand changed," I blurted.

"How?"

I made hooks of my fingers and growled.

"You were able to transform one body part and nothing else?"

"Yes."

"I've never heard of a werewolf being able to do that before." Will offered the talisman. "Show me."

I stared at the tacky white wolf for more than a minute before I took it. Closing my eyes, I thought of the moon. I waited for the icon to heat, shift, maybe whine. What I got was—

"Nothing." I opened my eyes. "You think I'm crazy?"

Will contemplated me without any expression at all. "I think it's daytime."

15

I glanced at the window to discover dawn had just broken.

"Duh," I muttered.

Will continued to study my face. "There's someone you should meet. Her name's Cora Kopway. She's very old. Very wise. A member of the *Midewiwin*."

At my blank expression, he elaborated. "Grand Medicine Society. Once, it was a secret religious fellowship devoted to healing through knowledge of the other world. Cora has spent her life studying ancient texts and conversing with the spirits in her visions."

For most people, meeting with a woman who received information from the dead would seem strange. But once you turned furry every full moon, strange takes on a whole new meaning.

"If anyone can tell us about the totem," Will continued, "Cora can."

The sound of a car on the street below drew Will to the door. "Jessie's back."

I glanced at my watch with a frown. She hadn't been gone all that long.

"Edward?" I asked.

"Not with her. Neither is Nic."

Even though I hadn't expected him to be, disappointment sparked.

"Let's tell her what you told me."

I followed Will down the stairs and across the alley. As soon as we entered the cabin, Jessie announced, "Mission accomplished."

I hadn't seen Nic for seven years, a few days in his company shouldn't make me bereft upon losing him.

Shouldn't, but did.

"Where's Mandenauer?" I asked.

Jessie looked confused. "I thought he was with you."

"He said he was going to help you."

"I never saw him."

An uneasy sensation tickled the base of my skull. "That's not good."

"Doesn't mean jack. Except I'm in deep shit because I didn't smell a tail."

"Where would he go?"

"Who knows with him? Either he'll show up, or he'll call. He always does."

My unease lessened, though it wouldn't go away completely until Edward walked through the door holding my research. There was always someone, or something, after him. That he'd survived this long was a miracle, or supreme luck. Sooner or later his luck would run out.

"Show her the totem," Will ordered.

Jessie stilled. "Another one?"

I dug the plastic out of my pocket and handed it over. She held the thing gingerly, her gaze shifting from the icon, to me, and then back again.

"Yours?"

"Not really."

Will filled her in on everything we knew and all that had happened.

Jessie closed her fingers around the plastic wolf. "I don't feel anything."

"Should you?"

"The last one was . . . creepy. Thing moved, slithered even."

Jessie referred to the black totem I'd been studying in Montana, which should be ashes but probably wasn't. The icon had borne the markings of the *matchi-auwishuk* manitou.

Technically, *manitou* means "mystery, godlike, essence." There are many such creatures sprinkled through Ojibwe lore. All are helpful but two—the *weendigos*, or Great Cannibals, and the *matchi-auwishuk*, also known as the Evil Ones.

One of Mengele's werewolves had used the *matchi-auwishuk* totem to become a wolf god, and had planned to rule the world.

What is it with ruling the world? Every nutcase wants to.

"This one moves for me," I murmured, and retrieved the wolf from Jessie's hand. "Growls and mumbles, too."

"Maybe I should hold on to that," Will said.

I shoved the tiny wolf back into my pocket. "The totem stays with me."

Jessie and Will exchanged glances.

"What?" I asked.

"The icon is making you stronger, better," Jessie said.

"That's a bad thing?"

"I'm not sure," Will admitted.

"How can stronger and better be bad?"

"You want a list?" Jessie muttered.

"If I hadn't been able to do a quick change when Billy attacked, both Nic and I would be dead."

Will and Jessie considered me for a moment, then Jessie shrugged. "Let her keep it. If I have to shoot anyone, better her than you."

She winked. I wasn't sure what to make of that.

Weariness washed over me. I had to get some sleep, even if it was six o'clock in the morning.

"Which room's mine?" I asked.

Jessie blinked. "You're staying here?"

"Of course she's staying here. Where else?" Will patted my shoulder and gave me a little shove toward the rear of the house. "Third one on the left."

"Thanks."

"Jess, give her something to sleep in, would you?"

I glanced at Jessie in time to see her scowl. When she caught me looking, she wrinkled her nose. "Come on."

She led me down the hall, stopping at the first door on the right. Inside was a king-sized bed, unmade, along with two suitcases, open and sitting on the floor. Jessie started rooting through a tangle of clothes.

"Did Nic—"

I broke off, mortified that I'd been about to ask her

if he'd said anything about me. If I wasn't careful, I'd be begging her to pass him a note in study hall.

"Did he what?" She withdrew a wrinkled, double-X T-shirt and tossed it across the space between us.

"Never mind." I headed for the door.

"He said to tell you, he'd see you again."

I spun around, annoyed at the way my heart leaped. "Were you going to relay that in this century?"

"Don't get snippy with me. I'm not the one who lied to him."

"I didn't lie."

"Omission."

"You think I should tell him, 'Oh, and by the way, I turn furry and snarl beneath the moon. I don't know if I'll ever be cured. I might get worse. And we can't have children. Let's get married'?"

I could have sworn I saw a flash of sympathy in her eyes, but the expression was gone so fast I knew I'd imagined it even before she sniped right back at me.

"Tell him *something,* Doctor. The man's in love with you."

"Is not."

My denial was automatic, even before I thought of Nic's words and behavior since he'd walked back into my life. There was something between us, but I doubted it was love—at least for him.

"You're right." Jessie let her gaze wander over me from the top of my tangled hair, to the tips of my filthy tennis shoes. "Skinny, blond eggheads probably aren't his type. I'm sure he loathes the very sight of you."

"He acts as if he does."

"And then, let me guess, he sticks his tongue down your throat."

I frowned. Close enough.

"That's what I thought." She drew in a deep breath. "You don't have much experience with men."

"You do?"

"I played with boys most of my life."

I lifted my brows.

"Get your mind out of the gutter, Doctor."

"Elise," I corrected. "*Doctor* makes me feel like I should ask you to bend over and cough."

She almost laughed, and I wasn't even trying to be funny.

"What did Edward say that made you tell Nic to go?" Jessie asked.

He knows the names of the people you've killed.

I couldn't tell Jessie the truth any more than I could have told Nic.

"He said Nic was up to something. That he couldn't be trusted. Someone could get killed."

"Knowing Edward, I'm sure he said that someone would be the G-man."

She knew him well.

"If Franklin was the enemy, he'd have killed you the first chance he got. Bad guys, contrary to most popular motion pictures, do not screw around talking their enemy to death or fashioning Batman-like death traps so the good guys can escape and win in the end. Evil people kill you, then they move on."

She was right; Nic wasn't up to anything but his job. A job that would get me a lethal injection or him a bullet in the head. Choices, choices.

"Mandenauer's probably worried you'll be overcome with lust. When that happens, his perfect world gets shot to shit. You know how he is about his agents having a social life."

Except in Edward's mind, I wasn't an agent and I didn't deserve a life, social or otherwise.

"G-man *is* pretty hot," Jessie continued. "How did you ever stay a virgin around that guy?"

Discussing my sex life, or lack of it, with a near stranger wasn't a place I was prepared to go. However, Jessie wasn't the type of woman to be denied an answer.

"Come on, tell the truth. You guys did it. You just didn't want Mandenauer to know."

I shook my head before I could stop myself.

Her snort of derision was almost as insulting as her words. "You really are an ice princess."

"Thanks." I headed for the door. "I needed that."

"Wait. Elise." She gave a short, sharp sigh. "Sorry. My mouth gets away from me sometimes. Playing nice is tough."

I glanced over my shoulder. She really did look sorry.

"I never had a girlfriend." She shrugged. "Until—"

"Leigh?"

"Zee. That didn't go well."

Which was putting it mildly. I was surprised Jessie had been able to bond with Leigh at all after the fiasco in Miniwa. Of course, they *were* two of a kind.

Still, knowing that Jessie had been as much of a social reject as I was helped. I understood her better. I even liked her a little.

"Was Leigh the same?" I couldn't help but ask. "Hard time making friends like . . ." I was going to say *us,* but I couldn't manage to articulate what a loser I'd been.

"Leigh?" Jessie laughed. "No. She was the duchess of pom-pom."

"I'm sorry?"

"The prom queen, the cheerleader, the quarterback's girl. I can't believe I didn't shoot her when I had the chance."

Jessie's words made me smile. Girls like Leigh had set my teeth on edge, too—back when such things had made a difference.

But once you knew what kind of monsters lived in the world, the petty nonsense of adolescence lost its power to terrify. One less thing.

"If Franklin shows up again, screw him."

I wasn't sure if she meant screw him . . . or screw *him.* Either way—

"Huh?"

"Have sex," she clarified with a roll of her eyes. "Maybe if you do, you won't be so damn annoying."

I'd thought we'd made a certain peace, yet here she was insulting me. I didn't get it.

"I can't," I said.

"You want to die without ever knowing what it's like to be with someone you love?"

"Who said I love him?"

"I may not be the most sensitive person on earth, but I do know love when I see it. What you feel is all over your face every time you say his name."

I mumbled something vile and kicked the door. Jessie snickered. "Men are dense. I don't think he knows."

"What about Will?"

"He's more with it than most, but he won't tell any-one."

We were back in study hall again. I felt like a fool.

"So whaddya think?" Jessie pressed. "If G-man shows up we can make ourselves scarce. I'll take Mandenauer on a wild-wolf chase."

I shook my head. "When I fell in love, my whole life changed."

"Falling in love will do that."

"Not the way it did for me. Who knows what I might become if I sleep with Nic?"

"You're a werewolf, Elise." Jessie spread her hands. "What more can the universe do to you?"

16

The woman had a point.

Kind of. Since we were dealing with werewolves, there weren't a lot of rule books. Nowhere did it say I couldn't become different, even from what I was. Damien had.

Of course, he'd been cursed. Blessed. Hell, I didn't know anymore.

But since sex is a normal, physical function of both humans and wolves, perhaps in abstaining, I'd done myself more harm than good.

See, I could rationalize with the best of them.

"Jess? Will called. "We're supposed to check in with Sheriff Stephenson."

"Keep your pants on, Slick." Jessie moved past me and into the hall. "Or maybe take them off," she murmured so only I could hear. "He looks much better that way."

A muffled thump at the front of the house announced they'd left, and weariness washed over me again. I stumbled into the room that was now mine, dumped my sweat-stained clothes, then crawled beneath the chilly sheets in nothing but Jessie's T-shirt.

The windows were covered with heavy curtains—a *Jäger-Sucher* staple, issued right along with silver ammunition and fake IDs, since most of them slept in the daytime and hunted all night.

Considering that, a vampire would make a great werewolf hunter, if you could trust the bloodsucking undead. I'm sure it goes without saying that you can't.

I awoke much later, rested but stiff. I'd slept so heavily my body was in the same position as when I lay down. Unusual for me. I was an active sleeper. Lucky I slept alone.

Except I wasn't alone. The instant I woke up, I heard someone breathing. The door was closed. I remembered leaving it open.

In an attempt to fool whoever had invaded my place, I kept my respiration deep and even. I moved nothing except my eyes.

Near the window stood a man.

I tried to pin his scent, but he'd showered so recently I caught only a whiff of soap and damp hair. New clothes that smelled of the plastic they'd come in, new shoes so fresh I could taste the rubber.

Best defense and all that, I bounded out of bed and had my elbow around his neck before he could turn. He tried to talk but I was cutting off his air.

This close I didn't need to smell him. I knew the shape of that body, the texture of the skin. I loosened my hold, and he turned.

"Miss me, sweetheart?"

It was a rare occasion when I didn't know who was coming after me long before they got there. Those few seconds of not knowing had scared me.

"Do you have a death wish?" I snapped.

I stalked across the room and tapped the reading lamp on the bedside table. The muted glow barely reached into the corner where he hovered.

"No one throws me out of town," Nic said.

"I think someone did."

His eyes narrowed. "I'm here, aren't I?"

"And when Edward sees you he'll have a temper tantrum. I don't want to watch."

Edward's temper tantrums usually consisted of guns firing, blood spurting, bodies bursting into flames.

Nic crossed the room and crowded into my space. The action should have been intimidating. I'm sure he meant it to be. Instead, I found his nearness, his attempt at dominance, arousing.

Why did he have this effect on me? I wished the desire would go away. I wished *he* would go away.

As if he'd heard my thoughts, he grabbed my arms, and gave me a little shake. My breath caught on a gasp, not of shock, but excitement. I was pathetic. Since when had I enjoyed being manhandled?

Since the man doing the handling was Nic.

"I'm *not* leaving."

His fingers tightened as I tried to get away. I could have, easily, if I hadn't been enjoying the struggle so much.

"What hold does Mandenauer have on you, Elise? What is it that he knows?" I froze, eyes going wide. "Who is he to you?"

"M-my boss."

"There's more to it than that."

He was right, but I couldn't tell him so.

"When you disappeared," Nic murmured, "I asked everyone if they'd seen you, but no one had."

Trust Edward to make sure of it.

"Except for the guy sneaking in from a night celebrating a solid C on his biology test."

Uh-oh.

"He saw a beautiful blonde leaving with a skinny, scary old man."

I swallowed. "So?"

"Now I've met the skinny, scary old man and I wonder . . . He wasn't your boss then, so why did you leave with him?"

My head tilted; my hair, loose and wild, brushed his arm and his nostrils flared, even as his lips thinned. He was furious.

And as aroused as I was.

"I left because I wanted to."

That much was true. I'd wanted to get away from a place where everyone had suddenly smelled like meat.

"You were . . . too clingy," I blurted. "You were pushing me into something I wasn't ready for."

Something sparked in his eyes, and for an instant I was afraid of him, which was foolish. He couldn't hurt me. At least not physically.

"You mean this?"

His mouth crushed down. Our teeth clashed. I tasted blood. Mine? Nic's? I didn't care. The taste, the scent, only tempted me to give in to the wildness I kept trapped inside.

My lips opened. I welcomed him in. Our tongues dueled—touch, spar, retreat. I shuddered, fighting the urge to draw more blood.

His fingers wound in my hair, pulling my head back so he could trace a heated path down my throat. His tongue pressed against my pulse; his teeth worried a fold of skin as his fingers stroked my already aroused nipple to an aching peak.

Had he come back for me, or for this? Didn't matter. I wanted him. Always had.

I needed to hold on to something or fall, so I clutched his shoulders, then became fascinated with the thin line of his collarbone and the shape of his biceps.

Somewhere along the line he'd discarded the suit and found a bright, white T-shirt and a pair of jeans; his holster and his gun were gone. The lack of dress-up clothes and a weapon—his new, yet somehow old, outfit—reminded me of the boy I'd fallen in love with.

Happier, more innocent times, when we'd lie on the couch all tangled together, studying, kissing, unable to resist the fury of first sexual awareness.

Nic's hands fluttered down my back, under the flimsy cover of the T-shirt, stilling when he encountered nothing but skin. His fingernails scraped the sensitive area where my thighs sloped into my rear, before he filled his palms and ground us together.

I wanted to wrap my legs around his waist and ride the tide. As if he knew my thoughts, he lifted me, settled my knees over his hips, and buried his face between my breasts.

I crossed my ankles behind his back and clenched,

pressing myself against him. Cursing, he whirled and dumped me onto the bed, then he lost the jeans and the T-shirt.

The lamplight turned his skin to gold. He'd grown in the years we'd been apart, and without his clothes he seemed taller, broader, stronger.

His shoulders were wide, his waist narrow, his legs long and taut. The light dusting of dark hair across his chest led down his flat stomach and fed into a curling frame around another part that seemed a lot bigger without clothes.

I'd touched him in college—my hand down his pants, his breath harsh and rasping as I worked him in my palm and made him come—but I'd never *seen* him.

I didn't get much time to see him now. One look at my face and he joined me on the bed. He didn't ask, didn't hesitate, and I was glad. If I'd had too much time to think, maybe I would have stopped him.

But I doubted it. I'd held Nic in my heart as the man of my dreams, the one I could never have, and if I couldn't have him, I didn't want anyone. So here I was, a twenty-nine-year-old virgin werewolf. Fat lot of good abstinence had done me.

If I lost my soul, so be it. They could always shoot me tomorrow.

Nic took my mouth; and then he took my body. One deep thrust and I was no longer a virgin. The werewolf thing was going to be a little bit harder to get rid of.

The pain was minute; I endured worse every full moon. However, Nic froze, then slowly lifted his head. The anger still lurked in his eyes, but there was wariness now, and a gentleness I hadn't seen since he'd returned.

"Why didn't you tell me?"

"You didn't ask."

His forehead dropped to rest against mine. "Elise—"

"Don't stop. If you stop, I just might have to kill you."

He gave a half-laugh, but I wasn't kidding. My body was on fire. My skin felt too small for my body. Every sensation bubbled in my blood.

My hands clutched his back, learning the swell of his buttocks, the curves and the dips. Urging him closer, I asked the eternal question and was answered with another fierce thrust.

The entire world narrowed to the one small area where we had joined. My virginity was history, and I was still a woman. Or as close to a woman as I got.

Jessie had asked: What more could the universe do to me? Right now, I only cared what else Nic could do to me and for how long.

I rose to meet him, and his body responded, pulsing within me to the beat of our hearts. Eyes closed, head thrown back, with every movement he reached deeper, loomed larger.

"More," I mumbled against his mouth, then bit his lip. "Harder."

"I'll hurt—"

"You won't." I clasped his hips and showed him what I needed. "You can't."

What had started out rough became rougher. The slide of flesh against flesh incited me. Arching, I offered my breasts, only Jessie's T-shirt was in the way. I tried to tug it free, but the material was sandwiched between us and there was no way we were going to separate now.

With a growl that seemed to reach all the way to my toes, he put his hand in the neck and tore the garment down the front. Lowering his head, he captured one nipple, then scored it with his teeth.

My body trembled, and I tightened around him. Shuddering, he suckled, his tongue pushing me against the roof of his mouth in a rhythm echoed by our bodies.

I could no longer keep my eyes open as a whole new world exploded in my mind. The forest, the trees, the sky—no moon, full moon—the answer to every question I'd ever had, right there, so close, I could almost hear the words, see the solution.

I was no longer divided but whole. Not woman and wolf, just me. Two become one in a rite as old as time, and then . . .

I climaxed with a startled gasp as he reached a place meant only for him. Over and over and over again, he moved within me, and the orgasm surged through us both.

When the last shudder fell away, and the air shifted from hot to cool, I ran my palm over his hair. My chest went tight. I wanted to both hold him close and fling him away.

Nic rolled from my body and onto the bed. He didn't speak; I wasn't sure what to say.

I felt both different and the same. How could that be?

"This isn't what I came here for." His voice was remote. I wasn't sure what I'd done, or maybe not done.

"No?"

He made a sound of disgust and sat up. "I didn't use

a condom. Dammit!" He scrubbed a hand through his hair.

I wasn't worried, since I couldn't get pregnant, and, since lycanthropy can heal a non-silver bullet to the head, STDs aren't even a blip on our radar. Too bad I couldn't explain any of this to Nic.

"I've never been so stupid in my life," he muttered.

Suddenly naked and alone, I glanced away and my gaze was caught by a smudge of blood on my inner thigh. Quickly I wrapped the covers around me so he wouldn't see.

"Thanks," I murmured.

"I didn't mean it like that."

"What did you mean?"

He lifted his hands, lowered them. "You confuse the hell out of me, Elise. I see you, and it's like you never went away. Everything feels the same, but we're not the same people."

He had that right. I wasn't even a people anymore. Had I ever been?

"You look as if seven days have passed, instead of seven years." He tilted his head, stared at my face. "How can that be?"

His words reminded me, if I'd needed any reminding, that we could never be together. Not really.

Sooner or later he'd find out what I was, what I'd done, and he'd hate me.

"I want to hate you," he murmured.

I started. Could he read my mind?

"You don't?"

His gaze wandered over the bed, then over me. "Did that feel like hate to you?"

"No."

He sighed. "But it wasn't love."

Then why had it felt like love to me?

My eyes burned and I stood. The languid, peaceful feeling fled, and as I paced the room, dragging the end of the bedspread behind me, a buzzing energy took its place.

Catching a glimpse of myself in the mirror above the dresser, I froze. My eyes had bled blue; not a hint of white surrounded the iris. Wolf's eyes, except for one difference.

Most laymen aren't aware that only puppies have blue eyes. So if you see a wolf in the wild with orbs of blue? Better hope you have a silver bullet handy.

Panic made my breathing shallow. When I was wolf, I had human eyes, so what did it mean that they had gone wolf when I wasn't? I doubted it was a good thing.

I glanced into the mirror once more. Nic was getting dressed. Convenient, since I had to get rid of him right now.

"You wanted me," I said. "You had me. Get out."

His head lifted, he turned in my direction. I ducked my face so my hair would cover my eyes. If he saw them I was doomed. Or he was.

"What?" he murmured.

Beneath the calm I heard liquid steel, red hot and bubbling.

"We both wanted to see what we'd missed." I inched toward the door with a shrug. "Now we know. It wasn't all that much."

"You lie almost as badly as you fuck."

I winced. He was lying, too. Despite my inexperience, even I knew what we'd just shared had been as far from bad as it had been from a common fuck.

I heard him coming after me but I didn't pause to see how close he was. If I could get into the hallway, he'd never catch me.

Yanking open the door, I nearly screamed as a large, dark shadow swooped close.

17

"Elise!"

Edward's voice. What had I said about being doomed?

The back exit was only a few steps away. The rear of the cabin stood very close to the forest, a convenience I hadn't noticed until now.

I tried to brush past Edward, reach the out-of-doors, where I could give in to the change pulsing in my blood like a full moon pulsing in the sky. Edward would keep Nic here; I could disappear out there. At least until Nic went away.

But Edward caught my arm, held on tight. He was strong for an old man but not stronger than me. Still, I had been raised never to hurt him, to obey him, so I paused and looked into his face.

He flinched when he saw my wolf eyes. "What is going on?"

"Yes," Nic said from the bedroom. "What's going on?"

Edward's face darkened, and he reached for his gun.

"No," I said, and my voice rumbled between human and wolf.

"Elise?" Nic asked, stepping forward.

"Stay back."

I should not be losing control; the full moon was days away. Even then, I could control myself better than this.

I'd thought having sex hadn't changed me, but maybe it had.

"What is he doing here?" Edward demanded.

I didn't answer. Wasn't it obvious he'd been doing me?

"Fool," Edward spat. "You have no idea what giving in to such urges might cause you to become. Was the experience worth dying for?"

I wasn't going to answer that since I kind of thought that it was—a fact I should never admit to Edward Mandenauer, who'd be happy to oblige.

"What's he yammering about, Elise?"

Edward drew his sidearm. I put myself between him and Nic, but I needn't have bothered. He pressed the barrel to the base of my throat.

"Outside." Edward shoved me toward the back door. I tripped over the trailing blanket. "You as well, Mr. Franklin."

Nic came without argument. He had to believe both Edward and I had lost our minds.

The moon spilled from the sky, cool, welcoming, lopsided. The wind lifted my hair. I smelled the forest, the earth, and I was drawn to them. I wanted to run through the trees, feel the breeze in my fur, chase something small and furry, catch it and taste its blood.

Usually, I found such thoughts disgusting. Tonight I was tempted. I'd taken one step toward the woods when Edward's voice made me pause.

"Prove you haven't given your soul to evil by giving your body to him."

"What in hell are you talking about?" Nic snapped. "Is he nuts?"

"You know what you must do," Edward murmured, ignoring Nic. "Show me."

I shook my head, confused.

"Shift and follow instructions," he whispered in my ear. "Change and do not kill."

"No problem."

I started for the forest once more. He yanked me back and pressed the gun to my spine. I growled, low and threatening.

"Behave yourself!" He jabbed me harder. "Change here. Now. For him and for me."

"No."

His sigh revealed his impatience. "There are two ways to ascertain he departs and does not return. Your way, or mine. Choose."

Edward's way was death—always had been. Mine? Easy.

If I showed Nic my true nature, he would run. He'd live—there was my reward. But best of all, if he told anyone what he'd seen, they wouldn't believe him.

A win-win situation. Edward's specialty.

I glanced at Nic from beneath the curtain of my hair. His expression reflected both fury and confusion. He had no idea what he'd stepped into when he'd insisted on accompanying me to Fairhaven.

If he stayed he'd be in danger from every monster, alive or dead, if they found out I loved him. I really didn't have much choice.

I moved into the silver glow from the sky. Spreading my arms wide, I threw back my head. Opening my mind, I let in the moon.

The power was a blinding white light pouring through me. I heard things no man could hear, saw worlds beyond imagination, caught the scent of wolves that couldn't be real, heard them, too, like a ghostly pack circling through the sky.

The moon filled me, caressed me, changed me. The bedspread fell away as I became a wolf. Strength, speed, agility were mine.

"The perfect animal," Edward murmured. "People brain, wolf body. They are very hard to kill."

I opened my eyes, and the first thing I saw was Nic. He'd fallen to the ground. His chest was heaving, and I feared he'd gotten sick, but he was merely trying to catch some air so he wouldn't faint.

I couldn't blame him. Not every day do you see a woman become a wolf. He took it pretty well.

"How?" he managed, then lifted his head.

I'd crept closer, and when he looked up, his nose nearly brushed my snout. He cringed, confusion flowing over his face.

"Sign of a werewolf." Edward's voice was far too jolly. "Human eyes. Makes the phrase 'never shoot until you see the whites' actually mean something, *jawohl*?"

I turned in his direction and snarled. Edward laughed. Nic skittered backward and to his feet. His hand reached for a gun that wasn't there, and my heart cracked just a little.

I hadn't realized until that moment I'd been hoping he could see the true me and not care. His arm fell to his side.

"*Jäger-Suchers* don't hunt rabid wolves at all," he murmured.

"*Nein.*"

"Then what?"

"Werewolves. Among other things."

For Nic, curiosity seemed to be taking the place of concern. However, I wanted to be a sideshow freak even less than I wanted to be a demon-possessed horror.

"*She's* a werewolf."

"Elise is a special case. The only—"

I woofed once.

"Oh, him." Edward shrugged, his expression reflecting his lack of enthusiasm in the matter. "Elise and *Damien* are the only werewolves in their division."

"Damien," Nic murmured. "Didn't see that coming."

"Neither did Leigh." Edward's tone was no longer amused. "It was most disturbing."

"I'll bet. What did you mean by 'other things'?"

"Different monsters, different needs, different divisions."

"Different *monsters*?"

Nic's face appeared a little green. I whimpered.

"I'm okay," he said. "What kind of monsters?"

"Anything that you can imagine and many that you cannot."

"You're sure you're not in the FBI?" Nic asked. "X-file division?"

"What is this 'X-file' I am always hearing about?" Edward glanced at me, but I was in no condition to explain.

"Television show," Nic said absently. "You probably wouldn't like it."

"No doubt. Television is an immense waste of time."

Edward's sources of amusement were few—guns, bullets, and death. What a life.

Mine hadn't been much better. Serums, antidotes, and werewolves.

Oh, my.

"Why are you telling me this?" Nic asked. "You planning to kill me?"

"Of course not, Mr. Franklin."

Both Nic and I let out a long sigh of relief, which ended with Edward's next words.

"I plan to let her do it."

Silence settled over the yard, lengthening uncomfortably.

Edward laughed. "Just kidding."

I emitted a low, rumbling growl, and his expression became one of mock surprise. "But you are always telling me I need to grow a sense of humor."

"You still do," Nic said.

"And therein lies the trouble. Humor is so subjective."

I considered knocking Edward to the ground and sitting on his chest—werewolf humor. However, he'd be more likely to blow my head off with silver than laugh.

Humor certainly was subjective.

"I do not plan to kill you, Mr. Franklin. As Elise has pointed out on several occasions, killing people who annoy me can be more trouble than it's worth. A dead FBI agent would be the height of trouble, I think."

"Then why are you telling me this?" Nic repeated.

"No one will believe you."

"They will if I—"

"What? Bring them Elise? You'd subject her to the questions, the government, the press? What about the tests, the injections, the blood work?"

Nic's eyes narrowed, and he muttered, "Bastard," so low only I could hear. Then his head tilted, as if he'd caught a whiff of something interesting. I could almost see the idea popping up in his head like a lightbulb as he turned to me.

"What were you up to in that secret compound, Dr. Frankenstein?"

I blinked. He believed *I* was manufacturing monsters?

I was suddenly tired of the questions, the secrets, the lies. Edward wanted Nic to know everything? Let Edward tell him.

The forest called to me, and I answered, loping toward the trees, leaving Edward, Nic, the world behind.

"Find Jessie and Will," my boss shouted. "They went searching for the sheriff far to the north, and they have been gone too long."

He had said I needed to prove I was still his instrument and not evil, but being told to fetch like a dog annoyed the hell out of me. Better annoyed than dead, I suppose.

In a tiny corner of my mind, I remembered the talisman had been in the pocket of my sweats and not in my hand when I shifted faster than a speeding bullet. What did that mean?

Was I losing control of my beast? If so, then why did I feel more in control, more powerful, more right than I had ever felt in my life?

Werewolves might have a people brain, but it was still hard to concentrate on the mystery of the instantaneous change with the sensory overload of a new forest surrounding me.

The desire to run was all-consuming. If I wanted, I could travel over a hundred miles in a day, chase a herd for five or six miles, and *then* accelerate. Werewolves don't need superhuman abilities when just being a wolf makes them more than a man, or in my case, a woman.

I headed north, trying to catch a familiar scent but having very little luck. The moon pulled at my soul; a howl pressed at the base of my throat.

I lifted my nose just as a crow swooped low and cawed, startling me so much that I yelped instead. Several others sat in a nearby tree. At my glance, they rose, like great, black bats and followed the first. They were trying to show me something.

A whiff of water reached me long before I stumbled across the creek. Splashing in, I dipped my muzzle to the bottom and let the chilly liquid ease the buzzing from my brain.

I drank until the burning thirst faded, but it wouldn't go away completely. Because the thirst wasn't just for water. The full moon was coming, and unless I made more serum, I was going to crave blood.

Edward and I needed to have a discussion. Where was my research? Had he retrieved it? And if not, why not?

The crows circled above me. I tilted my head. No, they circled above something else—over there.

As I shook my coat, I could have sworn I caught the scent of werewolf. But when I tested the air, I smelled nothing but trees. Nevertheless, I could no more have gone back to the cabin then than I could have ridden a bicycle, so I followed the crows to a clearing surrounded by towering evergreens.

In the center lay a body—the sheriff's, from the appearance of the uniform. However, there was no werewolf but me, no wolf at all, no human left alive.

The crows were gone, not a trace of them in the sky. *Strange*. Had they led me here to help or hurt me? Hard to say with crows.

I should check on the sheriff. Though I smelled death, maybe I was wrong.

Hey, maybe I wasn't a werewolf. Maybe this was all a dream and I'd wake up at Stanford in Nic's arms. A fantasy I'd tried on a hundred times before. I knew better.

So I circled the body, hoping for a hint of movement and finding none. Creeping closer and closer, belly to the ground, I stretched my neck, longer and longer, until it cracked with the strain, then I sniffed his hand.

And someone pumped a shotgun next to my head.

18

At first I thought it was Edward, and I knew I was dead. Then I saw the shoes next to my paws. Tennies, not combat boots. Girl feet. Jessie. That didn't mean she wasn't going to blow my brains out, but she might give me a chance to explain first.

If only I could talk.

"We were looking for Sheriff Stephenson," she murmured. "Guess we found him."

"Or what's left of him."

Will. Thank God, a voice of reason.

I whimpered and lifted my head. He shined a flashlight into my eyes and blurted, "Elise?"

"Where?"

The shotgun barrel tapped my skull. I wanted to shout: "Be careful with that thing!" Instead I growled.

"Shut up. I'll deal with you in a minute."

"That's Elise," Will said. "The wolf you're about to kill."

"What?"

At least she uncocked the gun, and I breathed a little easier. But she kept the barrel tilted in my direction. I could smell the silver shot inside. I really wished she'd aim that thing anywhere but at me.

I glanced up and she started. "People eyes always creep me out. Change back, Doc, you bother me."

I nudged the gun away with my head.

"Oh, sorry." She lifted the weapon and held it in a cradle carry across her chest. "What are you doing out here?"

Her attention went to the dead sheriff, then swiftly returned to me. Her hands tightened on the gun.

I didn't do it! I wanted to shout, but I could only shake my head.

"Right. Sure. Dead guy. Werewolf. You be the judge."

I looked at Will and he shrugged. I don't think he believed me, either. I needed words. But to speak, I had to shift, and then I'd be naked.

I'd never been easy with nudity. I always kept clothes in the forest when I changed. But tonight I hadn't had the time or the wherewithal to prepare.

Huffing, I paced, worried the ground with a paw, then glanced at Jessie mournfully.

"Take a hike, Slick," Jessie murmured.

"What? Why?"

"She's gonna be buck naked after she changes. Get my extra set of clothes and the blanket from the car."

"How about if I get the stuff, and then she changes?"

Jessie lifted a bland gaze to his. "How about I shoot you, too, if you don't move your ass?"

"Jealous?"

"You don't need to see all you're missing."

"I don't see anyone but you. Haven't for a long time now."

I snorted, and Jessie said, "Yeah, that was hokey, wasn't it?"

"I'd just like to see the change, is that too much to ask? I'm a scholar. It would be interesting."

"I bet."

"Elise would understand. Wouldn't you?"

I lifted my upper lip and showed him my teeth.

"I don't think she would." Jessie made a shooing motion. "Get going, Cadotte. I need to talk to the doc, and I'd like her on two feet when I do it."

"All right, all right." He stomped off in what I presumed was the direction of the car. "I never get to see anything good. Never get to have any fun. Never get to shoot anything, either."

"You don't like guns," Jessie shouted after him. "And you're too much of a pansy to kill anything."

"I might make an exception with you."

She laughed as he disappeared into the trees. His flashlight bobbed for a few seconds, then faded. For an instant I worried about whatever might be out there hiding, until I sniffed the breeze and got nothing but a whiff of dead sheriff, Jessie, and Will.

"He really is kind of sweet," Jessie murmured. "Never thought I'd go for a pretty boy with a gentle soul, but it takes all kinds."

She was talking to me like a friend, which was strange considering I was all fanged and furry. Maybe it was easier for her to connect when she didn't actually have to . . . connect.

As if realizing what she'd done, Jessie made a self-derisive sound, then yanked a smaller flashlight from her coat pocket. Turning the beam in my direction, she scowled. "You've got some explaining to do, Doc."

I'd told her to call me "Elise," but I was starting to like the way she sneered "Doc." Which only meant I must be losing my mind as well as my control.

Will returned more quickly than I would have thought. I hadn't heard a car approach earlier, but I'd been a little distracted by the dead body.

Jessie yanked the blanket from his hands and held it like a curtain. "Get going." She peeked over the top. "We don't have all night."

The last time, changing back had taken longer than changing forward. This time, I lifted my nose to the sky, and the next instant the breeze fluttered hair instead of fur.

"What the hell?" Jessie gasped. "No one can shift that fast."

"Where's the icon?" Will asked.

"Haven't got it on me."

"Obviously." Jessie's tone was dry and I snickered.

Her eyes widened as she handed me a spare set of jeans and yet another T-shirt. "What's with you? You aren't exactly a laugh-o-rama most days."

And I shouldn't be feeling so lively now with a dead man at my feet and a shotgun filled with silver so close to my heart, not to mention Nic no doubt breaking land speed records as he drove as far away from me as he could get.

However, the strength and power I'd experienced while running as a wolf remained. For the first time,

I missed being what I was, and I wanted to be that way again.

Jessie's gaze returned to the dead sheriff. "Thought you didn't need human blood."

"Wasn't me."

"Like I haven't heard that a thousand times before."

Suddenly I was staring down the barrel of a shotgun again.

"If you're going to keep threatening to kill me, we'll never get anywhere."

"If you're going to keep lying, I don't have much choice."

"Edward sent me to find you."

"I haven't needed a babysitter for a long time now."

"It was more of a test." I sighed. "For me."

She frowned. "We came back earlier, but you were sleeping. Then the deputy called and— What the hell happened that Mandenauer felt the need to test you?"

I glanced at Will, then back at Jessie. I didn't want to tell them, but better me than Edward.

Quickly I related the events of a few hours past— glossing over the experience with Nic as best I could.

"So you gave it up, huh?" Jessie smirked. "G-man any good?"

"Jess," Will murmured. "Not your business."

Jessie lifted a brow and I couldn't help but smile.

"That's what I thought," she said. "Guys like him almost make getting blown to hell by a silver bullet worthwhile."

A tug of camaraderie surprised me. One minute I was tempted to become a werewolf and run with the pack. The next I was pulled toward the sort of friendship I'd always longed for and never had. My dual nature had never before seemed so divided.

"How did the sheriff die?" Jessie peered at the body with the aid of her flashlight.

I guess bonding time was over.

"I didn't get a good look," I said.

"Seemed like you were looking pretty closely when we got here."

"Smelling."

"Gag," Jessie muttered.

"For a rough-and-tough, kick-ass *Jäger-Sucher,* you're awfully squeamish about details."

"Sue me." Jessie shined the beam across the sheriff's neck. "I'm not a medical examiner, but I'm pretty sure that was sliced neatly instead of torn by teeth."

I frowned at the mess. "That's neat?"

"For this kind of murder. Knife wound." She looked me up and down. "Which leaves you off the hook."

"I could have thrown the weapon into the bushes."

"With your paws? Besides, a wound like that, you'd be covered in blood."

"Ew."

"Now who's squeamish?"

"You're saying we got a plain, old, everyday murderer on the loose?" I asked. "No funny stuff?"

"Seems that way."

"Which means there's no reason for us to stay." Although where I was going to go, I had no idea.

Jessie's cell phone rang. Still staring at the body, she answered.

"Jessie."

I heard Edward's voice clearly, even though the

phone was pressed to Jessie's ear. My transformation ability wasn't the only thing that was getting better.

"Is Elise with you?"

Jessie glanced at me. "Yes."

"Has she exhibited any odd behavior?"

"Not unless you count changing from werewolf to woman in the blink of an eye."

I stuck out my tongue, and she grinned. But her smile faded as Edward continued to speak. "There is a serious werewolf outbreak I need you to attend to."

She paced to the far side of the clearing, and though I tried to hear what Edward was telling her, I no longer could.

"Where?" she asked. "Okay. But we've got a little problem with Sheriff Stephenson. He's dead." Pause. "Throat slit."

A garbled stream of words, most likely curses, erupted, but I couldn't make any sense of them.

"Tell Basil." Jessie sighed. "Fine. Have him bring the ME."

"Who's Basil?" I asked when she'd disconnected the call.

"The deputy." Her eyes drifted back to the body. "Make that the sheriff. Major pain in the ass."

I waited, and when she didn't explain, glanced at Will, who did.

"He's one of those who still think Indians aren't worth the bullet it takes to shoot them."

"Is he lost in a John Wayne movie?"

Will's lips twitched. "Maybe."

"Basil's bringing the ME?" I asked.

"No," Jessie said. "G-man is."

I gaped. "Nic's still here?"

"Apparently, and this is now his problem."

"Huh?"

"Try to keep up, Doc. Dead by knife wound." She indicated the body with the tip of her shotgun. "No werewolves but you, and you're off the hook. G-man's here, and he isn't in any hurry to leave."

Which was almost as big of a shock as the murder itself.

"He may as well make himself useful." Jessie looked me up and down. "To someone other than you."

"We're just going to leave and let the FBI handle this?"

"We are; you aren't."

"Huh?" I said again. I was so witty lately.

"Slick and I need to hightail it north." She lifted a brow in Will's direction. "Werewolf outbreak in upper Minnesota."

"What a shock," he muttered.

"And Edward?"

"He's going to retrieve your research."

"Where?"

"Got me. You're supposed to wait here for the ME and G-man, then get out of Fairhaven."

"But—"

Jessie and Will had already started for the car. Jessie turned back. "But what?"

"Where am I going to go?"

Jessie opened her mouth, then shut it again. "Mandenauer didn't say. Call him when you're done with the body."

Without another word, she and Will disappeared

into the trees. Seconds later the sound of their car starting, then leaving, drifted on the breeze.

Within half an hour, another car arrived. Moments
later Nic and a second man broke through the trees and
into the clearing.

Nic's gaze widened at the sight of me. Either he
hadn't expected to find me here at all, or he'd expected
to find me furry. His face hardened, his eyes cooled;
his only greeting was a nod.

I swallowed the thickness at the back of my throat.
How could he act as if we'd shared nothing, as if we
barely knew each other at all?

And they called me a beast.

I forced my attention to Nic's companion, an elderly
man, at least seventy-five, perhaps more, who peered at
me with eyes both dark and sad enough to belong on a
basset hound.

His hair was snow white—but at least he had some—
his face weathered from age and the elements. He appeared as if he spent hours on various lakes pulling fish
from both warm water and ice. Lord knows why.

"Hello," he greeted. "I'm Dr. Watchry."

"Sir, I'm with the—"

I broke off. I'd almost said *Jäger-Suchers,* but how
much did the man know?

Dr. Watchry glanced at Nic, then back at me. "FBI?"

I merely smiled, unable to give voice to that lie. Nic
didn't correct me, instead introducing me. "This is
Dr. Hanover. Research scientist."

"How interesting," Dr. Watchry murmured. "I've always been fascinated with research, but I haven't had
time to pursue any. I've been the only physician in

Fairhaven for nearly fifty years. Also the medical examiner for this county."

Whoa! No wonder he was sad.

"Shouldn't you have retired by now?"

"If there'd been anyone willing to take my place, I would have."

"No one wants the job? Seems like a nice enough place."

Hey, I'd seen worse.

"Sweet child." He patted my arm. "To me it is. But to a youngster, fresh out of college, with a spanking new degree and money at last, the appeal of work, work, and then some fishing isn't very appealing. Now, what do we have here?"

I was still stuck on *sweet child*. No one had ever called me that before. I liked it.

Nic cleared his throat.

"Oh! The sheriff. We found him like this."

Dr. Watchry tsk-tsked as he stood over the body. "There's never been a murder in Fairhaven."

"Never?"

I might live in the wilderness, but I watched television. Even I knew the lack of murder was a big lack— and an extremely pleasant one.

"Not here. I did investigate a few in my tenure, but nothing on this scale. Hunting 'accident.'" He made quotes around the word with his fingers. "Happens a lot. People hold grudges, then they're set free in the woods with guns. Usually the alcohol consumed before the season opens—as well as during—is the culprit."

"And the other incidents?" Nic asked.

"Crimes of passion mostly. Husband. Wife. A lover or two."

"Happens."

"Not here."

"What about the disappearances?" I asked, and Nic cut me a sharp glance.

I fought the urge to smack myself in the head. He didn't know about the people who had gone missing. Now I'd have to tell him.

"No bodies, no crime," the ME answered, then got out his equipment: gloves, a mask, disposable tools. The man knew his job.

"The coroner's van will be here shortly," he continued. "Of course, we don't have a coroner, just me. I'll do some preliminary testing, then have the attendants take the body to my clinic."

"Not the morgue?"

"We don't have one of those, either. With most deaths, the corpse is delivered directly to the funeral home. But if there's a need for further investigation, my clinic has to suffice. I've been provided with equipment and a storage facility."

Nic tugged a portable spotlight out of a case, setting it up so the doctor could see. The garish beam lit not only the sheriff's body but half the forest.

Then we stood around helplessly as he gathered evidence. Since the possibility of contamination was high, we kept back and let Dr. Watchry work.

"What disappearances?" Nic whispered.

Quickly I explained why the *Jäger-Suchers* had been called to Fairhaven.

"But you found no evidence of . . ."

Nic paused and glanced at the doctor, but he was well occupied and too far away to hear us, even if he'd been a spring chicken.

"Paranormal activity?" he finished.

I snorted at the euphemism. "As far as we can tell we've got standard disappearances and plain old-fashioned murder. Otherwise, they wouldn't have left an amateur like me behind."

"Something weird's going on. Blood but no bodies is *not* a good thing."

Since he was right, I didn't bother to comment.

"Where's the deputy?" I asked.

"Wasn't in. I left a message at the station."

"No dispatcher? No radio? No cell phone?"

"No. Maybe. I don't have the number," he snapped. "This isn't New York, Elise. Around here, decades go by without the slightest need for emergency services."

"Huh," the doctor murmured. "That's odd."

Both Nic's and my ears perked up. We moved forward.

"What?" Nic asked.

"There's a bite mark."

I stiffened, my gaze automatically going to the forest, searching for the telltale shine of werewolf eyes.

"Where?" Nic leaned closer.

"Back of the arm, under the shirt. Didn't see it at first. Barely broke the skin. But as the blood settles, the bruise becomes livid."

The doctor shifted the sheriff and tugged up his left sleeve. A strangled sound escaped my lips.

The bite had been made by human teeth.

19

Nic turned a bland gaze in my direction before returning his attention to the ME. "You can get a DNA sample from that, right?"

"Definitely."

Dr. Watchry went to his bag, changed his gloves, and removed the swabs and other necessary items. Silence reigned, broken only by the click and shuffle of the job being done.

"What's going on?" I whispered.

"Murder."

"The bite. That's just weird."

Nic lifted a brow. "Says someone who shouldn't throw stones."

My lips tightened. If he was going to be snotty, I was going to leave. As soon as someone gave me a ride. I could shift into a werewolf and run back to town, but why should I when I had nowhere to go and nothing pressing to do?

"There are a lot of cases like this," Nic continued.

"Not only defensive, where the victim bites the murderer, but offensive, where an attacker gets off on inflicting pain, exerting control, or marking the victim as his own."

"I guess we can't expect normal behavior out of a killer."

"Or anyone else, for that matter."

My fingers clenched, but I refrained from flattening him. I was so proud of myself.

"The bite will help you catch the guy, right?"

Nic shrugged. "Bite-mark evidence is more often used for conviction than apprehension."

In response to my frown, he explained further. "In order to match that bite we'd have to check the impression against everyone's dental records in Fairhaven. And if the culprit isn't from here, or hasn't been to a dentist—"

"You've got nothing but worthless information," I finished.

"Yeah. On the other hand, once a suspect's in custody, a match can be used to issue charges, maybe even result in a conviction."

"I've never dealt with bite-mark evidence before," Dr. Watchry murmured, still working. "But I have an acquaintance who's a forensic odontologist out of Madison. We've discussed the best way to record the evidence. Photos. Measurements."

"Is it better to get him here?" Nic asked quickly.

"The window for collecting saliva in a DNA test is very small. Plus, the skin slides on a corpse if you leave it too long. Shifts the tissue underneath, alters everything."

I refrained from making gagging noises. I was, after all, a scientist. I'd seen more disgusting things than a corpse. Remember Billy?

"Sooner the better with this kind of evidence," Dr. Watchry continued. "But I'll call and ask him for help. Odontology is a very specific science."

"That would be great," Nic said. "I suppose forensic dentists are few and far between out here."

"He's the only one to be had." Dr. Watchry got to his feet. "Thought the transport would be along by now. I should get this to the clinic."

"We'll wait for them." Nic helped the doctor pack the lights and gear, then escorted him to his car.

He returned with a phone to his ear. I wondered for a minute where he'd gotten it, since his had blown up along with mine in Montana, then decided *where* didn't matter. At least he had one.

Nic disconnected the call. "Still no deputy."

Silence settled between us, heavy with things neither one of us wanted to say. Or I didn't want to. Nic didn't seem to have a problem.

"Why didn't you tell me?"

"What good would it have done?"

"I loved you."

Past tense. I wasn't surprised. He hadn't spoken of love before he'd known of my affliction. Now, I was just shocked he hadn't declared his everlasting hate and blown my head off with silver. If he had any.

My gaze lowered to the gun he now wore and I wondered.

"Elise?" My eyes met his before he turned to stare at the trees. "What happened?"

"Edward didn't tell you?"

"Demons, Nazis, incurable blood lust. I think he was trying to scare me."

"Did he succeed?"

"Enough for me to put the silver bullets he gave me into my gun."

Well, that answered one question, anyway.

"I'm not like the others," I felt compelled to point out; I'm not sure why.

"You've never killed innocent people?"

I swallowed thickly. "I didn't say that."

And I wasn't going to say any more. If Edward had told him everything, Nic would be arresting me—or at least trying to. I'm sure my boss thought showing him I was werewolf would be enough to make Nic stay out of my life forever. Edward was no doubt right.

"There's a whole world out here no one knows about," Nic murmured.

"It's the *Jäger-Suchers'* job to make sure one world stays separate from the other."

Forty-eight hours ago Nic hadn't believed in magic, power, the supernatural. Of course, seeing goes a long way toward believing.

Suddenly he cursed. I moved forward, putting myself between him and the trees. No matter what everyone said—that this was a regular murder, no werewolves, nothing strange but a killer—I was still jumpy.

This place wasn't right. Something was out there. Or maybe, as Damien said, something was coming. Something always was.

"What are you doing?" Nic asked.

"What did you see?"

"My own stupidity."

Nic stared at me with a curious expression, which couldn't quite disguise the trickle of fear. "I didn't use a condom. What does that mean? Puppies? Cubs?"

I shook my head. "I can't."

He grabbed me by the arms, shook me once, hard. "You *will*. Tell me. I have the right to know."

"Let. Me. Go," I said quietly, prepared to make him if he didn't. There was only so much manhandling I would accept.

Nic did as I ordered with a shove that would have sent me sprawling if I hadn't had the reflexes of a wolf. My fingers curled into fists, but I didn't retaliate. I had to cut the man some slack, though not for much longer.

"I didn't mean I can't tell you; I meant I can't have children."

"Explain."

"I would have if you hadn't been so bent on mauling me. Do you get off on that now?"

"You know what I get off on. Or at least I did until I found out she wasn't human."

His voice was chilly and distant. I remembered the dreams we'd shared—the picket fence, the little kids, the life.

Had he still been dreaming those things? Had he been dreaming of having them with me?

I doubted that. Nevertheless, I did owe him an explanation.

"Cross-species impregnation is impossible."

"Cross-*species*?" His lip curled.

"I'm not human; I'm not a wolf. I'm both."

"Great. That's a load off my mind. Am I going to get

furry now that we've swapped spit and various other bodily fluids?"

"Could you be more graphic?"

My voice had gone cool and prim. Ice queen was back. I'd kind of missed her.

"Yes," he snapped.

I should just tell him what he wanted to know, then leave him in the woods. He wouldn't mind.

"Lycanthropy is a virus, passed only through saliva while in wolf form. You can't catch it from me. Unless I bite you."

"Great," he repeated.

"And just to set your mind at ease, since a werewolf can cure anything but silver, you don't have to worry about STDs."

"Gee, a technicality I'd completely forgotten about amid all the others."

Had I once considered him funny and smart? I couldn't fathom it.

"Your pals fled town," he murmured. "Why are you still here?"

"Batting cleanup." I pointed at the sheriff, then froze.

"Well, there's nothing supernatural about this, so you can get lost." Nic turned and saw what I had.

The sheriff's body was gone.

20

"Uh-oh," I murmured, staring at the empty grass where a body used to be.

The ground was still dark with blood. Otherwise I might have thought we were in the middle of a shared delusion, and there'd never been any dead sheriff at all.

"Where? What?" Nic drew his gun and turned in a slow circle, eyes searching the forest. "Who?"

"There's no one," I said.

"But—" He stalked around the body, took a few steps into the woods. "There aren't any drag marks. I didn't hear anything."

He was still thinking in human terms. I could hardly blame him.

"That's because no one dragged him away."

"They had to—"

"No, they didn't."

My insistence finally penetrated his confusion. He put away his gun. "What happened?"

"I have no idea, but I'm thinking supernatural. Can I use your phone?"

He stared at the empty space as if the body might appear as miraculously as it had disappeared. No such luck.

"Nic?" I pressed. "The phone?"

He handed it to me, then went back to staring.

I dialed Edward, got voice mail, left a message. "Call me at—" I frowned, then snapped my fingers in front of Nic's nose. "Number?"

He recited it and I did the same, then called Jessie and relayed the news.

"Guess that explains where the dead bodies have gone," she said.

"Where?"

Silence met my question. "Well, maybe it doesn't *explain* it, but— Hell, I don't know."

"Are you coming back?" I asked.

"Can't. According to the authorities I've talked to in Minnesota, they've got a major wolf problem only we can solve, if you get my drift."

"Leigh and Damien?"

"Serious shit going on in Washington, too. They've got their hands full. I'd swear there was a full moon."

I glanced at the sky where the silver orb wavered, appearing slightly off balance, not at all full. Weird.

"Did you call Edward?" she asked.

"Voice mail."

"Figures."

"What should I do?"

"Deal with it. You're a *Jäger-Sucher*."

"Not really. I've never had to handle a case."

"You do now. Just wing it."

"I'm not the winging-it type."

"Change." Jessie hung up.

"Hell," I muttered.

"What did she say?"

"Wing it?"

"Hell," Nic repeated.

"Yeah."

"I'd better contact the ME," Nic said, "tell him to call off the coroner's wagon. Although how I'm going to explain a missing body I have no idea."

I handed Nic his phone, then stared at the blood-drenched ground. I hadn't a clue where to start. A few minutes later, Nic joined me.

"What did you tell him?" I asked.

"The truth."

"What!"

"Not the whole truth. Take a breath." Nic shook his head. "I said the body was missing. Since that appears to be an epidemic around here, the doctor wasn't surprised."

Silence settled over the clearing, broken only by the sounds of the night.

"I guess you can go," I said. "Nothing natural here."

"No."

I glanced at him in surprise. "Why would you stay?"

"I don't leave the scene of a murder, even if the body does. That's not how we do things in the FBI."

"You come across a lot of disappearing bodies in the FBI, do you?"

"That's beside the point."

"You can't tell them what's going on here."

"No shit. I'd be on the next transport to a little white room."

In truth, I wanted Nic to stay. I had no idea what to do. Not that he'd know any better how to figure out why a body—or ten—had disappeared into thin air. But at least he was someone who had dealt with death before. Still, there were other issues we had to get straight before we could work together.

"We can't—"

"Sleep together anymore?" he snapped. "I figured that out for myself, Elise."

"I was going to say 'keep sniping at each other,' but that, too."

There was no way I would continue an affair with a man who found me disgusting—especially when I still loved him. I might be pathetic, but I wasn't stupid.

"Fine." His jaw tightened.

"We'll work together." I held out my hand. "But nothing else."

He stared at my palm for several seconds, then spun on his heel and headed into the trees.

"I'll take that as a yes," I shouted at his retreating back.

The ride back to Fairhaven was silent. We reached town about 3 A.M.

"Looks like the deputy's back," Nic murmured, eyes on the sheriff's office, where every light blazed.

"Guess we should tell him he's been promoted," I said.

"Mmm. He's not going to be happy."

"Why not?" I let my gaze wander over the quiet,

peaceful street. "Fairhaven seems a decent place to be a sheriff."

"It was."

"He's a cop. He'll do his job."

"I don't doubt he will. But small towns usually hire retired law-enforcement officers—old men who don't want any more hassles."

"Oh," I muttered, understanding why Basil might not be thrilled to learn of his sudden promotion to head cop of a town with serious troubles.

Nic stopped the car, shut off the motor.

"I don't think we're supposed to actually tell him what's going on," I returned.

"We don't know what's going on."

"Then there shouldn't be any problem. But werewolves, disappearing bodies. Let's just keep that to ourselves, shall we?"

"What if we just tell him what we know? As little as that is."

"Rule number one," I recited. "No truth for civilians. They panic, then they call the press. *The National Enquirer* would be a real pain right now."

"I suppose."

I got out of the car. Nic followed and together we climbed the steps to the sheriff's office.

"But I don't like keeping law-enforcement officials in the dark. This guy should know what he's facing."

I reached for the door just as it opened, and I nearly fell into the man on the other side. He wasn't old. Though at least twenty-one, since he was a deputy, Basil Moore appeared much younger.

His long, wheat-shaded hair was tied in a ponytail. His cheekbones were high and sharp, his eyes bright green. He could have been a model, except for the scar that bisected his right cheek. What a waste.

Then again, the scar gave him the air of a pirate in a modern world. The perfection's marring only seemed to highlight how perfect he was.

"Deputy." I straightened. "I'm Elise Hanover. This is Dominic Franklin."

"FBI," Nic said, offering his hand, and in doing so, including me as one of them.

I let it pass. If Basil thought I was FBI, that saved a lot of questions as to what I actually was.

"More FBI?" Basil asked, shaking Nic's hand, then nodding to me.

"More?" Nic asked.

"That tall gal and the Injun." His lip curled. "Too damned friendly, if ya ask me. What the hell's she thinking?"

I recalled Will's description of Basil—not an Indian lover. I'd heard people like him existed, but I hadn't really believed it.

Basil kept on talking in a striking bass voice that would have been lovely if he hadn't been such a racist. "They were FBI, too. Why on earth the government would hire a red man, I have no idea."

Nic glared at me and I shrugged. I wasn't surprised Jessie and Will and probably Edward, too, had identified themselves as FBI. We lied all the time so we could do our jobs with the least amount of questions asked.

Besides, our usual lies—we were with the DNR,

there was rabies, and so on—wouldn't work in Fairhaven. There weren't any wolves.

"Yes, well—" Nic cleared his throat. "Will and Jessie found Sheriff Stephenson."

"I'd hope so since I told them exactly where he was."

"You didn't tell them he'd be dead."

Basil blinked. "Dead?"

"As in 'not alive,' " I offered.

Nic threw me a quelling stare, and I shut my mouth.

"I guess that makes you the acting sheriff," Nic continued. "Where have you been? I've been calling since the body was discovered."

"I was talkin' to some folks around town. They're upset. People disappear, and they start whisperin' about black magic, Devil worship, witches." Basil's eyes narrowed. "You think something like that is going on in Fairhaven?"

"Nothing like *that*," I muttered.

"Should I grab Dr. Watchry and head to the crime scene?" Basil asked.

"The doctor's been there already. He examined the body. Before—" Nic broke off and Basil sighed.

"Gone again?"

"I'm afraid so."

"Don't suppose anyone saw who stole it this time."

"One minute it was there," I said, "the next, poof."

Nic lifted a brow in my direction. I ignored him.

People hear what they want to hear, and Basil was no different. "I wish I knew who this crazy was, and how he managed to steal bodies with no one seein' him."

"Mmm," I agreed.

"What was Sheriff Stephenson doing out there?" Nic asked.

"Report of a grave desecration. Happens sometimes, here and around. Usually kids."

"Has it been happening a lot lately?"

"No more than usual."

"And what's usual for something like that?"

"Now and again. Few times a year maybe."

"Hmm," Nic muttered.

I understood his concern. Anything odd, especially anything odd that had to do with the dead, was cause for inquiry—both in his world and mine.

"I didn't see any graves. Did you?" Nic asked.

I shook my head.

"There are graves all over the woods," Basil said. "Folks buried their dead wherever they dropped in the old days."

"That's true," I agreed.

"And this grave?" Nic pressed. "Whose was it? Who called and said it had been disturbed?"

Basil shrugged. "I didn't take the call, but from the location I'd say that was the Anderson homestead. You'd have to look at the plot maps to be sure."

"I'd also like to see the paperwork," Nic said.

"Paperwork?"

"On the grave desecrations. Just point me in the right direction."

"I can't think that there's paperwork on something so simple."

I understood Basil's confusion. Though murders were rare, mischief was not. Bored kids did a lot of drinking in the woods, at the end of dead-end roads, on dusty trails, then they got into trouble. Until recently, a little grave-digging was probably the most excitement anyone got in Fairhaven.

"I suppose this means you Feds are going to be taking over the case," Basil murmured.

Nic and I glanced at each other.

"Yes," I said. "That's exactly what it means."

21

"Let's regroup." Nic stepped out of the sheriff's office and headed for the cabin.

The door was unlocked. A note and the key lay on the kitchen table.

Don't forget to talk to Cora Kopway, I read in what I assumed was Will's precise scrawl. He'd also drawn a map to her cottage.

"Who's Cora Kopway?" Nic asked.

"Ojibwe wisewoman."

"And you're supposed to talk to her why?"

"Remember that talisman we found in Montana?"

Which reminded me . . .

I left the kitchen and ran into the bedroom, retrieved the icon from my sweatpants and returned with it in my hand.

Nic sat at the table, scribbling notes onto a notepad he'd produced from Lord knows where. He didn't even glance up when I entered. "What about it?"

Quickly I related what had happened since the icon

came into my possession, as well as Will's thoughts and the need to talk to Cora. At least he stopped taking notes.

"You're *more* powerful?"

"Yes."

"And you don't know why?"

"No."

He stood. "Let's go talk to her."

I glanced at the clock. Close to 4 A.M. now. "Isn't it a little early for visiting?"

"You said she was old. She'll be awake."

Since he was already headed through the door, I hurried to catch up.

The sun wasn't even a smoky glow against the eastern sky when Nic parked in front of a small cottage several miles outside of Fairhaven. But the windows were lit, and as we got out of the car, the front door opened. A young, beautiful woman stood on the threshold as if she'd been waiting for us to arrive.

Her skin was olive, not the cinnamon shade of Will's, but her hair was just as dark, flowing to her waist like a waving ebony river. Her eyes, black and heavily lashed, gazed at us curiously, but she didn't speak, she merely waited. Talk about aging gracefully; Will's ancient wisewoman didn't appear a day over twenty-five.

"We'd like to speak with Cora Kopway," I said.

"My grandmother joined the spirits last week."

Hell. We were SOL when it came to information if Cora was dead.

"I'm sorry to hear that. Will Cadotte said she might be able to help us."

"The professor!" An expression of pure delight blossomed. "Grandmother spoke of him often. He didn't come with you?"

"He was called away."

We stood silent, her on the porch, Nic and I in the yard.

"Well—" I began.

"Would you mind if we took a look at some of your grandmother's books?" Nic asked.

"Of course not. She'd be happy to help any friend of Professor Cadotte's."

The woman opened the door wider. When she moved, a sound, like faint jingle bells, ensued. Golden bangles circled her arms; red, blue, and yellow beaded earrings tangled with her hair, their colors a reflection of the calf-length skirt and frilly peasant blouse. I caught a glimpse of an ankle bracelet, as well as several toe rings on her bare feet.

"I'm Lydia."

"Elise Hanover," I replied. "This is Nic Franklin."

She nodded in welcome to us both.

The place was lovely, overflowing with Indian paintings and sculptures. Most were of animals: bear, moose, birds, coyotes, and, of course, wolves.

One table held dried bones and what appeared to be teeth. Candles of all shapes, sizes, and colors graced the room. Pottery bowls stood on each table; some held powders, some unidentified objects.

I smelled fresh-cut grass, sandalwood, and new snow on a crisp winter night. I was reminded of Montana beneath a full moon, and for the first time in a lifetime I missed the place.

Bookshelves lined the walls, filled to the ceiling with volumes whose spines reflected every shade of the rainbow. More cluttered the tables and the floor, some rested on furniture the hues of the earth and the sky at sunset: mahogany, sand, azure, burnt orange.

"It's beautiful," I breathed.

"Thank you." Lydia stepped into the room just behind me. "Grandmother left me the place, and I'm grateful. She'll be a great loss to the Ojibwe community."

"Will said she was quite knowledgeable."

"Very. She was teaching me, but there was so much to learn."

Here was good news. Maybe we weren't SOL after all.

"We're interested in information on shamanic totems with mystical power," I said.

"What kind of power?"

"Shape-shifting."

Her gaze sharpened. "Into what?"

"Wolf."

"Weendigo," she whispered, and one of the candles sputtered, then went out, leaving a trail of smoke behind.

"I always hate it when that happens," I muttered.

Lydia struck a match and relit the wick. The flame held steady and sure.

"What's a *Weendigo*?" Nic asked.

"The Great Cannibal," Lydia answered. "Ojibwe werewolf."

Nic cleared his throat, turned so Lydia couldn't see, then pointed at his teeth.

I frowned, considering. There'd been a bite mark on the single victim we'd seen. But human teeth, not wolf. No flesh removed.

What about the others that no one could find? For all we knew, they could have been sporting bite marks, too, or missing big chunks of skin—kind of hard to tell without the bodies. We had something to think about.

I shook my head, indicating we'd keep the information to ourselves for now. We were here to discuss the talisman, not the disappearances.

"Getting back to the totem," I said.

"A sacrifice would be required to imbue the icon with power."

"Rabbit," Nic muttered.

"Unusual choice," Lydia said. "But blood is blood. What is the totem made from?"

"Plastic," Nic blurted, before I could show her the thing.

He was right to be cautious. The icon was evidence—of what, we didn't know. But passing the thing around like a brand-new baby could be a mistake.

"Also unusual," Lydia continued. "But Grandmother always said it's not the vessel that matters but the magic. The power behind the plastic is what counts. A spell, correctly performed by a shaman, could make anything a conduit. However, there aren't a lot of people left with that kind of power."

"Could Cora have done it?" Nic asked.

Lydia cast a quick glance his way. "If she wasn't dead."

Nic dipped his chin in acknowledgment before

asking, "I don't suppose you know any others of Cora's stature?"

"No, but I can ask around."

"I'd appreciate it." Nic removed a card from his pocket and handed it to Lydia. "You can reach us at this number."

I glanced at the books. "Are there volumes on shamanic transformation?"

"I haven't seen any, but that doesn't mean they aren't there. Help yourself."

"I'll take a quick look." Nic headed for the nearest stack.

Silence settled between us. We smiled, glanced away. Now what?

I'd never been good at making friends. Becoming a werewolf and being relegated to a compound in Montana hadn't improved the skill.

Crossing to the window, I peered out. The forest came right up to the cottage. Most people would be claustrophobic, but to me the trees were soothing, both refuge and retreat.

"Sorry." Lydia joined me. "I'm not very good with people. Comes from spending too much time with just myself and my books."

She thought *she* was being geeky. Her insecurity called out to my own.

"I have the same problem," I said.

My gaze was caught by a shadow. Something slunk low to the ground. Something furry, with ears and a tail.

"Did you see that?" I asked.

"What?"

"There." I pointed. "A wolf."

"No wolves around here. Probably a coyote."

The shadow had seemed damn big for a coyote, but then, shadows were like that.

"You've never seen any wolves?"

"Not since I moved in. Coyotes, though. A lot of them."

And where there were a lot of one, there weren't any of the other. Wolves would tolerate foxes in their territory, but never coyotes. Another of nature's little mysteries.

"I've heard there are quite a few crows, too," I observed. "They usually hang around wolves."

"I read something about that in a book on Chippewa legends."

Chippewa being the misspelling of *Ojibwe* by the government on treaties and other official documents. The mistake had made its way into common usage.

"I meant *Ojibwe*," Lydia said quickly. "The author kept using the term *Chippewa legend.* I can't get it out of my mind."

She smacked herself in the forehead with the heel of her hand.

A second shadow skirted the cool confines of the forest, distracting me.

"What's so interesting?"

Nic stood behind us.

"Elise thought she saw a wolf."

He stared out the window for several moments. I held my breath. Did I want him to see a wolf, or didn't I?

"Nothing," he murmured.

"Must have been a coyote," Lydia reiterated.

Was I jumping at shadows? Probably. In my world, shadows often turned out to be real.

"We should go," Nic said.

"You didn't find anything useful in Grandmother's books?"

"No. But thanks for letting me look."

"Nice meeting you." Lydia followed us to the door. "Come back anytime."

I stepped outside and sniffed, but the wind blew toward the forest—the wrong direction for me to scent anything but grass and trees, a few squirrels.

The sun was just peeking over the horizon. Werewolves, for the most part, exist from dusk to dawn. However, the exact minute of dawn is hard to put a finger on without an almanac.

"What's the matter?" Nic asked as we climbed into the car and drove away.

I flipped my finger toward the sky. "Too close to sunrise to have been anything but coyotes. Or real wolves."

"Okay." Nic shrugged.

"Then again, maybe not."

"Because?"

"The *Weendigo* shifted anytime he wanted to, into any shape he saw fit. Luckily, he's dead."

Thanks to Damien and Leigh.

"There can't be another one?"

A cheery thought, however—

"No. Or at least not right now. A *Weendigo* is made between the harvest and the hunter's moon."

"Which means nothing to me," Nic pointed out.

"Harvest moon is in September, hunter's October. Since it's November we're headed for the beaver or the frost moon."

"Where do you get this stuff?"

"From books. The Indians coined names for each full moon. In November, the swamps freeze and the beavers wander. The People would set traps and make winter blankets of the heavy pelts."

"A kind of calendar—a way to mark time by the moon."

"Right. But I don't remember reading anything about the beaver moon and disappearing bodies. I'll have to talk to Will." I held out my hand. "Cell phone?"

"That's a for-sure thing? The moon influencing—"

"Werewolves?" I interrupted. "Oh, yeah."

"Okay." He gave me his phone. "So no *Weendigo*. But that bite mark on the body bugs me."

"Me, too. I think we should talk to the medical examiner."

Nic's fingers tightened on the steering wheel. "Me, too."

22

As Nic drove back to town, I placed another call to Jessie.

"What?" she snapped. "A little *busy* here!"

Gunshots punctuated her words.

"If you're that damn busy, why'd you answer the phone?"

"What do you want?"

"Will."

"Can't have him. Mine."

"I need to ask a question. Is he there?"

Her put-upon sigh was followed by Will's voice. "Hey! Do not throw the phone at my head unless you warn me first. Hello?"

I didn't bother with niceties. I figured he had places to go, werewolves to kill—or at least he needed to hold Jessie's ammo while she killed them.

"You know anything about the beaver moon?"

"It's in a few days. Why? Did you talk to Cora?"

"No." I hesitated, not wanting to impart bad news over the phone, but what choice did I have? "Cora's dead, Will."

He sighed. "Damn."

"What?" I heard Jessie ask. Either my hearing was improving or she was shouting—maybe both. "Why the long face?"

"Cora's gone," Will answered.

"Got on her broom and took off at last, huh?"

I guessed the two of them hadn't been pals.

"Cora took Jessie's voice away once," Will explained.

"Took away?"

"Purple powder. *Bam*. Jessie couldn't talk."

"Really? Can I buy that stuff?"

"Not for sale. I already asked."

"Funny. Har-har," Jessie said loudly. "Old bat."

"Have some respect for the dead, Jess."

"She's dead?"

"What does *gone* mean to you?"

"Left town. Took a trip. Not *dead*. Jeez, who taught you how to break bad news?" Her voice softened. "I'm sorry, Will. I know how much you liked her."

"Yeah. I did. And every time we lose an elder, we lose a lot of knowledge."

"Cora appears to have been teaching Lydia the old ways," I said.

"Who's Lydia?"

Quickly I filled Will in on what had happened at the cottage in the woods.

"No *Weendigo* this time," Will murmured. "I have to say I am *not* disappointed—even though we do know how to kill one of those."

"Returning to our present problem," I said. "Beaver moon, disappearing bodies. Ring any bells?"

"Not offhand. I'll check around."

Gunshots broke out on their side of the line.

"Gotta go," Will said. "I'll get back to you."

"Well?" Nic said.

He stopped the car in front of Dr. Watchry's clinic and shut off the engine.

"He'll get back to me."

"Okay. In the meantime"—Nic nodded toward the building in front of us—"shall we?"

Together we got out of the car and headed for the door, but before we reached the clinic a tiny, elderly woman tottered out of Murphy's—the tavern that was always open, or had been before the disappearances. Right now it appeared to be not only open but full.

The woman didn't waste any time with introductions. "What are you doing about our dilemma?" She waved a paper-white, heavily veined hand toward the bar. "We're concerned."

From the smell of her breath, she was drowning her concerns along with the rest of the population.

I peered up and down the street. All the other businesses had CLOSED signs in the windows; the road was deserted except for Nic, me, and the little old lady. Maybe everyone *was* in the bar.

"People disappearing?" Her voice became more loud and shrill with every word. "Sheriff Stephenson murdered. What kind of person would steal a body?"

Basil had been busy soothing the populace with our lie, or maybe the doctor had, although it didn't appear as if they were very calm.

"Have you seen any strangers in town, ma'am?"

I glanced at Nic. *Good idea.* He really was very handy to have around.

"Besides the FBI?"

"Yes."

"My eyes ain't what they used to be. There was a man come through." She frowned. "Reminded me of Thor the Thunder God."

Someone broke a glass inside the bar and the woman gasped, then put a palm to her chest. She was spooked. I could hardly blame her.

The town had never seen a murder, now they had several missing citizens, probably dead, and a dead sheriff, now missing.

"What is the FBI going to do about the latest murder?" she demanded.

"All that we can, ma'am." Nic attempted to guide her back into the bar, but she didn't want to go.

"Two in one night. What is the world coming to?"

Nic paused. "Two what?"

"Two murders. Try to keep up, boy."

"Two?" Nic glanced at me and I shrugged. "Sheriff Stephenson and . . . ?"

"Susie Gerant. The doctor's receptionist."

Nic and I left the elderly lady on the street as we ran for the doctor's office.

"He isn't there," she called.

We stopped, turned.

"He went to examine the body." Her face crinkled in thought. "Not sure where."

"Sheriff Moore?" Nic asked.

"Haven't seen him."

We checked the clinic anyway. Drab waiting room with stained carpet, uncomfortable chairs, out-of-date magazines, banged-up toys piled into a laundry basket in the corner. But no doctor, or anyone else for that matter, so Nic left a note on the desk.

The sheriff's office was just as empty. No sign of Basil, not even a message on the activity board.

Nic cursed. "You'd think he'd call and let us know there was another body."

"Or be kind enough to leave a map."

"Or that." Nic called Basil's cell phone, cursing at the voice mail.

"Sheriff," he said tersely into the phone. "This is Agent Franklin. We need to talk. Call me, or come to the cabin ASAP."

When he had disconnected we stood in the center of the room at a loss. Now what?

"Thor the Thunder God?" Nic murmured. "Who's that? A north woods bogeyman?"

"More like someone she sees after too many cocktails. Probably a Norse myth, since there are a lot of Norwegians around here, or so I hear. We could look it up, but I don't really care."

"Ditto," Nic said. "Maybe we should get some sleep."

"It's eight o'clock in the morning."

"You're not tired?" Nic must have seen the weariness play across my face because he didn't wait for an answer. "We might as well rest until the doctor or Basil gets back."

We crossed the short space between the two buildings, and after a quick, silent meal of eggs and toast, headed for bed.

My face heated as we neared my room. I glanced at Nic and saw only his back disappearing into what had been Jessie and Will's space.

My lips tightened. It wasn't as if I'd expected him to join me, but I still felt as if I'd been slapped.

"Idiot," I muttered, and slammed my door.

The cabin rental must have come with linen service, because my sheets had been changed, the bed made.

Thank God.

I doubt I could have slept on sheets that smelled of him. As it was, I tossed and turned as memories assaulted me. Both present and past. Real and imagined.

I'd known all along Nic wouldn't be able to handle what I was, understand what I'd become. That he'd hate me both for leaving him and the necessity of it. But I hadn't realized how much his rejection would hurt. Never suspected that I'd been harboring the hope, the delusion, that he could love me no matter what.

"Moron." I punched the pillow and tried once more to sleep.

I had a doozy of a dream.

The future was bright and sunny. House in the suburbs, flower beds, picket fence, really nice minivan. I was a doctor who had actual patients that were people. My husband was—

"Nic!"

"Sweetheart," he murmured, as he stepped out of the house, arms wide to welcome me home.

Love washed over me with a suddenness that made my knees weak. Luckily Nic was holding me up, his kiss making promises without saying a word.

He lifted his head. "The baby's teething."

"Huh?"

"I feel so bad for her."

From inside came the wail of a child. I glanced around the yard.

A bicycle, a bat and glove.

"Mommy," a voice squealed, and a blond whirlwind shot out of the house, giving my knees a quick hug before picking up the bat and banging it against the nearest tree.

I kind of liked this dream.

Or I did until the gate opened, and Billy walked into the yard. Why did he appear more frightening wearing clothes in a suburb than he had naked behind glass? Must be the blood all over his face.

"Why aren't you furry?" I asked.

"Don't need to be. Killing people around here is so damn easy."

I glanced up the block. Everything was far too still. A trail of red led down the sidewalk between each house, ending right behind Billy's shoes.

In the way of dreams, I was both experiencing the situation and observing myself from above. I remembered Billy telling me this story before.

He liked to go to nice suburbs in good neighborhoods where he could walk right in, door after door after door. He was so good at killing, most people didn't have a chance to scream. The neighbors never knew he was coming.

I shook my head, tried to clear the dizziness. I knew this was a dream, yet everything seemed so damn real. I could smell the blood, hear my son singing, the baby crying, see Billy right in front of me, so alive.

"You're dead," I said.

He smiled and his teeth were red. "Do I look dead to you?"

"Fuck," I muttered.

"Yeah, I thought we might. But first—"

Billy turned toward my son and I launched myself at him. He smacked me in the chest with one arm, swatting me away as if I were nothing more than an irritating bug. I flew into Nic, who'd been right behind me, and we tumbled to the ground.

I thought of the moon and got nothing, reached for a talisman that didn't exist in this dimension, and realized with dawning horror that in this happy normal world, I wasn't a werewolf.

So I could do nothing but die.

If it meant saving my family, I didn't mind. However, Billy was still insane, even without the fur.

He rounded on me, punching Nic in the face, sending him to the ground unconscious. My son, whatever his name was, continued to play as if nothing were happening. In the house, the baby wailed.

"You aren't normal, Doctor, and you never will be."

"I am. See?" I pointed to the house, the fence.

He laughed, revealing those disgusting teeth again. "I'm your future."

"You're dead," I repeated.

"I'll never really be dead, because I'm all of them. No matter how many you kill, there'll be more."

"What if I find a cure?"

"We don't want to be cured. We like the killing, the fear." He leaned over, nuzzling my neck with his rank mouth. "The blood."

I struggled, but it was no use. He was stronger, crazier, and this was a nightmare. I couldn't win.

Just like life.

Despair rushed through me. He was right; I'd never be normal, even if I found a cure. There'd always be more monsters. They'd always be after me. And I'd always carry the burden of the people I had killed.

Unlike Billy, who'd never given a damn, even before he was a werewolf.

"Well." He lifted his head, shoved me hard enough to send me flying several feet, where I landed in the flower bed. "First things first. Kill the family, eat the baby, *then* fuck you. Ready?"

His mouth grew fangs, his eyes went wolf as he fell on an unconscious Nic and—

I came awake, heart pounding, all sweaty and alone in the night. For a minute I thought Billy was there, in the room with me, and a sob escaped.

I stifled the sound. Billy would love my tears, had told me on many an occasion how he enjoyed licking them from the cheeks of his victims as they died.

I shivered and pulled the blanket to my chin, eyes searching the room, nose twitching as I tested the air. Billy wasn't here, of course.

He was dead. I had killed him.

The knowledge wasn't as comforting as it should have been.

23

The shrill ring of the phone nearly made me jump out of my skin. Following the sound into the hall, I snatched up the receiver. "Hello?"

Static came over the line, so loud I pulled the phone away from my ear.

"Hello?" I tried again.

"Junkyard."

Screeech!

"Edge of town."

More static.

"Edsel behind a blue school bus."

I could barely understand the words. I couldn't recognize the voice.

"What?"

Snap.

"Research."

Crackle.

"Serum."

"Edward?" I asked.

Pop.

The line went dead.

I hung up and considered what I'd heard. Edward hadn't called in, perhaps because he was back. In the junkyard. Waiting for me to come and get my research.

But what if that hadn't been Edward?

Shaking my head, I headed into the bedroom, got dressed, checked my pocket for the icon—still there—then grabbed my shoes.

Outside Nic's door, I paused and listened. I could hear him breathing, slow and steady. Asleep.

Good. I wasn't going to take him with me. Not this time.

I had to retrieve my research and create more serum, or I'd do a lot more than change. I'd kill. I wouldn't be able to stop myself.

I jogged north on Midtown Road. When the buildings ended, there was a junkyard. No fence encircled the area. If anyone wanted to drag away a wreck, more power to them.

I'd slept through the day dreaming of Billy, and the cool caress of the moon trickled over my skin. Only a few nights from full, the orb was growing along with my hunger. With that thought driving me, I waded into the jungle of metal.

For a tiny town, they had a lot of old cars. It took me ten minutes to locate a blue bus. Behind the vehicle, half-covered by the low-hanging branches of a very old tree, sat an Edsel. Or at least that was what the nameplate said. I'd never seen one before.

There was a bite to the night, a chill in the air. I could have sworn a ghostly howl rose toward the stars, but when I turned my face upwind, I smelled nothing but motor oil.

Edward was nowhere to be found.

Unease trickled over me. The darkness pressed down; a sudden silence seemed to pulse with secrets and questions. My shoulders twitched as if I had a neon bull's-eye painted on my back.

I walked around the Edsel. Where would I hide research, if I was the one doing the hiding?

I went through the car, the trunk, the glove compartment. Nothing there but leaves, so I crawled underneath, checked the carriage, the tires, the ground, but there was no sign of any recent disturbance. I began to get the drift that the phone call hadn't been on the up-and-up.

Crawling out from under the car, I jogged back the way I'd come. I'd reached the main thoroughfare through the center of the junkyard, little more than a large space between the wrecks, when I stopped.

Clouds danced past the moon, spreading a ghostly, flickering light. Shadows danced among the dead vehicles. Something slunk low in the tall grass at the edge of the clearing.

The breeze whispered, caressing my skin, making me shiver. Something was here. I turned in a slow circle and my fingers brushed fur.

Glancing at my hand, I scowled. I could still feel the tactile impression, but I saw nothing.

A body thumped into the back of my legs, sending me forward. I tripped over an invisible barrier and slammed into the ground.

Flipping onto my back, I tensed in expectation of an attack. None came.

More edgy than I'd ever been, I got to my feet. The hair on my arms and at the back of my neck vibrated with awareness. I couldn't run; I couldn't just stand here and let whatever was stalking me do its worst. I had power of my own, but in human form I was as helpless as everyone else.

As I tilted my face to the moon, Jessie's jeans split at the seams; so did her shirt. My shoes cracked open with an annoyingly ripe shriek, and I was free.

The odd, faint scent of wolf distracted me. I heard them growling, pacing, hunting, but all I saw were wisps and shadows.

Nothing concrete. If I hadn't smelled wolves, heard them, too, I wouldn't have been able to distinguish just what it was that wavered here and there like ghosts.

A slight movement and I spun just as a shimmering shade blew through me. I was cold, then hot. I heard the whisper of a voice I couldn't understand, caught a glimpse of . . . something I couldn't quite place.

As I turned slowly with a stiff-legged gait, wavering entities surrounded me. I darted at one, but it danced out of my way. Another levitated, then flew off into the trees. A third let me catch it, but when I encountered the strange cold spot, the whisper, I yelped and backpedaled with all my might.

"Who's out there?"

I froze at the strange voice and ducked behind a rusted pickup truck. A graying, grizzled old man wandered through the wrecks. The night watchman or maybe the owner, he carried a rifle; however, that wasn't what made the ruff on the back of my neck lift.

A low rumble spread across the night. A distinct

warning, which the man didn't appear to hear, even when the growl increased in volume and was joined by several others.

Shadows flickered, circled, converged.

Torn, I perched near the left truck tire, hoping whatever stalked the junkyard would go away. A pained whine erupted from my mouth, and the man's gaze swung in my direction. Me, he could hear.

I ducked low and hid behind the bumper. The shadows inched closer; the growls escalated to snarls. I had no choice.

Though the ghostly wolves might not be able to hurt me, they might hurt him. I couldn't let an innocent civilian be bitten or killed by Lord knows what.

Bursting from cover, I ran straight at the first shadow in my path. I braced for the disturbing cold spot; nevertheless when I thundered through it I lost my footing, then tumbled across the grass, snarling, snapping at half a dozen other cold spots.

I reached my feet, spun about, saw nothing and felt even less. Were they gone?

Panting, I paced. Too much power, too much adrenaline. I had to fight something. Kill it and now.

I caught a faint scent and followed it to the trees. Diving in, I sensed them all around me. My lip curled. I showed them my teeth.

Come on! I wanted to shout. *I can take you. I can take all of you.*

The foliage shivered. The odd smell faded. They had run because they were afraid, and I loved it.

Tingling, I shook my fur as if I'd just stepped out of

an icy river. Unable to contain myself, I tilted my nose to the moon and howled.

As the sound of my exultation faded, the wind whispered, and this time I understood the words.

Give in to the power. Embrace what you are and discover the secret you seek.

I contemplated the message as the rushing of my blood and the racing of my heart lessened. The air seemed cooler, the moon brighter, the trees taller, and the grass softer, more fragrant.

My head buzzed with the glory, the mystery, the strength, which was the only reason I forgot about the watchman until the squelch of a shoe against wet earth made me remember. By then it was too late.

He shot me.

24

His gun was filled with lead. Regardless, being shot hurt. Really, really hurt.

And he shot me in the butt. How mortifying.

I wanted to shout, curse, cry. Instead I ran.

At first all I could think of was getting away, so I accelerated in the general direction of Cuba. However, when my skin began to heal the hole with the bullet still inside, I detoured to the cabin.

Approaching from the rear, I sniffed the air and smelled nothing but trees, heard only the wind. Leaping onto the back porch, I imagined myself human and suddenly I was.

The talisman resided in the pocket of Jessie's pants back at the junkyard. Even though I didn't appear to need it anymore, I wanted the icon back. And I'd get it, just as soon as I removed the irritating bullet from my ass.

I could get used to changing back and forth in the

blink of an eye. The lack of pain and agony was a definite plus.

Making use of my suddenly opposable thumb, I turned the doorknob, slipped inside, then straight into the bathroom. The glare of the electric light made me flinch even before I saw myself in the mirror.

Dirt streaked my face; my hair was full of leaves and twigs; fiery red scratches marred my arms. Twisting awkwardly, I tried to see my wound, but I couldn't.

The bullet seemed to be scraping me from the inside out. What didn't kill me might just drive me mad. I was going to have to ask for help, and I hated that.

I opened the bathroom door, and yelped. Nic stood on the other side. One glance at my face and he cursed, then shoved his way into the room.

I snatched a towel off the rack and clutched it to my breasts. *Stupid.* He'd already seen and touched everything already.

"What the hell happened?" Nic demanded.

I wasn't sure where to start.

"I woke up and you were gone. No note. Nothing."

Nic shoved his fingers through his hair, making it stand on end, reminding me of the coarse blond locks of our dream child.

I shoved the image out of my head. That child wasn't real, could never *be* real, and I had to remember that.

Nic wore nothing but boxers. Too bad I didn't have time to admire his physique. Blood flowed down the back of my legs and dripped onto the floor.

"What the—"

Nic yanked the towel free and spun me around. I was so shocked, I let him.

"Who shot you?"

"Guy in the junkyard. The owner, or maybe the night watchman."

"I take it you were furry at the time," he murmured. "Or he and I are going to have a discussion."

I glanced over my shoulder and caught an expression of such violence cross his face I was shocked—and a little bit charmed.

I could take care of myself—bullet in the butt notwithstanding—but it was kind of nice for once to have someone else want to look after me.

Nic saw me staring and schooled his face into the stoic mask I'd come to loathe. "You'd better get in the bathtub. You're making a mess."

"Good idea." I climbed in.

"What were you doing at the junkyard?"

Quickly I explained about the phone call, the Edsel, the watchman, and the ghostly wolves. When I was done, Nic stared at me without blinking. "Ghost wolves. Are they something new?"

"I've never heard of them. But now I know why I saw wolf shadows at Lydia's and caught the scent of wolves when everyone else swears there aren't any. At least I'm not nuts."

"Just able to see, smell, and hear things no one else can," he said dryly. "Do you think the disappearing bodies are related somehow?"

I thought for a minute, then shook my head. "The ghost wolves didn't do much beyond bump against me and spread cold spots. I doubt they're killing people. Besides, Sheriff Stephenson was killed with a knife, then marked with a *human* bite."

"Which means we've got two problems instead of one."

"At least."

"So what's the deal?" He waved at my rear end. "I thought werewolves could heal damn near anything."

"We can. Trouble is, I'm healing faster than usual. You're going to have to dig that out."

He didn't argue. "Got any medical instruments?"

"Not anymore."

"Oh, right. Compound go boom."

Leaning down, Nic peered at my left cheek. Funny how a little bullet and a lot of blood took care of any sexual interest in my nakedness. Or maybe discovering my true nature had already killed that.

"Will left a few things," he said. "Hold on."

He returned a few minutes later with a small leather case. Inside were several lethal-looking blades.

"Filleting knives." Nic began to root around in the medicine cabinet concealed behind the mirror over the sink. "Will must like to fish."

"What are you searching for?"

"Alcohol."

I snorted. "As if I'll get an infection."

"Humor me."

Removing a clear bottle, he doused the smallest of the knives, then withdrew a tweezers from the cabinet and doused that, along with his hands.

"Turn around," he said.

"No problem." I didn't want to watch.

Nic splashed my butt with alcohol, and I nearly

jumped out of the tub. "Hey! What did I say about infection?"

"Can you promise I won't get furry if I accidentally cut myself with your blood all over me?"

"I told you. The virus is only passed through saliva when I'm in wolf form."

"But things can change."

He was right. I had no idea what was happening to me. The virus could be mutating, and then everything I knew, or thought I knew, would be wrong.

"Leave it," I said. "I'll live."

"I'm not lame. I won't cut myself. Besides, you've got the handy-dandy antidote. If I get infected, you can cure me."

Could I? I no longer had the formula, and it wasn't exactly simple enough to remember off the top of my head. None of them were.

I hadn't heard from Edward since he'd left town. I was starting to worry. If he were to disappear, along with everything I'd invented, the world, as well as me, was in big-time trouble.

Nic poked me.

"Ow!"

"Hold still or you'll have more holes than you already do." He punctuated his words with another jab. "I've almost got it."

I stared at the bathroom tile and waited for him to finish. Within three minutes, something pinged against the bathtub, then rolled toward the drain, coming to rest on top of the steel trap.

Nic picked up the bullet. "Constantly amazes me that something this little can do so much damage."

He lifted his gaze and in his eyes I saw many things. Relief, anger, wariness, fear, and something else I couldn't quite place before he turned away, tossing the instruments into the sink and dousing them again with alcohol.

"You'd better take a shower."

His voice was remote once more, and I had to wonder if I'd seen or only imagined the softer emotions crossing his face.

I turned on the water. Even if Nic could get past my being a werewolf, there were so many other things about me he didn't know and never could.

"The wound's already healed over," he murmured.

I couldn't see the hole, and I didn't really want to. Yanking the shower curtain closed, I let the heated water wash the blood from my skin. If only it could wash the blood from my hands—or should I say *paws*?

"You mind if I stay while you explain what's going on?" he asked.

"Suit yourself." I stuck my head under the spray.

"Who called you?"

"I thought it was Edward."

Now I wasn't so sure.

"Does he have your research?"

"I hope so."

"Not having it. That's bad?"

"You have no idea." I scrubbed soap into my hair, working the suds from my scalp all the way to the ends. "Not only is the formula for the antidote gone, but so is the formula for me."

Nic yanked back the shower curtain. "What happens,

exactly, if you don't take your medicine? I thought you were different."

"I am." I pulled on the plastic. "You mind?"

He scowled but drew the curtain across the rod with a shriek of metal rings, and I began to rinse my hair.

"Werewolves can't help but change under the full moon," I explained. "There's no resisting its pull. I've tried to cure the transformation, but I've never been able to."

"So if you have to change, how are you different?"

"I was never possessed by evil—what we call the 'demon.' Killing people sickened me."

Nic had never been dumb. He heard what I wasn't saying. "You never *liked* to kill, but you did."

"The first time, the transformation is frightening, maddening."

The power is exhilarating.

The words whispered through my brain. Was that my thought or someone else's?

Someone else's?

I must have lost too much blood.

"The hunger," I whispered. "I can't describe it."

The agony in my belly, the pounding of my pulse, the shrieking in my head. Despite the steamy heat surrounding me, I shivered.

"You'll do anything to make the torment stop. Anything."

Silence from the other side of the curtain spoke louder than words. Nic was wondering why I hadn't eaten a silver bullet rather than a person. I'd wondered that myself. At least he didn't ask.

"If a werewolf doesn't partake of human blood on the night of the full moon, what happens? He dies?"

"No such luck."

If it were that easy, Edward could just lock up all the werewolves and forget about the key.

"Only silver ends a lycanthrope's existence. Or being killed by another werewolf. However, that's rare."

I'd found it bizarre that a lycanthrope would murder a human, yet balk at killing another werewolf, but no one ever said they were logical.

"Why is it rare?"

"There's a fail-safe, for want of a better term. Maybe a taboo, I guess, against killing our own kind. My personal theory is that the fail-safe is part of the demon."

"Which you don't have," Nic said slowly. "And neither does Damien."

Damien's curse had taken away not only his demon but any lingering concern about the werewolf rules. He'd also discovered that killing other werewolves took the edge off that pesky need for human sustenance. Convenient for him, since he hadn't had access to my serum.

"What about that *Weendigo* you and Lydia were discussing? The Great Cannibal?"

"I've known one—Hector Menendez. He was demon personified, and he had no problem killing werewolves."

"Which screws up your personal theory."

I'd thought a lot about Hector. Probably too much in the dark of the night.

"Since Hector had no problem breaking human taboos—" I began.

"Such as?"

"Eating people when he was still a people."

"I thought he was a werewolf cannibal."

"With Hector we got a twofer."

"A cannibal in both forms," Nic murmured, "so all of his fail-safes were broken."

I'd always enjoyed talking with Nic. He was so quick and bright, he'd often finish my thoughts before they came out of my mouth. That hadn't changed, even though almost everything else had.

"That's my theory," I agreed.

"But Hector's a little too dead to ask about it."

"Exactly."

"With regular werewolves, those with the demon and no access to your serum, what happens under the full moon?"

"The madness takes over. If they don't shift voluntarily, they'll do so automatically."

I closed my eyes and let the water beat down on my face, but nothing could make those memories go away.

Nic remained silent for several minutes. When he spoke again, I understood why. "Mandenauer told me you experienced your first transformation at Stanford. But why then?"

Hell. Trust Edward to tell Nic just enough to make him curious and not enough to make him stop questioning me.

I shut off the shower, then wrapped myself in a towel before opening the curtain.

Nic leaned against the sink, arms crossed over his

bare chest. His biceps bulged; his stomach was hard and flat, his legs long, muscled, and lightly covered with hair. I remembered what his hands felt like, what his skin tasted like. I forced myself to walk away, but Nic followed me into my bedroom and brought with him his questions.

"Was it the moon? Your age? A spell?" He made a disgusted sound. "A spell. I never thought I'd hear myself ask that."

I moved to the window, pushed the curtain aside, and let the silver soothe me. Funny, the icy glow that beat down from the sky, to me as strong as the sun in the middle of July, used to upset me. Now I was drawn to it.

"Does it matter?" I asked. "There's no going back."

Nic came up behind me, and I caught the scent of his hair, felt the heat pulsing off him like steam.

"Tell me," he insisted. "I deserve to know."

He did, although I didn't want to be the one to tell him. Too bad I was the only one here.

"Love," I said. "Love changed me."

"I don't understand."

I wasn't sure what else to say, so I hesitated. He lost his patience, not that he had much to begin with, and grabbed me by the shoulders, spinning me around.

"Tell me," he ordered through gritted teeth.

"Fine," I spat, through teeth just as tight. "Dopamine rushing through the brain, adrenaline making the heart pound, phenylethylamine creating the feeling of bliss, oxytocin bringing about sexual arousal."

My tone was clinical. I refused to look Nic in the eye. He released me as if I'd suddenly sprouted horns.

Maybe I had. "Falling in love with *me* made you a were-wolf?"

"No. My mother being bitten by a monster was what made me a werewolf. The virus was there waiting. It was only a matter of time."

"And the right person."

I shrugged and turned back to the window.

"You changed and then you disappeared. But what happened in between? You said the hunger was too much to bear the first time."

"It was."

"You killed someone?"

"Yes."

"And then?"

I stared at the moon, the trees, the night, and I remembered.

Then Edward had locked me in a cage.

25

"Elise?"

"Mmm?" I murmured, overcome by memories I'd tried so long to suppress.

"I never heard about a murder on campus."

"Edward can cover up anything. That's what he does."

And speaking of Edward—

I brushed past Nic to get to the phone in the hall. This time when I dialed Edward, he answered.

"Where are you?" I demanded.

"Taking care of business."

"Have someone else shoot them. I need my research."

"I am taking care of actual business, Elise. We have no command center. *Jäger-Suchers* from all over the world have been frantically calling my cell phone since you are no longer answering at headquarters. They are quite panicked."

"Nice to be loved."

"I do not think it is your absence that has upset them, but rather the loss of what is familiar."

Trust Edward to burst any bubble I might have blown.

I was somewhat concerned to realize that I'd completely forgotten my job. I wasn't a field agent. I was a lab geek. The organization queen.

I collected the reports, kept track of the agents, their assignments, while I tried to find a cure. All it had taken to forget my responsibilities was a little explosion and some great sex—or had that been a little sex and a great big explosion?

I glanced at Nic as he came into the hall. His hair was still mussed, his chest bare, he was getting a five o'clock shadow. I wanted to feel the scrape of his whiskers on the inside of my thighs.

Gritting my teeth, I turned away from temptation. Why didn't the man put on some *clothes*?

"When are you coming back to Fairhaven?" I demanded of Edward.

"You are still there?"

I'd forgotten; he didn't know, so I filled him in.

"Ghost wolves," Edward mused. "So many years and yet I have not heard everything."

"Amazing, isn't it?"

My sarcasm was lost on him.

"*Ja*. Why on earth would you go to the junkyard? I would never leave something so important to be easily found."

"Ever heard of hiding in plain sight?"

"That would not be hiding."

I sighed. Why did I even bother?

"You will have to deal with things as best you can. Everyone else is busy. Has the FBI left?"

"Not hardly. He's on the case."

Nic snorted from behind me. I didn't turn around.

"You have told him all of your secrets?" he demanded.

"Some."

"Have you no brains?"

"*You're* the one who started it, sir."

Edward went silent. He did that a lot when I was right.

"I cannot return to Fairhaven just yet," he continued. "There is someone after me."

"Again?"

Most of the monsters who'd met Edward face-to-face were ashes, but word still got around. They'd been sending assassins after him almost as long as he'd been sending *Jäger-Suchers* after them.

I wasn't sure if Edward lived a charmed life, or if he was as good at killing and evading as he claimed. I kind of thought it was both.

"I need that research."

"Would you like me to send everything in a Federal Express packet?"

"No!" I shouted.

Anyone could grab it then.

"That is what I thought." Edward sounded smug.

"You have everything with you?"

"Your formulas and serums could not be safer."

Unless whoever was chasing him this time actually caught him. Then I might as well eat a silver bullet, before I started eating my way through the citizens.

"I will be back before the full moon."

"You swear?"

"Have I ever broken a promise, Elise?"

As far as I knew, he'd never made one.

Before I could point this out, he hung up. I couldn't recall the man ever uttering the word *good-bye*, or *hello* for that matter.

Nic was no longer in the hall. I followed the sound of tapping into the kitchen and discovered him hunched over a laptop. He still wore only his underwear. Was he trying to kill me?

"Where'd you get that?" My voice was more shrill than I would have liked.

Nic didn't seem to notice. He didn't even look up when he answered. "I think it's Jessie's. I doubt Will's capable of leaving a computer behind. I've started an Internet search on ghost wolves."

Why hadn't I thought of that?

My gaze dipped to the flat, brown circle of his nipples surrounded by soft, curling dark hair.

Why did I continue to ask such stupid questions?

I listened to Nic tap on the keys, as I shifted my eyes to the wall and my mind off his body. A few moments later he grunted. "There's an Ojibwe legend about ghost wolves. They're called 'witchie wolves.' "

"Ojibwe," I murmured. "Not much of a shock."

"No," Nic agreed, before he continued to read. "Witchie wolves are said to protect an ancient burial ground on the eastern shore of Lake Huron. I wonder if they can exist anywhere else."

He typed in a few more commands, then squinted at the screen. "Huh."

"Let me guess. They can?"

"According to this, witchie wolves can be raised to protect the resting place of any ancient warrior against those who desecrate it."

He lifted his gaze. Together we muttered, "Grave desecrations."

"Let's see if there's an ancient warrior buried in Fairhaven," Nic murmured. "Although I kind of think that there is."

I moved closer, leaning over him as he tried the computer again. I caught the scent of his hair, my arm bumped the bare skin of his back. He jumped, but he didn't jerk away, so I stayed where I was, pretending to watch the computer screen when all I could see was him.

The machine whirred. "I'm not getting anything," he said.

"With Indian records that doesn't mean much. A lot of their history is oral."

He shot me a quick glance, and I swallowed a sudden burning in my throat. That *had* sounded a bit suggestive. I straightened so I was no longer pressed against his back, and coughed.

"We need to talk to a townsperson, an elder. Probably Lydia."

Nic looked at the clock. "Two in the morning. I don't think we'll have much luck right now."

"The doctor never got back to us about the second murder."

I didn't like that at all.

"Never heard from Basil, either," I continued.

"I'm starting to think he's avoiding us."

"I guess we can ask about stray Ojibwe warrior graves in the morning. Not like they're going to move or anything."

"True."

Silence settled over the room, broken only by the waiting hum of the laptop.

"Uh, anything else?" I flicked a finger at the computer.

"Huh?"

Nic's eyes were on my chest. I'm sure my nipples were hard and thrusting against the thin material of my shirt, as usual. I really needed to buy a bra.

"More info?" I waved in front of his face.

"Oh." Nic cracked his knuckles. "Let's see."

Clatter-tap-tap.

He sat back and waited. "I cross-referenced witchie wolves and werewolves."

I lifted my brows. "You're really good at this."

"Among other things."

He surprised a laugh out of me. I was even more surprised when he grinned in return. But his smile faded quickly as the computer beeped. He peered at the words. "You aren't going to believe this."

"Wanna bet?"

"Witchie wolves are considered werewolves because they were human once."

"Looks like the sheriff called in the right people after all."

"Human in life, they're cursed to run as wolves in death, a transformation of sorts."

"Why are they cursed?"

"Doesn't say, but—"

He tilted his head. I could see an idea flickering to life in the same way answers spilled from the Internet and onto the computer screen.

"Wanna share?" I asked.

His gaze lifted to mine. "We've got dead people and ghost wolves."

"Two dead people."

"And a lot of missing ones who've left blood behind. Considering the sheriff's disappearing act . . . You do the math."

"You think our disappearing bodies are becoming witchie wolves?"

"Yeah," Nic said. "I do."

I did, too. But I wasn't sure what we were going to do about it.

"I'll call Lydia in the morning," Nic continued. "Ask if Cora had a book on witchie wolves."

"That would be a good place to start."

Silence fell between us. Nic and I glanced at each other, then away. Now what? A whole night stretched in front of us with nothing much to do.

"I'll see you then." He stood and practically ran out of the room.

At loose ends, I sat in front of the computer. I accessed my credit card account, requested a replacement, and wrote down my number. Then I amused myself for an hour surfing the Net and ordering new clothes. Jessie had left most of hers, and they'd hold me over, but I'd lost everything in the compound explosion. Sooner or later I'd have to buy new. Why not now, if it kept me from going after Nic and begging him to touch me?

When that was done, I wandered the cabin. No television. What kind of place was this?

Vacation home. Still, what was more relaxing than TV?

I glanced longingly down the hall toward Nic's room. I could think of a few things.

Eventually the boredom dragged on me and I yawned. If I could fall asleep, morning would come so much quicker. I stripped, then checked my wound, which was already nothing more than a small scab.

I'd just reached for Jessie's sleep T-shirt when my door opened. Nic stood on the threshold. I couldn't fathom the expression in his eyes. Desire warred with fear, lust pushed at the boundaries of sadness. He wanted me, though he shouldn't. He longed for the past, yet feared the future. And below everything I detected a smidgen of guilt, which was exactly what I hadn't wanted him to feel. None of this was his fault.

"If you could have known what would happen to you," he murmured, "you never would have spoken to me that first day."

I tilted my head. The library at Stanford. He'd dropped his book on my foot, then apologized so profusely, so sweetly, I'd let him carry mine home. We'd spent the night talking, the dawn kissing, and from that moment on we'd been together.

"I would have talked to you even if I'd known," I said quietly. "I couldn't have stopped myself from loving you even if I'd tried."

I still couldn't.

"Having the memories of you kept me sane, Nic."

When I'd been in that cage and after, when I'd lived in a stone compound with no one for company but guards and the likes of Billy, I'd taken out the memories, and I'd found a little bit of peace.

He stepped into the room, still wearing nothing more than his boxers. I clutched Jessie's T-shirt to my breasts.

He flicked off the light and darkness descended. Nevertheless, I could see him inching closer, and the scent of desire, of danger, wafted over me.

"You make me insane, Elise. I should hate you, but I can't. You should disgust me, but you don't."

He stopped so close his erection brushed my belly. I dropped the T-shirt, and when it draped over his penis instead of falling to the floor, he tossed the garment aside with a growl.

I took one step backward before he grabbed me, yanking me onto my toes. "I swore to myself I'd never touch you this way again, but all I do is think about it."

"Me, too," I whispered.

"I've rationalized everything. The horse is out of the barn. No more virginity and you didn't go all demon on me. Can't get pregnant, no STDs. Perfect world." He shook his head. "Or as perfect as it's going to get now that I know all that lives in it."

"Nic—"

"Shut up."

His hands tightened. I shut up.

He was angry. What else was new? Though there were times I missed the boy from Stanford, I had to admit, this man excited me more.

He inched back, and his eyes glittered in the small amount of light from the hallway. "Just sex, right? No strings. When we're through in Fairhaven, we're through."

Though a part of me died at his words, I knew it had to be that way.

"Right."

His mouth met mine with both fury and passion. The clench of his fingers on my arms would have caused a bruise in a normal woman. One of these days I was really going to have to make him stop treating me like this.

But not today.

He captured my tongue with his teeth and tasted the end. Pleasure and pain at war, I clutched his shoulders and surrendered.

My fingers drifted across his bare chest. His heart pounded first against my hand, then against my mouth. I trailed my lips down to his belly until I encountered the waistband of his boxers, let my tongue slide beneath the material and tease just a bit before I yanked them away with a violence to match his own as my knees met the floor.

Edging forward, I pressed a kiss to the inside of one leg. His penis leaped against my cheek, and I turned, capturing the length of him in my mouth.

The heat, the strength, the taste drove me wild. He wrapped my hair around his wrist and showed me the rhythm. A little rough, I didn't mind. Knowing he couldn't hurt me only excited me more.

My teeth scored the tip; he hissed, then moaned, not pulling away, instead urging me closer. Pleasure, pain, so close, so different and yet the same. I laved the tiny hurt with my tongue and got back to business.

I felt him growing, coming, and he pulled away, lifting me to my feet and melding his lips to mine.

He was frantic. So was I. Our tongues tangled, our hands fluttered here and there, stroking, teasing, testing.

The curling strands of his chest hair seemed to scrape my sensitive nipples, but I rubbed myself against him anyway. I had to have him inside of me or die of it.

"Now," I murmured.

He must have agreed that now was best, and the bed too far away, because he lifted me onto the dresser, stepped between my legs and drove home.

The chill of the wood at the base of my spine was a welcome contrast to the heat wherever we touched. His palms at my hips, he pulled me closer. His thumbs stroked my thighs, urging my knees wider, so he could travel deeper with every thrust.

The drawers rattled, the mirror thumped against the wall; I found the sounds almost as arousing as the slide of his body into mine.

I was almost there. I only needed a little something extra to shove me over the edge into orgasm. He nuzzled my breasts, licked my nipple just once, then blew on the moist imprint left by his mouth.

My shudder of reaction caused me to tighten around him, the gentle yet intense movement inciting his release and fueling my own. Grasping his shoulders, I held on as together we came apart.

Both energized and relaxed, I lost track of how long we stayed there, all tangled together on top of the furniture. I felt so glorious. How had I ever survived celibacy?

Of course, I hadn't known what I was missing.

Glancing down at his dark head against my pale skin, I touched the shorter length of his hair. The shearing of the soft strands, combined with the specks of gray, reminded me that years had passed, wars had been fought—both in his world and my own—changing everything.

This was just sex, not love. Could never be love, and I had to remember that. Nic was going to leave, if I didn't leave first, and there was always the possibility one of us would die.

How was that for a cheery after-orgasm thought to ruin the mood?

Nic straightened. The loss of his heat, the moist memory of his mouth, caused a shiver. He moved away, his body leaving mine. I suddenly felt exposed, naked, a little slutty.

The chill had returned to his eyes. How could he look at me like that after what we'd just shared?

Except this hadn't been sharing but sex. I'd thought I could handle that, but maybe I'd spoken too soon. I loved him, so our being together meant something to me, even though it meant nothing, *I* meant nothing, to him.

I glanced at the bed, enjoyed a vision of cuddling close to Nic's side, my head on his shoulder, the sheets and bedspread creating a warm cocoon all around us.

But we had no dreams to share, no future to speak of. Getting in that bed would lead to one thing—several times.

I didn't think I could do it anymore.

I mean, I could, but I didn't want to.

Wait—I wanted to, but I shouldn't.

Every time we had sex, I remembered the love, the hope, the dreams, and I ached for what we'd lost. I might be a werewolf and a murderer, but I had feelings, too.

Really.

I turned to tell Nic we could never do this again, but he was gone. His door closed and silence settled over the house.

I guess he'd already decided the same thing.

26

I slept a bit, coming wide awake several hours later, with one thought. The talisman was still at the junk-yard.

Throwing on Jessie's clothes, I cursed as I remembered I'd split my tennis shoes the last time I'd changed.

"Dumb, dumb, dumb."

At least the lack of them made it easier to sneak out. I could have woken Nic, taken him along, but why?

He couldn't help if I ran into ghost wolves, and in truth, I didn't want to see him right now.

Just sex? Sure. But what were we going to do about the embarrassment that came from sharing bodies and not hearts?

He'd said when we were done in Fairhaven, we'd be done. Nic might not have a problem with that, but I would. He was my first, and even if I didn't love him, such a thing would be hard for me to forget.

I hurried through the chilly darkness in bare feet. No

one was out this early, or was it late? Lucky for me, because when I reached the junkyard I found something strange.

My stuff was gone—clothes, shoes, or what was left of them, and the talisman, too. I'd have thought the watchman cleaned up a bit, but—

I glanced around at the tangle of metal. Really, why?

I continued to search in larger and larger circles until I reached the damp earth at the edge of the grass. There I found a footprint.

Make that a paw print. Too big to be a dog—hell, too big to be a coyote; too real to be that of a ghost wolf, unless they could become unghostly, too. And wouldn't that be special?

My neck prickled as a howl rose toward the sky. The first I'd heard in Fairhaven, the call tempted me.

Wolves howl for many reasons: to assemble the pack, warn of danger, locate one another, communicate. Each animal has his own pitch, and a pack can harmonize, making it seem as if there are twenty wolves, when there are only three or four. What sounded like a lot from a distance could be a lot, or only a few.

But this was one, and that in itself was strange, considering the pack nature of both species. Which of the two was calling me now, I couldn't say. I'd only be able to tell if I saw the beast up close.

A breeze swirled in from the west, lifting my hair, fluttering the ends; my skin seemed to buzz.

Embrace what you are.

I was getting a little tired of the wind being so chatty, however, I had no problem doing what it said.

Lifting my face, I barely thought of the moon before I changed.

My clothes tore and fell away; the night came at me like a lover, surrounding me, caressing me, making me his. Strong, free, in command, the change now brought power with none of the pain.

If Edward or Jessie were here, we'd have trouble. They wouldn't trust me. They'd want to kill me, or at least lock me up until they knew what was happening, and I hadn't even told anyone about the voice yet.

The breeze brought not only a message, but the trace of another like me. Maybe just a witchie wolf or two, I couldn't tell, but I followed the scent into the forest.

Squirrels skittered out of my way and up the trees. Small furry things ran into the bushes with a screech. Because I was wolf first in this form, I became distracted by their movement, their smell, and I lost the trail.

Retracing my path, I lifted my nose and sniffed. Nothing. Growling, I pawed the earth just as a crow swooped low, nearly clipping my ears with its wings.

Wolves have been tracking crows for so long the behavior is ingrained in our DNA. One glance at the bird's flight pattern, and I adjusted my direction.

A few hundred yards away, I stumbled on a ravine encircled by brambles. From deep within came a moan. Was someone hurt? Bitten? Dying?

Bracing myself against the inevitable scrape of the thorns, I put my belly to the ground and crawled closer. The earth tilted downward. I continued to inch along, stopping at the edge of a culvert.

I heard voices along with the moans. The latter had taken on a distinct tinge of pleasure, not pain. I knew what I was going to see even before I stuck my muzzle over the edge.

Bodies entwined on a soft bed of moss; the moon flowed through the branches speckling the man's skin with silver. His buttocks tightened and released in an age-old rhythm as he pumped himself into the body of the woman beneath him.

Her long, tanned legs wrapped around his back, tugging him closer. Fingernails digging into his shoulders, she urged him to greater speed. When she left red welts on his skin, he emitted a rumble that was half growl, half purr. The sound pulled at my belly, made my skin tingle and my fur stand on end.

I'd never watched anyone have sex before—except in a movie. I shouldn't be watching now.

Carefully I inched away, but my claws freed a waterfall of stones and dirt down the side of the crevice.

The man and the woman froze. I ducked my head against my paws, flattened my ears and tried to get small.

Caw!

Caw, caw!

I didn't dare lift my head, but the flutter of wings told me I'd been saved by the crows, even before the man murmured, "Just a bird, baby. Don't get distracted."

I knew that voice. If I hadn't been so interested in the mechanics of the act, I'd have recognized his hair.

As it was, when I peeked again, the man had turned his face to the side, the better to nuzzle his partner's breast. The scar that bisected his cheek was a dead give-away.

No wonder the deputy hadn't returned to Fairhaven. Basil Moore was otherwise occupied.

I craned my neck higher as the rhythmic thud of flesh on flesh and the accompanying moans recommenced. The woman now had her ankles crossed behind Basil's neck.

I tilted my head. She must take yoga.

Basil lowered his face to her breast again, tongue flicking one nipple, before he took it in his teeth and tugged.

The woman arched, cried out, and he stiffened, yanking her body against his and slamming into her one last time.

I shuffled backward, uncaring if they heard me now. I doubted they'd give chase. Even if they did, I could definitely outrun them.

Besides, I'd seen too much. Not only Basil, naked, but his partner, too.

Lydia Kopway.

The crows flew off. I was on my own as I attempted to pick up the stray werewolf scent again, even as my mind mulled over what I'd observed.

Why had Lydia and Basil been doing it in the woods when they had a perfectly good house for such things?

Why did their liaison bother me? They were young, attractive, single, as far as I knew. Maybe they had an outdoor-sex fetish—there were worse things.

Nose to the sky, I gave a snort of annoyance. The

scent I'd tracked was gone. Frustrated, I headed for the cabin.

Taking the long way, I skirted the woods, hugging the shadows. What was it about the deputy and Lydia that kept nagging at me? Merely embarrassment at observing a private moment, even when that moment had been performed in public? Or something else?

On the back porch I had no choice but to change, unless I wanted to scratch at the door and wait for Nic to let me in. Not.

I imagined myself a woman, and I was. Turning the doorknob, I slipped into the cabin, then into the bathroom, just as it hit me.

According to both Will and my own observations, Basil didn't like Indians. But if that was true, why was he screwing one?

A puzzle: maybe nothing more than a bigot who made himself feel superior by sleeping with those he considered inferior. However, I didn't think Lydia was the type of woman to give someone who looked down on her a minute of her time. She definitely wouldn't allow him free use of her body.

Of course, I hardly knew her, or him. I could be wrong about them both.

Footsteps sounded in the hall. I wrapped a towel around me just as Nic appeared in the doorway.

"Where have you been?" he asked.

My feet were grubby, my fingernails, too. I'm sure there were leaves in my hair and quickly healing bramble scratches all over my body. Did I really have to answer that question?

I tilted my head and saw comprehension dawn in his eyes. "Oh. Why?"

I filled him in on my excursion, the loss of the talisman, the werewolf scent that came and went, and the free porn in the forest.

"You watched?"

"I was stuck."

"I bet." He inched closer and pulled a leaf from my hair. "Did you like it?"

My gaze lifted to his. "Not exactly."

"Liar," he whispered, and kissed me.

My skin still buzzing from the change, my body aroused from the power and the real-life adult video in the woods, I let him.

Hell, I let him do a lot more than kiss me.

What had happened to "never again"? The vow flew out the window the instant Nic touched me.

My back against the wall, my legs around his waist, his body again buried deep in mine, I came screaming. I wasn't going to be able to give him up. I was addicted.

This time, instead of leaving me alone without a word or a even a kiss, Nic brushed my brow with his lips and turned on the shower.

"Who do you think has the talisman?" he asked.

"No idea. The junkman could have thrown my clothes into the incinerator."

He glanced over his shoulder. "But you don't think so?"

"It's a junkyard. Why clean up?"

"True."

"I don't like not knowing where the icon is," I said,

"but I don't need it anymore, and, according to Will, the thing shouldn't work for anyone but me."

"He's sure about that?"

"As sure as you can be with magic."

Nic nodded, as if he discussed magic every day. He was fitting amazingly well into my world, which should be disturbing but wasn't.

"We need to talk to the ME," he continued. "And Basil, if we can find him."

"I don't know if I can look the man in the face."

"You're gonna have to."

He offered me first dibs on the shower with a lift of his brow. I shook my head, as I wrapped the towel around my body. Despite the steamy heat filling the room, I was chilled. Losing my fur always had that effect.

"You think you smelled ghost wolves?" he asked.

"Maybe. Probably. I don't know."

"I left a message for Lydia asking if she had a book on witchie wolves."

"Isn't it awful early to be calling people?"

"I woke up and you were gone."

He went silent for a minute and I frowned, wondering if he'd thought I'd left. If he'd cared.

Had that been what the sex, the kiss, the gentleness had been about? He didn't want me to leave any more than I wanted him to? At least not yet.

I couldn't ask, couldn't take the risk that he'd laugh and walk away. I still needed him. Not only for the sex but for the job. I wasn't up to solving this case by myself.

"I wanted something to do," he continued. "So I called Lydia. But she wasn't there."

"Obviously."

Nic shut off the shower and whipped open the curtain. Any other words that might have come to my lips died at the sight of his body streaming with water.

His muscles appeared bigger, polished and smooth, the curls that covered his chest, his legs, his genitals, had darkened. With his hair slicked away from his face, he seemed younger, again the boy I remembered, the one I'd lusted after so completely. I wanted him all over again. Hell, I wanted him all over me.

Nic grabbed a towel, started rubbing himself down, which only excited me more. Turning away, I grabbed my toothbrush, then forgot what I was supposed to do with it.

"We need to get moving." Nic handed me the toothpaste. "Sun's up. Day's a-wasting."

I nodded and climbed into the shower, taking the toothbrush with me. The air of domesticity—sharing a bathroom, a shower, the toothpaste—was both disturbing and comforting. Which would I miss more, the sharing of our bodies or the sharing of everything else? That I couldn't decide was more upsetting than the decision itself.

Half an hour later, Nic and I strolled along Midtown Road. We checked the sheriff's office—no Basil, no kidding—then headed for the clinic.

The door wasn't locked. Nic walked in first. Practically on his heels, I smelled it right away.

Fresh blood.

I shoved Nic to the ground, nearly ran over his back. "What the hell, Elise?"

"Stay down," I shouted, and the rear door slammed open as someone ran out.

I followed, taking note of a dead Dr. Watchry as I went past. One step outside and a brick landed on my head.

Or at least that was what it felt like. I fell to my knees, then onto my face. By the time I glanced up, the assailant was gone and Nic was there.

"Person or werewolf?" he asked.

"Daytime."

"Which only means a person at the moment."

He was catching on. To discern a werewolf in human form I had to touch them, and they hadn't waited around long enough for me to get a good grip. I wasn't thinking clearly. I blamed the brick in the head.

Nic helped me sit up, touched the knot on the back of my head, mumbling, "Sorry," when I winced.

"Man? Woman?" Nic lifted me to my feet, and I wobbled.

"No clue." I put my fingers to the throbbing ache, and they came away wet with blood.

"We should probably get that stitched," he said.

"By who? The damn doctor's dead."

Which really pissed me off. I liked Dr. Watchry. He'd called me "sweet child."

"Unless he hit me with a silver brick, I'll heal fine on my own."

Nic picked up a fist-sized rock lying near the building and shrugged. "You're safe."

"Swell."

"Come inside," he murmured. "We shouldn't be out in the open right now."

"If he wanted me dead, he'd have shot me with silver."

Which meant this assailant and the one in Montana were not the same. Yippee.

"He?" Nic asked. "I thought you didn't see anyone."

"He, she, it. Whatever. Let's get inside."

"Try to be nice to someone and they bite your head off," he muttered.

"Watch it or I will."

Nic actually laughed. Was he getting used to what I was? How could he, when I wasn't?

He tugged me into the clinic, slammed then locked the door. I collapsed on a stool next to the work station.

"You okay?" Nic asked. "I'm going to take a look at him."

I nodded, then regretted the movement as agony sliced through my brain. Nic knelt next to the doctor, checked his pulse, then sighed.

"How did he die?" I wondered.

"Skull bashed in. Assailant probably had the same thought for you, except your head's too hard."

"Ha-ha. Is there a bite mark?"

Nic stood and found a pair of gloves. Snapping them into place, he proceeded to search. My eyes were caught by the microscope nearby. The doctor appeared to have been using it recently—perhaps when he died—since there was a slide on the stage. I inched closer and read his notes.

"There was a bite mark on the doctor's receptionist, too." I leaned closer and read a notation to the side. "Body *stolen,* like the sheriff's."

Nic grunted as he continued to check the doctor for evidence.

"According to Dr. Watchry the same set of teeth was used for both bites."

"We kind of figured that," he said.

According to the notes, the slide held a saliva sample from the bite mark on Sheriff Stephenson. Curious, I peered through the lens. At first I merely stared, then I lifted my head, blinked, rubbed my eyes and tried again. The specimen on the slide remained the same.

"Nic," I murmured.

"Give me a minute. He's dead weight."

"Nic!"

He heard the urgency and stopped what he was doing to join me. "What is it?"

"The slide." I pointed at the microscope, but I couldn't force the words from my mouth.

He squinted into the lens, then shrugged. "Means nothing to me."

"This is saliva from Stephenson's bite. I've seen it before."

Nic's gaze sharpened. "You know who the sample belongs to?"

"No. But—"

"Where did you see it?"

"In my lab."

"The bite mark is human. How can that be werewolf saliva?"

"It isn't."

"Explain. Slowly. For those of us without the doctorate."

"When a person is bitten their chemistry changes. Even when they're human, they're different."

Nic stared at me, and I could see from the tightening of his mouth that he knew what I was going to say before I said it.

"The sample on that slide is from a werewolf in human form."

27

"You can't tell whose saliva that is?" Nic flicked a finger toward the microscope.

"Only if I'd seen it before and I had my notes. But really, what are the odds that one of those I've examined has turned up here?"

"Pretty damn slim," he agreed.

Sure, the werewolves in the basement could be free, but they'd also been locked up when the disappearances began.

"Did the doctor have a bite mark?" I asked.

"No. Which leads me to believe the making of a witchie wolf involves the bite of a werewolf in human form," Nic said. "How about you?"

I contemplated the body, which was still quite visible. "I'm thinking that, too."

"We still don't know why."

"No."

"Maybe Lydia will find a book, and it will explain everything."

"Including how to get rid of them."

"Wouldn't that be nice?"

"Mmm," I murmured, still staring at the doctor. "Do you think he was killed because he was on to something?"

"If the bad guy meant to keep his identity a secret, why leave the evidence behind?"

"We interrupted him." I reached out and plucked the slide from the stage and the notebook from the table. "Just in case."

"Maybe I should send that stuff to the crime lab. Free service for all U.S. law enforcement agencies."

"I don't think so."

"But—"

"Can you imagine what would happen if a government scientist got a gander at the saliva of a werewolf in human form?"

"I doubt he'd know what it was."

"Exactly. So what good would showing him do?"

"None." Nic sighed. "And then we'd have FBI all over the place, asking questions."

"Getting eaten by werewolves they didn't know about."

"Chaos. I see your point."

"We should just handle this on our own as we've been doing."

"Right." Nic glanced at the doctor. "We'll need to get someone to take care of the body. Leaving it here isn't practical."

"Damn," I muttered.

"What's the matter?"

I waved a hand at Dr. Watchry. "I'm not used to this."

"Death?"

No, *that* I was used to.

"People I've just met, and liked, getting killed the minute I turn my back."

"Oh." Understanding spread across his face. "Happens."

"How do you stand it?"

"By pushing aside useless emotion and focusing on what's important."

"Important?" My voice rose several levels in pitch and volume. "What could be more important than someone's murder?"

"Finding the one who killed them and making them pay."

All the righteous indignation went out of me like the air out of a popped balloon.

"Okay."

Nic smiled. "We'll handle this."

Unspoken was the word *together,* but I heard it nevertheless.

"Let's find Basil," I said. "Tell him about the doctor's death."

"And ask him about stray Ojibwe warrior graves. I could also use a list of the missing. Any connection between them could give us a clue."

Thoughts like those were why I kept him around.

My gaze wandered over the biceps that stretched the seams of his T-shirt. Among other things.

We locked the clinic behind us—didn't need any

citizens stumbling over the body—then headed for the sheriff's office.

The place was still empty. Nic strode over to the desk and started rooting through the paperwork.

"Hey, can you do that?"

"I'm a Fed. I can do anything."

"Thinking like that is usually what gets you guys in trouble."

He ignored me. I had to say I found his take-charge attitude attractive. What *didn't* I find attractive about him lately?

"Ah-ha!" He held up a sheet of paper. "List of missing persons."

A quick glance around the room, and he located a Xerox machine, made a copy, and slipped the original back into the file. "He'll never know I was here."

I opened my mouth to ask why all the secrecy, and the door burst open. Both Nic and I turned in that direction with welcoming smiles, which froze on our faces when we didn't recognize the man who ran inside.

I'd seen a few survivalists in Montana. This guy must have been one of their friends. Beard, long hair, jeans, boots, and a flannel shirt. He was young, perhaps twenty-five, no more than thirty. Might even have been handsome without all the hair and the dirt.

"I need the sheriff," he announced.

"The dead one or the new one?" Nic asked.

"Basil."

"Not here."

"Who are you?"

"FBI."

An expression of relief filled his eyes. "I found a body."

Hell. Another one?

Nic grabbed a pencil and a sheet of paper. "Where?"

"Out on the old highway. Anderson homestead."

Nic and I exchanged glances. "Where Sheriff Stephenson's body was found?"

"Yeah. *Exactly* where his body was found."

"A second body? Left in the same place."

"Not left. The grave was dug up."

"Grave desecration," I muttered, and smacked myself in the forehead.

My only excuse for not seeing the connection earlier was that I'd been focused on finding an Ojibwe warrior's grave, not that I would have known what one looked like even if I'd seen it.

"What?" Nic asked.

"The reason the sheriff was at the old Anderson place was that there'd been a report of a grave desecration." I turned toward the mountain man. "But we didn't see anything disturbed."

"There is now. From the paw prints in the dirt, I'd say dogs."

Maybe. But doubtful.

"They probably couldn't help themselves," he continued. "The body was pretty fresh."

The room went silent.

"You mean skeleton," Nic said.

"No. Definitely a body. Newly dead. I'd say no more than a week or two."

"Could you guess at a cause of death?" Nic asked.

"I'm thinking the large, gaping knife wound at the throat had something to do with it."

"You're sure?"

"I've seen a few."

Nic and I exchanged glances again. I really didn't want to know where this guy had seen death by knife wound to the throat.

"We need to get another ME from . . . anywhere," Nic muttered. "We have to find out who was in the grave."

"A woman," Mountain Man stated in a dry, clinical tone. "Native American. Pretty old."

"Hell!" Nic muttered at the same time I kicked the desk. Mountain Man stared at us as if we'd lost our minds.

"Uh, yeah. Thanks for coming by." Nic ushered him to the door. "We'll send someone out as soon as—"

"We find someone," I said.

Nic closed the door and turned to me. "I guess an Ojibwe warrior isn't necessarily a man."

"No. I'm betting it's Cora."

"Lydia said she passed away."

There'd been no mention of throat cutting—an item that would have topped my list in any conversation about a dead grandmother.

"Lydia said a lot of things," I pointed out. "We'd better talk to her."

"Yeah. Gramma passing away is a whole lot different than Gramma getting her throat slit and being buried in the woods."

"Why would Dr. Watchry insist there'd never been a murder in Fairhaven?"

"Perhaps Cora didn't die in Fairhaven."

"Who knows anymore?"

"Did you get a read on Lydia?" Nic asked.

"She seemed nice enough."

"I meant, did you bump against her when you passed or at least shake her hand?"

"You think she's a—"

"Someone is."

I went over the meeting with Lydia in my mind. "I never touched her. Never thought to."

Nic's face hardened. "Let's go touch her now."

28

"That was a bust," I muttered.

We'd gone to Lydia's without calling first—no reason to give her a heads-up—but she hadn't been there. So we'd driven to the crime scene.

Mountain Man's description had been correct. Ancient Native American woman with a throat wound. Lots of paw prints. But not from a dog. There were also old bones mixed in with the earth, which led us to believe the grave had not been Cora's originally.

Had she even been there when the sheriff was killed? Had he been killed because he found her? Hard to say.

Nic spent a lot of time on his cell phone asking *hypothetical* questions of FBI contacts. He'd even managed to get a hold of Basil once.

The new sheriff promised to find another ME, somewhere, and send him to the crime scene. He also promised to send someone to deal with the doctor's body.

Then as soon as Nic got to the interesting questions—*bam*—Basil's cell phone went out. When Nic tried to call him again, all he got was a busy signal.

We drove into Fairhaven as night threatened. A car was parked in front of the cabin. I caught sight of Lydia walking around the far side of the building.

"Looks like she got your message," I said, as we followed.

"Miss Kopway," I greeted, just as she knocked on the back door. "Nice to see you again."

"Oh! I went to the front, but no one answered, so—" She shrugged.

Nic and I climbed the porch and I offered my hand. Her gaze lowered and she smiled, then gave me hers. I braced myself for the pain. Nic slowly reached for his gun. Our skin touched and—

Nothing.

I frowned and glanced at Nic.

"Is something the matter?" Lydia asked.

"No." I tucked my hand into my pocket. "Everything's great. So how did your grandmother die?"

Nic choked, then turned the sound into a cough. Lydia stared at me as if I'd just belched in church. You'd think I was Jessie the way I blurted things out.

"My grandmother was murdered in her own home by an unknown assailant." Lydia took a deep breath that shook in the middle. "She never hurt anyone. Why would someone hurt her?"

Nic gave me a quelling glare, then set his hand on Lydia's shoulder. "I'm sorry. How was she killed?"

Lydia, who had been staring at the ground, slowly lifted her gaze to mine. "Her throat was slit."

Bingo, I thought. But I kept my mouth shut.

"I had her buried behind the cottage," Lydia continued. "That was what she wanted. But then someone took the body. I heard the same thing's been happening in Fairhaven."

"Mmm," I said noncommittally.

Cora hadn't truly disappeared as the others had. But did Lydia, or anyone else, know that?

"Does the FBI have any new information on my grandmother's killer?"

"Not really," Nic answered. "But we're trying to cover every angle."

"You'll let me know if you discover anything?"

"Of course."

I surmised we were keeping the recovery of Gramma's body to ourselves. Probably not a bad idea considering we didn't know what was going on, who was lying and who was not.

Lydia handed Nic the book she'd brought. "What's your interest in witchie wolves? They aren't a common legend."

"No?" I asked.

She glanced at me. "They exist on the shores of Lake Huron, protecting the graves of the warriors buried there."

We already knew that, so I didn't comment.

"Obscure mythology is one of my hobbies," Nic said.

"Like the professor?"

"Sure."

"I just found it odd that you would ask about witchies when I had another request for the same information not so long ago."

Both Nic and I stilled.

"Who?" I demanded.

"The deputy. Well, I guess he's the sheriff now."

"Basil?"

"Yes, that's the one," she said, as if she didn't know him.

"You two are friends?" I asked.

"Not really. He had questions; I had Grandmother's library. I just found it strange that the deputy would be interested in an obscure Ojibwe legend when I hear he's been extremely *uninterested* in Ojibwes for most of his life."

He hadn't appeared too uninterested from my point of view, but I didn't want to bring that up. The book incident at least explained how the two of them had met. More than that, I probably didn't want to hear.

"I'd better get back," Lydia said. "Nice seeing you two again. Keep the book as long as you like."

We made the appropriate bye-bye noises, waiting until her car pulled away before we spoke.

"She's lying," Nic murmured.

"You think?"

His eyes narrowed at my sarcasm, but he chose not to comment. On that at least. "Although, I have to say, if my grandmother was murdered in such an ugly way, I wouldn't want to discuss it, either. Dead is dead."

"Not really."

He blinked. "No?"

I was having a hard time remembering what Nic knew and what he didn't about my world. Edward had given him the basics, but what, to Edward, was basic?

"If a werewolf bites but doesn't eat, new werewolf within twenty-four hours."

"What if the victim dies?"

"Then things get ugly. The dead rise, people start screaming, the tabloids show up. Messy. That's why it's our policy to shoot the bitten with silver, even if the body isn't breathing."

"Thanks for the tip."

"Anytime."

"What about Basil?" Nic murmured. "Why did Lydia pretend she didn't know him?"

"Maybe she's embarrassed."

"Or he is."

The wind stirred my hair, and a slight sound made me glance toward the woods. I caught the glint of the moon on metal.

"Get down!" I shouted a millisecond before the crack of a gunshot.

A bullet passed through the air where my head had been, then thunked into the side of the cabin. I was getting really sick of being shot at.

I waited for more gunfire; instead I heard the thudding retreat of footsteps. Nic started to rise, gun in hand, and I yanked him back down. "I'll go."

Before he could argue, I moved to the edge of the porch, thought of the moon, and shifted. The scent of werewolf invaded my nose, and I leaped from the steps, then raced into the woods.

The aroma tickled the edge of my brain. I wasn't certain if it was just the smell of werewolf that was familiar or this *particular* werewolf. Even so, I couldn't get a fix on the identity.

I didn't get very far before the scent of death over-powered that of wolf. I nearly stumbled over Basil's body. His eyes stared sightlessly at the sky. Most of his throat was missing.

I growled low—a sound of both warning and un-ease. Who had done this? Lifting my nose to the night, I howled, waiting for an answer, getting none.

The smell of werewolf was all around Basil. A trail led into the forest, growing fainter and fainter, then disappearing altogether. When I heard Nic calling me, I hurried back. I didn't want him unpro-tected beneath the moon while an unknown werewolf roamed.

I burst through the foliage on one side just as Nic did on the other. His gaze went from the mutilated body to me, and he lifted his brow. I shook my head and pawed the earth.

"That's what they all say." Nic tossed a blanket be-hind a bush. "Thought you might need that."

I took advantage of the gift and the foliage, chang-ing with the swiftness that now seemed to be mine for good, then I wrapped myself in the sarong and re-turned to the clearing.

"What happened?" Nic was already examining the body.

"There was another werewolf."

He lifted his gaze. "No human bite mark. Maybe he didn't have time to shift back and finish the job."

"Maybe," I murmured.

"First rule of a murder investigation," Nic recited. "Extreme violence, injury to the face or the throat equals personal."

"Which brings us back to Lydia. Boffing Basil. Mighty personal."

"Lydia isn't a werewolf."

"Maybe she was sleeping with one."

"Two-timing Basil with a lycanthrope?"

"She might not know that," I said.

"We'll have to talk with her again." Nic sighed. "And now we've got another body. I don't know who to call anymore."

"How about the mayor?" I suggested.

"What the hell?" Nic threw up his hands.

We headed back to the cabin and Nic opened the door. I hung back, frowning at the bullet hole that had plowed into a log.

"Why would Basil shoot at you?" Nic asked.

"A better question"—I reached out, yanking my fingers away when they burned—"is why would he shoot at me with silver?"

Nic blinked. "He did?"

I nodded, thinking. Could Basil be—

"The traitor."

"What traitor?" Nic asked.

Quickly I filled him in on what had been, a few days ago, my biggest problem next to Billy.

"Someone's been selling information?"

"Yeah. Although I don't know how they could have found out about me. No one knows but Edward, and there certainly aren't any personal records with the box 'werewolf' checked."

"More people than Edward know."

"You." I frowned. "You wouldn't."

"You're very trusting, Elise."

I tilted my head.

"But you're right. I wouldn't, even if I knew who to sell you to. But what about the others?"

"Others?"

"Jessie, Will, Leigh, Damien."

"They'd never—"

"You're sure?"

I didn't even have to think about it. "Yes."

They might not understand me. They might not even like me. But *Jäger-Suchers* stuck together. We had no one else.

"*Someone* sold you out."

"Not necessarily," I said. "Maybe Basil just knew there were werewolves, so he loaded his gun with silver bullets. They work on anything."

"But why shoot at you? What did you ever do to him?"

"There is no telling," a voice murmured.

I didn't jump, or gasp, or spin around. I knew that voice as well as I knew my own.

Edward was back.

29

"Perhaps you killed someone dear to him—by accident or design."

Edward stepped out of the cabin. Nic backed up, putting himself between me and my boss.

"When did you get here, sir?"

"Not very long ago. Imagine my surprise to hear gunshots, find out that once again, strangers are shooting at you with silver. Are there no secrets anymore?"

"Apparently not. I see you managed to escape from the latest round of people who were trying to kill you."

"*Escape* makes it sound as if I were running away. I ran to them and now they are . . . gone."

I knew what *gone* meant, so I let the matter drop.

Edward's gaze wandered from the top of my wild and tousled head, past the sarong blanket, down to my dirty toes. He said nothing, but I felt his censure just the same.

Edward turned to Nic. "Why are you still here?"

"We've been working together," I said.

"Is that what they call it nowadays?"

Nic's hands curled into fists. I touched his shoulder and slowly his fingers relaxed.

Edward saw the interaction and scowled. He believed that the fewer attachments *Jäger-Suchers* had, the less they had to lose. And a person with little to lose was much more dangerous than one who had everything. That he allowed Jessie and Will, Damien and Leigh, to work together, to be together, meant he was softening.

And the idea that this man was a softer version of the one he'd always been was a frightening thought, indeed.

"Now that I am back"—Edward gave Nic a hard stare—"you can go away."

"We already played that tune, Mandenauer. I'm not leaving."

"Just because Elise has shown extremely bad judgment in letting her personal feelings interfere with her job does not mean that I will."

Edward stalked into the cabin. Nic followed, ignoring me when I plucked at his sleeve.

"Shouldn't we go see Lydia?" I asked.

"Soon."

Nic sounded distracted. I had no choice but to trail them both into the living room where Edward turned to me. "Make him go away or I will."

"Wait." I jiggled my ear. "Time warp. We're having the same conversation twice."

"Sarcasm does not become you, Elise."

Huh, and I thought I was getting the hang of it, too.

"We will not have the *same* conversation, either." He lifted a yellowed brow.

"What more can you tell me?" Nic asked. "She's a werewolf. I don't care."

I glanced at him in shock. "You don't?"

He shrugged. "I'm getting used to it."

"She has not told you of her other hobby."

I stilled. Nic might not care that I was a werewolf, but I doubted he could as easily forgive my being a murderer.

"You have to go," I blurted.

Nic merely rolled his eyes.

"That list of names?" Edward murmured. "She killed every one of them."

Instead of drawing his gun and arresting me, Nic merely appeared resigned. "Is that true?" he asked.

"Yes."

He nodded slowly. "You're not just his right-hand woman, you're an assassin. And a damned clever one, since you're freaking hard to kill."

I didn't bother to answer what hadn't been a question.

"You do not seem upset, Agent Franklin. You are not horrified to discover you have been sleeping with a killer?"

"The people on that list were monsters," he said. "The world is a much better place without them in it."

My eyes widened. I wasn't sure what to say.

"Such an attitude for a law enforcement officer." Edward tsk-tsked.

"Sue me." Nic kept his gaze on my face. "He sent you after them on the nights of the full moon, didn't he?"

I nodded.

"He's using you."

"It's all right."

"It isn't. Killing upsets you." He narrowed his eyes, tilted his head. "A lot more than it's ever upset me."

The travesties I'd read about in Edward's dossiers . . . Rapists, serial killers, child molesters, scientists experimenting with new ways to birth ancient horrors—both monsters and monster makers. They'd have given me nightmares if I hadn't ended their existence myself. Hell, they did anyway. Nevertheless—

"Who are we to play God?" I murmured.

"Better us than Mengele," Edward snapped. "Or another like him."

"He has a point," Nic agreed.

Instead of being thankful for the support, Edward merely scowled. "I am going to take care of the latest body in the woods."

He slammed out of the cabin.

Nic crossed the room, pausing right in front of me. I tensed, not exactly sure what he planned to say or do. Though he hadn't flipped out at the news I was an assassin, as well as a werewolf, that didn't mean he wouldn't. Nic was an FBI agent; he should arrest me. Or have someone else do it. Instead, he leaned down and softly pressed his lips to mine.

The embrace was completely different from most of those we'd shared since he'd walked back into my life. On almost every occasion he'd been angry with me, furious at himself for wanting me. So what was the matter with him now?

Nic lifted his head. "I was scared."

"Of me?"

"No." He straightened. "Never."

"Never? You're not as bright as you look."

His lips tightened. "Don't try to push me away, Elise. I know all there is to know about you, and I don't give a flying fuck."

He was mad again. I couldn't win.

"What exactly *is* a flying fuck?"

Nic made an annoyed sound, pushing past me and into my bedroom. I stood in the living room alone for a minute, then followed.

A box lay on my bed. A glance at the label revealed the clothes I'd ordered online had arrived. The only way for that to happen so fast was if Edward had made some calls. I didn't bother to wonder how he'd known about the order. Edward knew everything.

Nic plucked at the tape on the box. "That bullet barely missed your head."

"Oh," I said, as understanding dawned. "You didn't seem scared."

"I'll let you in on one of *my* secrets." His eyes met mine. "When I seem the least scared? I'm terrified."

His gaze returned to the box. "I know everything now, don't I?"

He didn't know I still loved him—always had, probably always would—but I planned to keep that to myself. As previously noted, I *was* brighter than I looked.

"I think you've heard all the secrets," I said. "Yep."

The box popped open and brightly colored clothes tumbled out. I snatched up a fuzzy sweater in neon green and a pair of bright blue sweatpants.

Had I ordered items so vibrant? They were so unlike me—or maybe they were perfect for a new me.

I dropped the blanket and got dressed without concern for my nakedness. The wild, tangled length of my hair cascaded down my back, brushing the swell of my rear. I hadn't braided the strands since leaving Montana.

I wasn't the woman I'd been at the compound, and I was glad. I'd been hiding inside those stone walls, hating what I was, constructing a life that wasn't really a life.

In Fairhaven I'd been almost happy and that was strange. People were dying; I'd stopped fighting my werewolf nature, pretty much embracing it, inching closer to the beast and further from the woman, and Nic didn't seem to care.

"You aren't scared I might tear out your throat when you aren't paying attention?" I asked.

Nic picked up a lock of my hair and tugged. "Should I be?"

Hell. There was one more secret I'd neglected to tell, not only to him but to anyone.

"I heard a voice," I said.

"Just now?" He glanced around the room with a frown.

"No. On the wind."

"What was it telling you to do?"

"Give in to the power. Embrace what you are and discover the secret you seek."

"Doesn't sound like bad advice," Nic murmured.

"Unless Satan's giving it to me."

Nic lifted a brow. "You really think Satan's speaking to you?"

"Stranger things have happened."

"I'll have to take your word on that."

"I'm stronger since I came here."

"Because of the talisman?"

"No. Yes." I threw up my hands. "I don't know. Either way, I don't need the icon anymore to do amazing things."

"What's the secret you seek?" he asked.

"The cure?"

"You don't sound convinced."

"If the talisman increased my power—or at least began this change—and tempted me to become more of a wolf, why would it tell me to seek a cure?"

"Who said the voice and the talisman are connected?" he pointed out.

"I'm getting a headache." I pushed my thumb against the throb in my temple.

"Get in line," Nic muttered.

"Maybe the talisman didn't make me stronger. Maybe it's just that I'm not fighting what I am anymore. Now that everyone knows and they haven't shot me—" I broke off.

"What? You can tell me, Elise."

I stared into Nic's eyes, and I realized that I could. He'd heard the worst, and he hadn't run screaming.

"I don't hate what I am so much anymore," I murmured. "There are times I even like it."

"You're basically the perfect werewolf," he said. "Power without pain, strength without evil."

He was right. Why hadn't I seen that and accepted it before? Because of one thing I could never make right.

"At Stanford, I killed someone who just happened to

be in the wrong place under the wolf moon. I can never forgive myself for that. I can never forget it."

"You shouldn't. That you can't makes you human, not an animal. Do you think the monsters care who they've killed? Do you think they spend their lives atoning for their mistakes?" Nic shrugged. "Except for Damien, I guess, though when he did those things he was as evil as the rest. You were just out of your head."

"Not guilty by reason of insanity?"

"It's a credible defense, Elise."

"And used far too often to excuse the inexcusable."

"You need to put the past behind you, look forward, finish what we've started in Fairhaven, then focus on a cure."

"And then?"

The words left my mouth before I could stop them.

What did I want him to say? That we could be together forever as we'd once dreamed of being? We couldn't.

I wasn't human, and I might never be.

30

"Let's take this one day at a time," Nic said.

A good idea. Lord knew what tomorrow might bring.

Nevertheless, I was disappointed. Where once sex with no strings hadn't sounded bad, now it no longer sounded good.

Nic lifted my tangled hair from my neck and pressed his lips to the sensitive skin at the curve.

Or maybe it did.

"For years I thought you were dead. Now I'm so scared you might end up that way, I can't sleep at night."

Not exactly a declaration of everlasting love, but it was something.

"I don't kill easily," I murmured.

"Maybe I should sleep in here from now on."

His mouth drifted lower, hovering just above mine.

"Maybe you should." I lifted onto my toes and kissed him.

He tasted both familiar and new, the past and the present in just one man. Everything I knew of sex and love, I'd learned from him.

I wanted him now as I'd wanted him then, loved him the same, if not more. Could I hope again for a future only to have it snatched away? Was it better to dream the impossible than never to dream at all?

Regardless of what tomorrow brought, we had tonight. I planned to make the most of every opportunity.

Hooking my ankle around his, I tumbled us onto the bed. We fell in a heap of limbs and new clothes with me on top. Nic laughed, and I stared down into his face.

"What?" His laughter faded, leaving a puzzled smile in its wake.

"I haven't heard you laugh like that since—" I broke off.

"Stanford?"

I shrugged.

"I don't laugh much anymore. Life without you hasn't been very funny."

With me wasn't going to be too ha-ha, either.

He touched my cheek. "Stop."

"What?"

"Thinking so much." He slipped his hand around the back of my neck and tugged. "Come here."

I went gladly, touching my lips to his. But when I tried to deepen the kiss, he wouldn't let me, instead making the embrace more tranquil than arousing, more gentle than passionate. That single kiss, which went on and on, moved me more than the sex ever had.

"Elise!"

Edward slammed the door, and I scrambled off Nic as if I were fifteen years old instead of twenty-nine.

He appeared in the doorway, lifting his brows at the sight of my tangled hair and twisted sweater. I smelled smoke—he *had* taken care of the body in the woods— then his gaze went past me to Nic, and he grimaced before turning away.

"Kitchen," Edward snapped.

I turned to see what had annoyed him this time and had to hide a smirk. Nic might have been kissing me gently, but he still had a hard-on that was clearly visible beneath his jeans.

"If he thinks he's going to force me out of town again," Nic said, "I'm going to kick his bony ass, then shoot him. With silver, just to be sure."

I started to laugh, then I choked as a thought hit me, sending a nasty chill from head to toe.

"Stay here," I said, and followed Edward into the kitchen.

He'd set a package on the table—my research, thank goodness. One less thing to worry about. On to the next.

I crossed the room, hesitating as I neared him. Could I shoot Edward? He could certainly shoot me.

I touched his arm. He jerked back, nearly knocking over a chair in his haste to get away. But it was enough. I glanced at Nic, who had followed despite my orders.

When our eyes met, I shook my head and he lowered his hand from his weapon. I took comfort from the knowledge that he would have shot Edward if I couldn't.

"You thought I was bitten?" Edward asked.

I shrugged. "Better safe than sorry. You *have* been acting odd lately."

"How can you tell?" Nic muttered, earning a glare from Edward.

"I would shoot *myself* if I was infected."

"You know damn well if you were bitten you wouldn't be you anymore," I said, "you'd be them. Or us. Whatever."

"Don't you have an antidote?" Nic asked.

"Only if the victim is injected before the first change."

"A concoction that would be more useful," Edward pointed out, "if it did not spoil within twenty-four hours of mixing it."

In that moment I understood that nothing I ever did would be enough for him. And suddenly, I didn't really care.

"Getting back to our present troubles," Edward continued briskly. "I did not know this Basil Moore."

"Why would you know him?" Nic asked.

"To be a traitor, to know some of the things our enemies now do, the culprit would have had to be one of us once."

"Rogue agent," I supplied. "Once *Jäger-Suchers*, until fired by Edward for inappropriate behavior."

"What kind of nutcase do you have to be to get ousted from a monster-hunting society?"

"I have rules." Edward sniffed. "If they are not followed, out you go. If you are lucky."

Unlucky people disappeared.

Many former J-S agents were adrenaline junkies. They couldn't give up the danger, or hold down a regular job, so they went hunting on their own. After searching out and destroying monsters most of mankind didn't even know about, it was kind of hard to adjust to life as a librarian.

"But since Basil was not one of us," Edward reiterated, "he could not be a traitor, though he may have bought information from one who is."

"And now we'll never know, because someone killed him," I said.

"A werewolf, not a someone," Edward pointed out. "Now tell me what you have learned about witchie wolves."

Lydia's book lay on the table. Nic picked it up and started paging through as I filled Edward in.

"Have you spoken with Jessie's lover?" Edward asked.

"Why do you call him that? He has a name."

"What is it again?"

I rolled my eyes. He knew damned well what Will's name was.

" 'Witchie wolves sleep in the sun until dark moon,' " Nic read.

Edward and I glanced at each other, then at Nic.

"And what do they plan to do under the dark moon?"

I frowned. "What's a dark moon?"

"I have never heard that term before," Edward said.

"We should really call Will."

"Wait." Edward went into the hallway and came back with his briefcase. He pulled out an electronic device I'd never seen before.

"Speaker phone?" Nic asked.

"Of a kind. This is a prototype. Not only can those

we call hear all of us, but it magnifies the other line so we can hear them."

Edward was provided with the latest technology from the U.S. government—usually double-nought spy stuff like this.

"It will be easier to discuss the case, *ja*?"

"*Ja,*" I said. "I mean yes."

Edward hooked the contraption to the phone line, then dialed Jessie's number.

"This had better be good," she answered, the slur in her voice making me glance at my watch.

Midnight. Why was she asleep?

"We need to have a conference," Edward said. "Set the phone on a flat surface so we might hear both you and your—"

He broke off, glanced at me, scowled and muttered, "Cadotte."

"My Cadotte? Well, he is kind of mine." The phone clunked once. "Okay. Go ahead."

"How up-to-date are they?" Edward asked.

"Werewolf in human form biting the dead, disappearing bodies, invisible ghost wolves—"

"Whoa!" Jessie interrupted. "I never heard anything about ghost wolves."

The rustle of sheets preceded Will's voice. "Are you talking about witchie wolves?"

"We think so."

"They're supposed to live—well, not live exactly, exist, I guess—on the shores of Lake Huron."

"Apparently they don't know that, because they're here."

"Fascinating," he murmured.

"Off he goes," Jessie said. "Computer Boy to the rescue."

"Hold on, Will," I ordered. "Have you ever heard of the dark moon?"

"No," Will said. "Where did you hear it?"

"In a book Lydia gave us. 'Witchie wolves sleep in the sun until the dark moon.' Mean anything?"

"Not yet."

Sounds of a computer turning on, booting up, came over the line. This prototype phone was pretty cool.

Tap-tap-tap.

"There's an Ojibwe expert on witchie wolves," Will said. "He doesn't live too far from here. He wrote a book."

Nic turned the cover so I could read the title. "*Witchie Wolves of the Great Lakes* by Raymond Banks?"

"That's the one. He's very knowledgeable about obscure legends. I'll head over and talk to him in the morning."

"Can't you call him?" Jessie asked. "Send a fax? How about E-mail?"

Will coughed.

"He lives in a cave, doesn't he?"

"Wigwam."

"Same difference," she said. "Why can't your people step into the twenty-first century?"

"Most of us did, and it wasn't all that different from any other."

Silence ensued. I felt compelled to fill it, so I told them all we'd learned about the mystery in Fairhaven.

"The witchie wolves come to power under the dark

moon." Will tapped on the computer some more. "Then their army rules all until the end of days."

"I always get nervous when the end of days comes up," Jessie said.

"Armageddon. Apocalypse." Edward sighed. "I have thwarted a hundred of them."

"Let's make it a hundred and one," Nic said.

"Another werewolf army," Jessie muttered. "Can't they find a new tune?"

"Why?" I wondered. "When the old one plays so well."

"If the witchies are the brave new army," Will continued, "you could be in big trouble if you don't find out who plans to command them before the deed is done."

"We always are," I said.

"Whatever happened to the totem you found in Montana?"

Everyone went silent.

"It's gone," I said. "Not sure where."

Edward scowled.

"I had pocket issues. Sue me."

"Let's not worry about the totem now," Will interjected. "You haven't needed it since the first time."

Who knows?—maybe I hadn't even needed the icon then.

Nevertheless, I wished I had the thing in my possession or at least knew who did. But if wishes were horses, et cetera, et cetera.

"I'll talk to Mr. Banks in the morning."

"We'll talk to him, Slick. Together."

"He may not speak freely with a stranger there."

"You're a stranger."

"We're of the same tribe. Never strangers."

"Whatever."

"You could head back," Will suggested. "They might need you in Fairhaven."

"I'm not letting you traipse off alone to meet some guy we don't even know. He could turn into anything. Sheesh, you think I'm an idiot?"

I glanced at Nic to find him staring at the copy of the victims' list we'd taken from the sheriff's office. In all the excitement, I'd forgotten about it.

"We have a list of the victims," I announced.

"Why didn't you say so?" Jessie asked. "Read them out. Will can probably find something."

Nic was already booting up Jessie's laptop. He cracked his knuckles and winked at me. This sudden, yet familiar, lighter side of him was almost as fascinating as the darker, sexy side.

"It'll only take me a minute. You wouldn't believe what the FBI can find out about people."

"I'd believe it," Will muttered.

Will had been an activist before he was a *Jäger-Sucher*. His name was on a whole lot of watch lists. The FBI's certainly.

While Nic clattered away, I checked my research. Not only were my formulas and notes on a disc, but there was an emergency dose of serum, which was going to come in handy far too soon.

I pocketed the vial, just as Nic murmured, "Hello."

"What?" Jessie, Will, and I asked at the same time. Edward merely waited.

"All the people who've disappeared owned their own homes, businesses, or a plot of land in Fairhaven."

"Each victim owned a part of the town?" Jessie asked. "And they died for it. Why?"

Nic typed in a few more words, then squinted, straightened, and said, "Uh-oh."

"What is 'uh-oh'?" Edward demanded. "I *hate* 'uh-oh.' "

"Fairhaven was built on top of an Ojibwe burial ground."

"There are more graves than the one where we found the sheriff and Cora?" I asked.

"According to this, the greatest concentration of bodies is in a ravine right outside of town."

I'd been to that ravine, along with Lydia and Basil. Coincidence? *Nah.*

From the glance Nic threw my way, he didn't think much of the coincidence, either.

"Why are so many bodies buried there?" Nic murmured.

"Because rather than bury them individually," Will spat, "they tossed everyone into a hole. Much easier that way, and really, why spare the time for some Injuns?"

"Massacre?" Jessie asked.

"Probably."

Will sounded disgusted. I couldn't blame him.

"At least we know why the witchie wolves are here," Will continued.

"We do?" I glanced at Nic, who shrugged.

"They protect the burial mounds of warriors from desecration."

"What desecration?" I asked. "I don't see any turned-up earth or ancient bones dragged around."

"To buy their graves, to own the land—which isn't for sale—is desecration enough."

"Everything's for sale, Slick. Get used to it."

"You can't buy the earth. Or purchase a bird, a stone, a tree."

"He gets like this sometimes," Jessie muttered. "Give him a minute, he'll find the right century."

"Building a Pizza-Rama, or a Super-Mart, or a Gas-and-Dough on someone's grave . . ." Will paused. "They were just asking for it."

"Oh, yeah," Jessie said. "Begging."

Will ignored her. "You've theorized that the bite of a werewolf in human form causes the dead to shift into ghost wolves." He began to type again, talking at the same time. "The theory makes even more sense if the victims are doomed to protect that which they have desecrated."

"And the punishment shall fit the crime," Nic murmured. "But if they've desecrated an Ojibwe burial ground, wouldn't it follow that the murderer is—"

"Ojibwe," Will finished.

"Well, yeah."

"We're back to Lydia again," I said.

"Why would she give us a book on witchie wolves if she was raising them?" Nic asked.

"The book is pretty vague."

"Ojibwe legends often are," Will agreed.

"Which is why the werewolves use them, Slick. They can easily manipulate vague into evil."

"Except Lydia isn't a werewolf," I felt compelled to point out.

Silence settled over us, broken only by the clatter of Will's fingers on the keyboard. "I can't find anything concrete about the dark moon, but I'm betting it's when the moon is darkest, or new. Since tomorrow night is the full moon, we'll have two weeks before the witchie wolf army gains power."

"Then we've got plenty of time to figure out what they're planning," I said. "Who knows, we could even stumble over the werewolf tomorrow night, blow his brains out, and be home free."

Both Edward and Nic turned a bland gaze on me.

"I know." I sighed. "Like that'll happen."

31

We spent the rest of that night trying to discover something more about the dark moon, witchie wolves, even Lydia. According to Nic, she existed, but he couldn't find out anything else about her, which made him nuts.

The man wouldn't get off the Internet. Around 3 A.M. I fell asleep on the couch, only to be awoken by Edward several hours later.

"Dawn approaches," he said. "Let us go and question the native woman."

Mr. Politically Incorrect. I was going to have to watch what he said to Lydia.

From the bloodshot appearance of Nic's eyes as the three of us climbed into Edward's Cadillac, he hadn't slept at all. Shortly after the sun rose, we reached Lydia's.

She stood on the porch as we climbed out of the car. The smirk on her face was disturbing. The way she stared at Edward even more so.

"Lydia," Edward said. "It has been a long time."

"Wait a second." I glanced from Edward to Lydia and back again. "You know Cora's granddaughter?"

Edward snorted. "She is no more Cora's granddaughter than she is mine."

"Who is she?" I asked.

"Lydia Lovell. A familiar."

"Familiar with what?"

"The werewolves." Edward made an exasperated sound and turned to me. "You know what a familiar is."

I did, but how was I supposed to know Lydia was one?

Traditionally, familiars took the shape of black cats, dogs, or wolves, going places no human could go. The concept of the helpful spirit being is believed to have originated with the totem animal guides of the shamans. However, since the werewolves were already animals, their familiars took the form of humans.

"She said she was training to become a Chippewa—"

"*Chippewa?*" Edward interrupted. "She said *Chippewa?*"

"Yes. Then no. She corrected herself. Why?"

"I've learned a few things from Cadotte, and no true Ojibwe would ever use the word *Chippewa*."

Nic pulled his gun and pointed it in Lydia's direction.

"Not yet," I murmured.

The gun didn't appear to make Lydia nervous, which only made me more so. Either she didn't plan on any of us living long enough to stop her, or her nefarious plan was too far along to thwart.

Was there a door number 3?

"Herr Mandenauer is right. I work for the were-wolves. But soon they will work for me."

"You're raising a witchie wolf army," I said.

Lydia inclined her head.

"But how? You aren't a werewolf."

"Are you certain?"

"Yes," I said firmly, even as my mind doubted.

One thing I'd learned as a *Jäger-Sucher*, the rules applied only until someone or something changed them.

"You don't sound very confident. But I've spent a lot of time and money to make all of you doubt what you know and who you trust."

Money? The light went on in my head.

"You bought information from the traitor."

Lydia laughed. "There isn't any traitor—or at least not in the technical sense of the word. None of your own betrayed you."

Good to know. Really set my mind at ease.

"If not one of us, then who?"

"Do not waste your time," Edward said. "She will not tell us." Edward turned his attention to Lydia. "I am afraid your lover is dead. Will that destroy your plans, I hope?"

"My plans are right on schedule."

"You *wanted* Basil dead?" I asked.

"Not particularly. He was an incredible lay. He'd do anything I wanted, anywhere. All day, all night. The boy was amazing."

"Way too much information," Nic muttered.

"He follows orders amazingly well. 'Kill Dr. Hanover,' I said. Next thing I know—*bam, bam.*"

"Actually, it was just *bam* for him, right, Nic?"

"Yeah. Then he ran away like a girl."

"Hey!" I protested.

"Sorry. How about we try *bam-bam* on Miss Familiar?"

Lydia laughed again. Why did she find Nic's threats of shooting her so amusing? Maybe she couldn't be shot.

"Why is she so smug, Edward?"

I needed to know what I was facing before I could face it with any sort of strength. Even then . . .

I glanced at the sun sparkling through the trees. I wasn't going to be able to do much damage at this time of day.

"Lydia is a descendant of Gypsies," Edward answered.

"Romania, tambourines, fortune-telling Gypsies?" Nic asked.

Lydia snorted at the same time Edward said, "Hardly. Gypsies are the traditional companions of werewolves. Familiars. They protect them and in turn are paid handsomely."

"You didn't know this?" Nic asked me.

"I knew."

"Gypsy? Werewolves? You weren't a little suspicious?"

"She said she was Ojibwe. Why shouldn't I believe her?"

"You couldn't tell the difference?"

"Have you ever seen a Gypsy?"

"I'm not sure."

"Exactly. They're a little hard to peg in the wild."

"There are very few with pure Gypsy blood left," Edward said.

"Why is that?" Nic inched forward; I elbowed him back. Who knew what kind of powers she had?

"Hitler killed four hundred thousand in his death camps," Lydia snapped. "He labeled us nonhuman."

"I hate it when that happens," I muttered.

Lydia shot me a glare. "Mengele loved to experiment on the Gypsies as well as the Jews. When he concocted monsters, he made them from bits and pieces of other things."

"His werewolves have Gypsy blood," I guessed, and Lydia dipped her chin in acknowledgment. "But if they're your cousins or brothers. Children . . . whatever—"

"You say *they* as if you aren't one of them."

"Fine, if *we're* related, then why do you want to rule *us*?"

"Someone has to. If the werewolves banded together, had a leader with half a brain at the helm, someone who didn't get distracted by a demon, or the full moon, or blood on the breeze, they could become so much more than what they are."

Edward had always feared just such an occurrence. If all the werewolves joined forces, what was to prevent every other monster from doing the same? Pretty soon people would be in the minority—if they weren't already.

We had to stop her. If only we knew what she was up to.

Why did she need a witchie wolf army? What could they do? More importantly: How could we kill them?

Hard to say. Hard to ask, too, since I doubted she'd tell us.

"Why get rid of Basil?" I pressed. "Especially if he was so gifted."

"Well hung, you mean?"

I hadn't but . . . I shrugged.

"I didn't kill him."

"I did."

That voice. It couldn't be.

I turned toward the sound just as a figure stepped from the woods and pressed a gun to Edward's temple.

Oh, jeez! Oh, shit! Oh, *hell*!

"Billy."

32

"You're dead," I said, echoing the protests of my dream, which, in retrospect, appeared to have been a vision.

"Not quite."

"I ripped out your throat."

"Not completely."

"You healed."

"I'm very old." Billy smiled, and the expression was more frightening than a scowl. "I can heal just about anything. Except silver. Which is something we have in common. I always wondered what it was about you that bothered me."

He'd found some clothes—Lord knows where since there weren't any outlets for the big and tall in this neck of the woods. The jeans and sweatshirt almost made him appear normal.

Almost. A single glance into his eyes and no one would mistake Billy Bailey for anything other than an escaped lunatic.

"Thor, the Thunder God," Nic murmured.

Double damn. Had the old woman seen Billy? If I'd known that, I could have exited Fairhaven screaming a long time ago.

"Toss your weapon into the trees," Billy ordered.

Nic complied, and Billy shoved Edward forward so he could keep the gun trained on all three of us. I didn't care for his expression when he glanced at Nic.

"You're screwing my girl," Billy murmured. "I don't like it."

I froze as all of the horrible things Billy planned to do to me when he got out of his cell flooded my mind.

I needed to kill him, *really* kill him, and quick.

"Mandenauer."

Edward, who'd been inching toward the rifle propped against the rear bumper of the Cadillac, stopped. I managed to sidle in front of Nic while Billy's attention was on my boss.

Billy didn't want me dead. Not yet. But I had a feeling he wouldn't feel the same way about the others. Though why he hadn't just shot them first and done his talking later, I wasn't sure, and I didn't plan to ask.

"If you don't want a taste of what you've served up so freely," Billy continued, "you'll move far away from that gun."

Edward scowled but did as he was told. Unfortunately, he arrived at my side talking. "You didn't make sure he was dead, then burn the body? Have you learned nothing?"

"Guess not," Billy murmured.

I still couldn't find my voice through the fear.

"You're the werewolf in human form," Nic said. "You killed all those people."

"Actually, that was her." Billy jerked a thumb in Lydia's direction. "Except for Basil. That was me."

"Why?"

"He tried to shoot Dr. Hanover." Billy's eyes narrowed on Lydia.

If that gaze had been fixed in my direction, I certainly wouldn't have tossed my head and shrugged. Why wasn't Lydia afraid of him?

"You promised I could have her when you were through," he said. "That was our deal."

"True." Lydia examined her fingernails. " But I never promised she'd be alive."

Billy growled and the hair on my arms lifted.

"He's really very good." Lydia glanced at me. "If you like your sex extremely rough."

Something wasn't adding up, but I was still too frightened to do the math.

"Don't look so scared. You'll be dead by then." Lydia returned her attention to Billy. "I didn't think you'd mind."

"We've discussed this." He gave a long-suffering sigh. "I fuck her until she dies, and then I do it some more. A deal is a deal."

"That just isn't going to work for me. Sorry."

Billy swung the gun in her direction, and Lydia disappeared.

Nic and I stood gaping at the place where she'd been an instant before.

"I hate it when she does that," Billy muttered.

Edward had been creeping forward while Billy's

attention was elsewhere. Almost as an afterthought, Billy's elbow shot out and clipped the old man in the mouth. Edward's head snapped back and he fell to the ground, but he didn't pass out. Sometimes I wondered if Edward was human himself.

Billy shifted his icy stare to mine. "Soon, Doctor. Remember everything I ever told you."

Black spots danced in front of my eyes. When they went away, so had Billy.

Nic was at my side. I couldn't help it, I turned my face into his neck and hid. Even with ancient Ojibwe women buried in shallow graves, murder, mayhem, and a ghost wolf army on the rise, the world had still been a much cheerier place without Billy in it.

"I'm okay."

I'd found my voice. *Hallelujah.* So why wasn't I screaming mindlessly until someone locked me in a nice, safe, impenetrable white room?

Because having Nic here helped more than I would have imagined. He was steady and sane—which put him two steps ahead of Billy. Sadly, Billy was about two hundred steps ahead when it came to strength and power. We just couldn't win.

I took a deep whiff of Nic's scent, trying to clear any remnant of Billy's. Then I brushed my lips against his chin and lifted my head. Nic gazed at me with concern.

"So that was Billy Bailey," he said. "Creepy son of a bitch."

"Let's kill him." Edward struggled to his feet.

"You neglected to mention that Gypsies have superpowers, too." I looked at Nic. "*That* I did not know."

"It explains how she found out about you."

"How?" My mind wasn't keeping up very well—too full of Billy.

"If she can disappear and appear at will, she could know anything."

I saw Nic's point. Lydia didn't need to tap our phones or pay our enemies for information. All she had to do was become invisible and walk inside the compound.

"Why didn't she kill me before now?"

"She needed you here for . . ." Nic shrugged. "Something?"

"Terrific." I glanced at Edward. "So explain why Gypsies have superpowers."

"Most do not."

"Did she, or did she not, just go poof?"

"She did." He sighed. "Lydia is not only a Gypsy but a witch."

"Witch?" Nic asked. "Since when are there witches?" He turned to me. "Did you know there were witches?"

"Yeah."

"And you didn't tell me?"

"You want a rundown on every supernatural creature we've encountered?"

He thought a minute, then said, "Yes."

"If we're still alive next week, remind me to make you a list." I turned my ire on Edward. "Why didn't you tell us she could disappear?"

"Even if I had known, what good would it have done to tell you? Could you have prevented the disappearance?"

I rubbed my forehead. "What *do* you know about her?"

If I focused on Lydia, maybe I'd quit seeing Billy's eyes fixed on me. I doubted it, but anything was worth a try.

"Her grandmother was removed from one of the death camps and sent to Mengele."

"Her grandfather?"

"Was also at the laboratory in the Black Forest."

"And then?"

"They were released, along with the werewolf army."

"That's all?"

He shrugged. "Witches are hard to identify. They do not sprout tails. They do not suck blood. They do not rise from their graves. They are just magic."

Just?

"Does anyone find it odd that the usual familiar *helps* a witch, but a werewolf familiar *is* a witch?" Nic pointed out.

"Not all Gypsies are witches," Edward said. "Only the pure have magic—*witches* for want of a better term. Mengele used that blood to concoct his werewolves."

"Magic Gypsy witch blood to make werewolves," I muttered.

I did remember something about that in my notes, but since I'd doubted it would help me find a cure, I'd pushed the information to the back of my mind.

"Where did you meet Lydia?"

"I was acquainted with her grandmother." Something flickered in Edward's eyes, and he looked away. How well had he known the woman?

I considered the suspicion. Edward could no more have an affair with a werewolf familiar than he could . . . what? Employ a werewolf?

"You didn't think it was a good idea to keep track of these people?" I asked.

"Of course. But as they are magic, they have a habit of slipping out of our reach."

"And the name Lydia didn't set off any alarm bells?"

"It is a common enough name."

"If you're lost in the forties," Nic muttered.

"I will admit, I made an error not keeping better track of the witches." Edward steepled his fingers. "But let us discuss *your* error, Elise."

"Mine?"

"Billy isn't dead."

Oh, that error.

"Get over it," Nic interjected.

"Excuse me?" Edward lifted a brow.

"He isn't dead, but he will be as soon as I find him." Nic reached for his weapon, frowned. "And my gun."

He started off in the direction of his pistol, then stopped and turned back. "I'm confused. To make the witchie wolves, dead people need to be bitten by a werewolf in human form?"

"That's the theory."

"As near as we can tell, the bites were all from the same mouth."

I nodded, though he knew this as well as I did.

"A mouth we'll assume to be Billy's since there isn't a pack of werewolves in Fairhaven—unless you count the ghost wolves."

"There is a point soon, correct?" Edward murmured.

"People were disappearing before we got here, and we have a lot more ghost wolves than two, so how could Billy have bitten anyone if he was locked in a compound in Montana?"

From the silence that settled over the clearing, no one had a definite answer for that, but Edward usually had an educated guess. Today was no different.

"Perhaps another werewolf came first. Once Billy arrived, he killed him."

"That *would* be a Billy thing to do," I agreed. "Except Damien said there was no werewolf here but him until I arrived."

"Damien could have been wrong," Edward pointed out.

Could have been, but I doubted it. Damien had been a werewolf for nearly sixty years; he knew how to identify another like himself.

"Let us find Billy, ask him, then kill him," Edward suggested. "Or just kill him."

"You know what my vote is," I said.

"Why did they let us go?" Nic asked. "Billy could have killed any, or all, of us. Lydia wants you dead, Elise, yet she took off. Why?"

"They must realize we will come after them," Edward continued. "The full moon is tonight. Billy will have to change."

"And I'll be waiting for him," Nic murmured.

"Wait." Edward held up a long bony hand. "If they want us to hunt under the full moon, we will not."

"Wrong," I said, at the same time Nic snapped, "Like hell."

Edward and I turned to Nic as he lifted, then lowered, one shoulder. "I don't like how Billy spoke to you, Elise."

"You should have heard him in the compound," I muttered, then shivered again at the memory.

"I did not say we would not hunt." Edward sounded exasperated. "Nor that we would not kill him and anything else that gets in our way."

"What *did* you say?" Nic asked.

"Silver works on werewolves in the daytime as well as the night. In human form as well as the form of a wolf."

Understanding spread across Nic's face, followed closely by excitement. "We'll shoot him in the daylight. He won't even know what hit him."

"Only this one time," Edward ordered. "Billy is a special case."

Edward frowned on us shooting people with silver in broad daylight, no matter how certain we might be of their true nature. In his defense, flaming humans were a lot harder to explain than flaming wolves.

"Fine. One-time deal only. Now where's my gun?"

"You will need a rifle, as well," Edward said. "I have an arsenal in the trunk."

He always did.

Nic practically skipped off to shop at the firearm bonanza, as I stalked toward Edward. I did *not* want Nic going after Billy. Billy was insane.

"Nic isn't a *Jäger-Sucher*," I whispered. "Since when does he get to pick a rifle and join the party?"

"Since we are shorthanded, and you are nothing short of horrific with a gun."

My chin went up. "I have other talents."

"Not in the daytime. Besides." Edward nodded toward the Cadillac. "I doubt you will be able to stop him."

Nic was going through the rifles with an ease born of practice. His face held a determination I recognized. He wouldn't be dissuaded from hunting Billy.

"Fine." I threw up my hands. "But he goes with you."

"Not you?"

"You're the best. Except for Leigh."

Edward scowled but didn't argue since I was right, then he stomped over to the trunk, yanked out his favorite rifle, and began to bark orders. "Franklin, you are with me."

"But—" Nic glanced in my direction, and I shrugged as if I had nothing to say about anything. Though I didn't want Nic out of my sight ever again, he'd be safer with Edward. Especially since Billy seemed to have a hard-on for me.

"We will meet at the cabin before dusk. If one of us has accomplished the task, fire three rounds into the air, then return to town."

I glanced at the Cadillac. "What about the car?"

Edward's long-suffering sigh made me want to melt into the earth with shame, same as it had when I was three.

"Drive the vehicle back to town. Walk out from there, Agent Franklin and I walk in from here. We will flush him from his hiding place."

Was I supposed to know this trick without ever having been told? Apparently.

Edward moved toward the trees. Nic stepped after him, then glanced in my direction and paused.

Though it was the height of unprofessionalism, I went into his arms. Edward didn't even bother to snicker, snort, or be snide. He must think we were all going to die.

"Be careful," I couldn't help but murmur.

Sure, he was an FBI agent, but this was a *Billy* and Lord knows what else.

"You won't be safe until he's dead." Nic released me with a final squeeze.

I tried one more time. "Maybe you should go—"

"Where? I think I'm better off with Mandenauer and enough guns and ammo to outfit a small country than I am at the cabin alone or on my way to the airport in a flimsy steel car."

He was probably right. Nevertheless, I didn't like this at all.

"Meet you in Fairhaven before dusk, if not sooner."

I nodded, then glanced at my boss as Nic joined him. The old man acknowledged my query with a single sharp nod.

Billy would not get to Nic. Not while Edward was alive.

Of course, Edward being dead was just another one of my mountain of worries.

33

The wind suddenly whispered in Lydia's voice. *He'll do anything to keep me from sharing his secret.*

I remembered another time, another place, another message. Had the voice been Lydia's? I didn't think so. How many voices were there?

I glanced at Edward, but he was oblivious to any whispers on the wind. Which was probably the entire idea.

I opened my mouth to call out to him and the trees murmured: *I'll tell you the truth about your mother.*

My teeth closed with an audible snap. I knew the truth about my mother. Didn't I?

"What about Lydia?" I blurted.

"Kill her."

"Sir?" I blinked. "She's a—"

"Murderer? Witch?"

"We shoot monsters, don't we?"

"You do not think she is a monster?"

I wasn't sure.

"Shouldn't we find out what she's done and how to undo it?" I asked. "If she's dead that could be tough."

"Do what I tell you, Elise. Or must I use that silver bullet I keep solely for you?"

Nic made an involuntary movement of denial, which Edward ignored. I kept my gaze on my boss.

My eyes narrowed; so did his. I was half-tempted to shift and chase him around the yard; too bad it was daytime. Too bad he'd kill me without so much as a bat of his nearly invisible blond eyelashes.

See? said the breeze through the leaves. *He doesn't want you to know.*

I glanced away. I might be an alpha wolf, but in the human world, Edward was king. Besides, with him hanging around, I'd never find out if what I'd been told about my mother was the truth. If Lydia could be trusted to tell the truth.

Probably not. Nevertheless, I found myself sympathizing with Eve in her garden. All that knowledge just waiting in a tree—all she had to do was listen to Satan.

The wind fluttered the ends of my hair, the silence so loud it pulsed with unanswered questions. When I looked back, both Edward and Nic were gone, so I chose a weapon, shut the trunk of the Cadillac, and headed in the direction of the voice—conveniently in the opposite direction of the others.

I had my orders. Despite my unease about killing Lydia, I'd killed people before. Just not with a gun.

Besides, who knew? Maybe eliminating Lydia would also eliminate the witchie wolves she'd raised and the coming Armageddon.

Two birds, one stone. I'd always loved that.

I followed the wind. Every time I hesitated the breeze murmured, drawing me farther and farther away from the cabin and closer and closer to—

Coming around a crop of low spruce bushes, I slid to a stop at the edge of the ravine. The scent of wolves washed over me, so strong I could distinguish it even in human form.

I paced back and forth until I found an opening big enough for a woman instead of a wolf, then inched through the brambles. Peeking over the rim as I'd done once before, I discovered nearly a dozen ghost wolves lolling on a grassy knoll.

The witchie wolves were werewolves, down to the human eyes. No longer shadows, they weren't solid either, since I could see the grass right through their hides.

"I've been waiting."

I spun toward Lydia's voice, half-expecting to find nothing but the rustle of a nonexistent breeze through the trees. But she stood a few feet away in a flowing skirt and peasant blouse of muted colors—violets beneath a spring rain, the sky just before a storm.

All of her bangles—wrists, ankles, feet—were in place. How had she snuck up on me? She must be able to appear as easily as she disappeared.

She held a gun in one hand, which looked suspiciously like the one I'd chosen from Edward's car. Glancing at my holster, I saw she'd disarmed me as easily as she'd snuck up on me. Edward would have a stroke.

Lydia tossed my weapon into trees, then lowered two fingers into the valley between her breasts and withdrew the icon, strung on a leather strip around her neck. "Remember this?"

I nodded.

"You hand over the power; I'll tell you all about your mother. What do you say?"

I wasn't going to agree, especially since I had no idea how I could hand over anything. But if she was inclined to chat, I was inclined to ask questions.

"You made the talisman," I murmured. "Why?"

"To steal your magic." She rolled the icon around in her fingers. "But you're stronger than I imagined."

"How could that thing steal my power when lycanthropy's caused by a virus?"

"Is it?"

"Yes."

Her smile was secretive, smug, and I stifled the urge to beat every tidbit of information out of her. All in good time.

"Cora told me I could capture the essence of a werewolf, contain it in the icon and transfer the gift to myself."

"I never heard of such a thing."

If I had, I'd have bottled up my magic and given it away long ago.

"You've been barking up the wrong tree, pardon the pun, for a while now. Concentrating all your efforts on science: tonics, balms, cures. But there's more than one answer to every question."

"Is lycanthropy caused by a virus or isn't it?"

"Both. Mengele manufactured a virus through magic."

Which was interesting, but didn't really help me much with the cure.

"If you wanted to become a werewolf," I murmured, "all you had to do was ask one of your pals."

"As if I wanted to be insane, ruled by the moon and my rumbling, blood-seeking belly." Lydia grimaced. "I want the power without the demon. That's what the old one promised."

"And then you killed her?"

"Well, I didn't need her anymore," she said matter-of-factly.

I had news for Lydia. She was already a stark raving lunatic, even without the demon.

"How was the talisman supposed to capture my power?"

"I don't know *how,* only that it would. Cora did some mumbo jumbo, told me to purify the talisman with the blood of a sacrifice, and when you changed the first time after touching the icon, your abilities would leave you and fill it." She scowled at the plastic wolf. "The bitch double-crossed me. Instead of stealing the magic, she made you stronger."

Bless the old woman I'd never met, had she given me the ability to defeat her own murderer? I had to think so, if I could only figure out how.

"So now I've got to kill you," Lydia continued.

"Whoa! What? Why?"

"Cora said sacrifice. I didn't realize she meant you. I should have."

Well, she *was* delusional. Who knows, maybe she was even right.

However, since I'd come to Fairhaven, I kind of liked my power. Even if I didn't, I certainly wasn't going to give it to her.

"If you didn't want me dead in Montana, then who blew up the compound? Who tried to shoot me with silver?"

Maybe if we kept talking, I'd stumble over something I could use.

"The idiot werewolves." She shook her head in disgust. "Sometimes I swear only morons are bitten. They really do need a leader."

She glanced at the forest as if searching for someone, then gave an impatient huff before turning back to me.

"I sold the information about your true nature before I figured out how I could use it to my advantage. Some ambitious werewolf decided to make everyone happy by eliminating you."

"What the hell did I do?"

"Who knows when you might stumble onto a cure, and then their fun is over." She waved her hand. "But I discovered their plot, and I saved you."

"Saved me," I repeated stupidly.

"I knew you'd come outside to check on your wolves, so I upset them."

My eyes narrowed. I opened my mouth, then shut it again, deciding I didn't want to know what she'd done.

"You came out; the bomb went off—"

"Then someone took a shot at me."

"He'd have gotten you, too, but I bumped him." She winked. "He never saw me coming."

"Okay." This was all making a sick sort of sense. "Then—"

"The idiot got spooked by your FBI friend and took off. I heard you say you were going to the shed, so I killed the rabbit, planted the icon—"

"And the rest is history."

"Except the damn thing didn't work." She stared into the hokcy jcwclcd eyes. "Yet."

Lydia pocketed the totem. "Once I figured out Cora had double-crossed me, I headed for Fairhaven so I could regroup before you got here."

"How did you know I'd come?"

"The compound's dust; someone's trying to kill you; traitor in the ranks; strange and bizarre occurrences in Fairhaven."

I started to see where Lydia was headed.

This had been a setup from the beginning.

34

"You raised witchie wolves to bring the *Jäger-Suchers* to Fairhaven?"

"Of course not. There's a reason for everything I've done. When the dark moon comes, all will be clear."

"As mud," I muttered.

"I knew you'd come to Edward. Then I'd have to get the others to leave so you'd be alone." Lydia spread her hands. "Werewolves popping up all over the place, and *wham,* the good doctor is on her own."

"But I'm—"

"Not. I know. I didn't figure on the FBI showing up and refusing to leave. Some idiot werewolf again—giving the Feds a tip, trying to screw up your life and instead screwing up mine. Heads are going to roll once I'm in charge."

I could imagine.

Lydia glanced at the sky, then into the trees. "Come on."

She shoved me farther into the ravine. As we walked

through the sleeping ghost wolves, they awoke and milled around our legs. The sensation was creepy—like a chilly brush of wind that scrambled straight through my bones.

A rustle from the forest was followed by the murmur of voices, the measured tread of human feet.

Edward and Nic pushed their way through the brambles at the edge of the clearing. They gaped at the witchic wolves. Their ability to see them made me uneasy. When they caught sight of Lydia, they pointed their weapons at her head.

"Just in time to watch the show." She put a knife to my throat.

Silver, it burned like fire. Smoke rose in an unpleasant stream in front of my face.

"We will kill her to get to you," Edward murmured. "It is our way."

"Not *my* way."

Nic stepped forward and the ground shifted. The witchie wolves howled so loudly my ears rang, then as one they stood and encircled the ravine. Nic's cell phone rang, the sound shrill and alien in the warm, waiting silence.

"Could be Will," I managed.

With information that wasn't crap. Nic punched the on button.

"Stay out of the woods."

I heard Will's voice as clearly as if the phone were pressed to my ear. This increased-power deal was very handy.

"Too late," Nic said.

Will cursed. "Definitely stay away from that ravine

where most of the bodies are buried. The greatest concentration of spiritual power is there. The witchies will protect that ground, since it was by far the most desecrated. It's where they'll come to power."

"In two weeks?" Nic asked.

" 'Fraid not. In some legends the dark moon is when the moon is new. In others, the dark moon shares the sky with the sun. The moon is always there, you just can't see it in the daytime."

"The dark moon is now," I whispered.

Nic's gaze met mine. Understanding filled his eyes, and his grip tightened on the phone.

"The witchie wolf army can't be killed," Will continued. "They're already dead. You need to stop Lydia from . . . whatever it is she's going to do."

"How?" Nic asked.

"The most powerful shaman commands them."

"Lydia's not an Indian."

"Shit," I muttered, as I remembered Will's explanation about shamans. "Blood has nothing to do with it."

"You're wrong." Lydia pricked my neck. "Blood has everything to do with it."

The ground trembled, and Lydia released me. I spun as she lifted the talisman, marked with my blood, toward the sun-drenched sky. "Blood to the earth, flesh to the flesh, spirits arise."

"Go!" I shouted to the others. "Run."

Nic snorted. "I don't think so."

"I live for this," Edward said.

The two started forward, and the witchie wolves snarled. Both men shot at the nearest wolf. Their bullets went right through the bodies and into the ground.

"Uh-oh," Nic muttered.

Together they turned their weapons on Lydia and the wolves charged.

"No!" I shouted, but they didn't seem to hear.

Instead they knocked the men to the grass. Considering how the bullets had gone through them, the witchies were awfully solid. One wolf sat on each of their chests, while two others yanked their weapons away and dragged them into the trees.

"Keep everyone out." Lydia lowered her arms. "Now it's just you and me."

The witchie wolves howled. "And them. They want to be led. They don't know what to do all alone."

Lydia inched closer. "I need more blood. I'm thinking, all of it."

Fury shot through me. What good were years of lycanthropy if I couldn't defeat one crazy witch?

With anger came strength, and energy rumbled along my skin like a flaming wind. I couldn't prevent the growl that tickled my throat from coming out of my mouth.

The sun was shining. I should not feel the call of the moon, but I did.

"Don't fight it," Lydia murmured. "Shift. In the daylight. You'll feel a whole lot better."

"That is what she wants," Edward shouted. "Do not do it."

Lydia's laughter tickled my spine like a feather. "Aren't you tired of him telling you what to do?"

"No," I lied.

"If you knew everything there was to know, you'd change your mind."

"I doubt that."

"Let's find out."

I blinked, and she was gone.

"Do you know who your mother was?" Her voice seemed to come from everywhere. The trees, the sky. Where the hell was she?

"She was a werewolf," I answered. "Edward killed her."

"Yes, but do you know why?"

"She was a werewolf."

"Not why he killed her; why she was a werewolf?"

"Bitten."

"Because of who her father was."

My mother's father. My grandfather. Who had he been? I'd never asked. No one had ever offered. I was an orphan, my entire family wiped out by werewolves. Maybe that was true. Then again, maybe it wasn't.

"They came after him, but they found her." Lydia's whisper was like a serpent hissing in my ear. "Death was too easy after all he'd done. Edward arrived too late to save his daughter, but he managed to save you."

I glanced in his direction. The witchie wolves had moved back, allowing Edward and Nic to sit up but not to stand. The old man stared across the ravine. One look was all it took to see the truth.

Edward Mandenauer had killed his own child—my mother—then raised me as a charity case, without love or affection or honesty. I couldn't believe even he could be so cruel.

"That's it." Lydia's voice tempted me. "Get mad. Get very, very mad. Shift in the daylight. Imagine the power."

"How do you know so much?" I managed, my voice more a beast's than a woman's.

"My grandmother and Edward were . . . close."

"Maria?"

"Maria was his wife. My grandmother knew him first, loved him best, but then he left her in the lab with Mengele and married Maria, a slut from the city. Granny made sure she discovered all of Edward's secrets. Which she shared with me."

Fury, red, hot, and bubbling, bolted through my blood, giving me strength, lending me focus, a clarity beyond anything I'd ever known. I felt the moon, despite the sun, because the moon was there, but it was dark.

Opening my mind, I embraced the ebony sheen. I welcomed the darkness, both in the sky and in me.

My hands became paws, claws shooting from my fingertips like razor blades. The hearing, the sight, the speed of a wolf was mine. When she spoke again, I was ready.

"Secrets are always useful. Eventually."

My arms shot out. A pained gasp whistled through the ravine. I opened my eyes and saw her. My claws around her throat, I'd made kind of a mess. She wasn't going to die from that wound, but she sure was going to bleed.

She moved her mouth, pointed at her throat. I was loath to release her in case she disappeared.

Wait a minute. Why *didn't* she disappear?

As if in slow motion, I watched a drop of blood fall through the air, soak into the dirt, as the witchie wolves howled.

The ground rippled like water, then spilled outward like the Red Sea. I saw skulls and bones unearthed. Talk about desecration.

Blood to the earth, flesh to the flesh, spirits arise.

That damn incantation.

I looked at the witchie wolves. They were really wolves now. I could no longer see through them, and according to Will, they were unstoppable.

Lydia began to struggle, and her peasant blouse shifted, revealing the talisman.

"Mine," I growled.

Tangling a paw through the loop, I yanked, then tossed Lydia across the ravine. She hit the ground and lay still.

Suddenly everything was quiet. I glanced at the others. Edward winced. I looked at Nic. He pointed toward his eyes, wiggled his fingers.

My eyes, my hands, were still wolf, so I took a deep breath, imagined myself human, and I was.

The talisman's rope was wrapped around my wrist. I left it there.

"I have never seen such a thing in all of my life." Edward stared at the witchie wolves. They were frozen, uncertain.

Nic crossed the ground in four quick steps and yanked me into his arms. Edward went straight to Lydia.

"Is it over?" Nic asked, his lips against my hair.

"Not quite."

Billy strode into the ravine, along with several other men. I recognized them. The werewolves from the basement disarmed Edward.

"Is there anyone not after you?" Edward snapped.

Before I could answer, Billy grabbed Nic by the back of the neck and tossed him away as easily as I'd tossed Lydia.

"I promised you the flesh of the *Jäger-Suchers,*" Billy said. "Take him, too."

I started to go after Nic, and Billy backhanded me across the face. "It's our time now."

Before I could think, concentrate, shift as I'd done with Lydia, Billy hit me again. Then he grabbed me around the waist, yanked me against him and kissed me, sucking the blood from my lips.

The guy was just not right in the head.

I struggled, but Billy was both a very large, muscular man and an ancient and powerful werewolf. He lifted his head and stared into my face. "I've been waiting so long for this."

I closed my eyes against the madness in his. I couldn't feel the moon, couldn't concentrate past my fear.

His body against mine, his scent filled my nose. His teeth nibbled at my throat as his hands clutched my breasts. There was no way I could focus well enough to marshal the power needed to defeat him, and Billy knew it.

Sounds of a battle rose nearby. Edward was fighting the basement werewolves for his life, and I couldn't help.

"I knew you'd kick Lydia's ass," Billy said. "Then I'd kick yours, and the army would be mine."

A chill trickled over my skin. Billy in charge of the witchie wolf army? The world would no longer be fit for anyone or anything. I doubted he'd care.

"The witchie wolves."

The voice was Nic's—faint, groggy, but alive.

Billy snarled and turned toward him.

"No." I grabbed Billy's arm.

He punched me, right in the nose, and I flew across the ravine, hitting the ground so hard my teeth rattled. But I'd gotten my wish, he came after me instead of Nic.

I tried to get up, but my head spun. My nose bled. My teeth felt loose. Billy grabbed me by the shirt and slammed me into the ground.

"Lydia was right. I'll just do you when you're dead." He wrapped his huge hands around my throat. "You'll be a lot less trouble that way, and really, I could care less what I fuck."

I tried to speak, but he was squeezing too hard, so I grabbed his fingers and pulled. He laughed. "You aren't strong enough. You never were. Hell, you killed me once, and it didn't stick. You'll never get another chance."

"You're wrong," I managed. "I am stronger."

Billy smirked and released me. "Prove it."

I didn't have to fight him. Nic's words had made me remember. Only the most powerful shaman commanded the witchie wolf army. But a shaman's power had nothing to do with physical strength and everything to do with magic, mystery, and belief.

I captured the icon between my fingers. Either this worked, or we all died.

"Kill him," I whispered.

Then, as the witchie wolves howled and understanding rolled over Billy's face, everything went black.

35

Embrace the power. Complete the quest. The answer lies in you.

The words came out of the darkness, in a voice I didn't recognize. I awoke to a whole new world—a beautiful place, full of color and light and scent. People and animals meandered about, enjoying the sun that sparkled on clear water. The lion with the lamb, black people with white, I even saw a coyote resting his head on the feathered breast of a chicken.

"Where am I?"

"You are in the Land of Souls."

A woman separated from those lounging near the water and walked toward me. Tall, slim, her hair was flowing black with only a trace of silver. Her face defied time; her eyes were dark, clear, and honest.

Her white T-shirt was tucked into a long colorful skirt. She wore a ring on each finger and on two of her toes. Three earrings hung from each ear and bracelets jangled around her slim wrists.

"Am I dead?"

"No." Her smile was gentle. She took my hand. "But I am."

"You're Cora." Her brows lifted. "Will spoke of you."

Her expression became both fond and sad. "He's a good boy, and I miss him. Tell him all that I have is his."

"He'll like that." I considered the beautiful, dead old woman. "You engineered everything, didn't you?"

"Lydia told me what she had planned." Cora shrugged. "I planned better."

"You gave me strength."

"No. The strength was always yours. The talisman was merely an instrument that allowed you to access it." She brushed her hands together. "Now, I promised you the truth."

"You did?"

"Embrace what you are, discover the secret you seek."

"That was you?"

She nodded.

"Why didn't you just tell me who the bad guys were?"

"The Land of Souls doesn't work that way. Only through accepting yourself could you ever become whole and learn the truth."

I wasn't sure I could handle any more truth.

"Because you defeated the one who ended my days, I can grant you the answer to a single question. All you need do is ask."

There was only one question I'd ever wanted the answer to.

"What is the cure for lycanthropy?"

"You don't wish to know how to cure yourself?"

"Isn't it the same thing?"

"The cure for one will not cure the other. You are different. You must choose."

Myself or all the werewolves? Once the decision would have been easy. I had loathed what I was, would have done anything to remove the curse, cure the virus. But I'd learned a lot in the past few days.

Edward might hate me, but that was his problem. I no longer did. I could help people, save lives.

Nic hadn't run screaming. Yet. However, he could when he discovered I might never be cured.

I paused to think, but I didn't really have to. I couldn't choose an easy life over hundreds, thousands of deaths. I just couldn't.

"Them, not me," I said.

"You wish to have the power to remove the demon and make werewolves human again?"

"Yes."

"A sacrifice," Cora murmured. "For the good of mankind. In the end, you will be blessed."

She took me by the hand. When she released me, a pentagram remained, stark black against the pale of my palm.

"Mark of the wolf," she told me. "The power to heal."

"How?"

"The gift was always in you. You fought what you were. You refused to embrace the beast. Relying on science to turn back the tide of magic." Cora shook her head. "There is no cure that comes from a bottle."

"But science made the monsters. Or at least some of them."

"Hate makes monsters. Those who worshipped the

sign of the beast attempted to bring about Doomsday, and they failed."

"Nazis? The swastika?"

"No one should call forth powers they do not understand."

"I'll be able to cure werewolves now?"

"You are woman and wolf—human and inhuman. Only you can touch them and make them whole."

The Land of Souls shimmered, faded, and was gone.

"Elise?"

I opened my eyes.

Either the sun was setting or a storm was coming. The ravine was shadowed, cool, a bit spooky. I could smell blood, a lot of it, along with wolves, people.

How long had I been—

Where had I been?

Nic, who was on his knees at my side, leaned over and kissed me. A thorough kiss, both sweet and seductive. I lifted my arms and wrapped them around his neck.

"Can we save the pornographic video for later? I got questions."

That was Jessie's voice. When had she gotten here?

Nic lifted his head, touched my cheek. There were shadows in his eyes that hadn't been there before.

"What's wrong?" I asked.

"You were dead."

"Was not."

"You didn't have a pulse." Jessie leaned over and put her finger to my neck. "You do now."

I slapped her hand away. "I saw Cora in the Land of Souls."

Everyone went silent. Jessie and Nic exchanged

glances. I could tell by their expressions they thought I'd lost my mind. Maybe I had. I'd been hit hard enough to jiggle my brain.

"Cora," I began, but stopped when Jessie pointed her .44 at my head.

"What's on your hand?"

I blinked at the black pentagram glistening starkly in the half light. The Land of Souls hadn't been a dream after all.

"Cora touched me and there it was."

"Last time there was a tattoo like that it was on a *Weendigo*," Jessie said. "I hate those guys."

Nic slid in front of Jessie's .44. "Put the gun down."

"Hey!" I tugged on his arm. "She isn't going to shoot me."

"Damn straight I will, Doc. I'm not going through that *Weendigo* shit again, even for you."

"A pentagram with one point ascendant represents good." Edward's voice—my grandfather's voice—drifted across the ravine. "Two points ascendant means evil."

Jessie leaned in close, squinting at my palm. "One up—guess you aren't Satan's handmaiden after all."

I rolled my eyes, wincing at the pain the movement caused in my head. Struggling to sit, I glanced in Edward's direction.

All of the werewolves from the basement, save one, were on the ground, dead bodies still smoking. Edward guarded the remaining lycanthrope, rifle nearly touching the guy's nose.

"How did you manage to arrive in the nick of time?" I asked Jessie.

"Will had a bad feeling." She shrugged, kicked the ground. "His feelings come true a lot. When he went to talk to the wigwam guy, I headed here." She lifted her gaze to mine. "Lucky I did."

The witchie wolves surrounded what was left of Billy. Even though he'd deserved what he got, my eyes still shied away from the remains.

Wait a second. Someone was missing.

"Where's Lydia?"

"Poof," Jessie said. "We got a little busy with . . ." Her nod indicated the werewolves, Billy, me. "When we looked, she was gone. Though Edward did find something interesting in her pocket before she left."

Jessie held out her hand. In it lay a set of dentures and a bottle of clear liquid.

"Okay, I'll bite."

Jessie snorted at my pathetic pun.

"What the hell is that?"

"We couldn't figure out how the bodies were being bitten by a werewolf in human form when Damien said there was no evidence of a werewolf in Fairhaven."

"How were they?"

"They weren't—not really. We think Lydia made an impression of Billy's teeth, collected his saliva, then did the deed herself."

"Why Billy?"

"The usual reason, most likely, power. He was loaded with it. I figure Lydia didn't want to release him if she didn't have to. That guy was whacked."

"But the compound blew up, he got out, came here, and she had no choice but to work with him."

"Great minds," Jessie agreed, and glanced at the

bloody grass. "Guess we'll never know the truth for sure, but it all fits."

"Lydia's going to try and rule the world again," I said.

"They always do. But we'll be here to stop her. Unless I have to shoot you in the head. Tell the tale, Doc."

Quickly I explained my journey to the Land of Souls.

"You've been wasting your time and the government's money? All you had to do was touch them, and they'd be human?"

"Not exactly." I frowned. "I've touched a few werewolves. Got a headache. Never cured one."

"So what's special now. The mark?"

"No." As my mind cleared, everything Cora had said began to combine with all that I'd learned, all that I knew. "Not the mark, but what it represents. Embracing my power, the magic, and my beast gave me strength and led me to the truth."

"I guess that makes as much sense as anything," Jessie said. "So why don't we find out if that brand-new fashion accessory works?"

I followed Jessie's gaze to the werewolf Edward held under the gun. "Okay."

"Wait." Nic put a hand on my shoulder. "Maybe you should rest first. Who knows what might happen?"

"Exactly, G-man. Who knows what might happen? She's the most powerful werewolf now. I don't know about you, but that makes me mighty nervous."

"She was the most powerful werewolf all along," Nic said.

I glanced at the witchie wolves. "He's right."

Jessie aimed her gun and so did Edward. No moss on them.

"What the hell?" Nic asked.

"She commands the witchie wolf army," Edward murmured. "They are indestructible."

"So if I'm of a mind to rule the world—"

"You can," Jessie finished.

However, I'd never been big on world domination.

"Wait for me in the Land of Souls," I said.

Before the last word left my mouth, the witchie wolves began to fade. Flesh and bone became ghost, ghost became shadow, and then they were gone.

"Oookay," Jessie muttered. "They can't be killed, but they can be commanded to wait in heaven. Works for me." She lowered her gun. "Let's move on. I want to know if that pentagram is good or evil—"

"She just proved she's not evil," Nic said. "She got rid of the witchies."

"That proved she's the most powerful. I don't like it."

"I'm not wild about it myself," I murmured.

"And if she's evil, you shoot her?" Nic asked.

Jessie merely turned a bland gaze in his direction. Stupid question.

"I won't let you."

"You won't have anything to say about it."

Nic's hand crept toward his gun and I put mine on his. "I'm not evil. She won't kill me. And this is going to work. Watch."

I got to my feet, managed not to wobble. This day, this week, hell, this life, was taking a lot out of me.

I crossed the ravine, skirting the mess that had been

Billy. The last werewolf from the basement, Jack Mc-Grady, stared at me in fear.

"No!" He tried to skitter back.

Edward thrust him forward. "Do it."

"I don't want to be human," Jack shouted.

"Would you rather be dead?" Edward shoved the barrel of a rifle into Jack's ear.

Jack was just a kid. He'd had his whole life ahead of him—in 1955. Since then, he'd made a career of ending other kids' lives. I didn't feel an ounce of guilt over using him as my guinea pig.

Reaching out, I placed my tattooed palm against his forehead.

36

I braced for the ice pick of pain. Instead, all I felt was darkness—like a blanket over my mind.

Somewhere in that darkness, the soul that had been Jack at eighteen whimpered. A tiny light became brighter and brighter, and suddenly the shadows were gone.

Jack stared at me in confusion. He appeared exactly the same as he had when I'd touched him. He hadn't aged fifty years. He didn't sport deadly wounds he could no longer heal. The only thing that was different were his eyes. There was no longer a demon panting to get out.

"Who are you?" He glanced around the clearing, flinching at the carnage. "Where am I?"

"Get him out of here," I told Edward.

"Not so fast," he murmured. "Perhaps we should perform one final test."

"What kind of test?"

"The full moon comes."

I glanced up. Night approached. I had been in the Land of Souls longer than I'd thought.

A hum filled my head, a desperate need; thirst pressed at the back of my throat. I was both different and still the same.

Fumbling in my pocket, I found the spare vial of serum and drained it in one long pull. The pulsing call of the moon and the intense craving for blood receded.

"When the moon hits the sky, if he doesn't change, he is healed." Edward glanced at me. "If you have cured him, you will have more work in your future than you will be able to manage. You will not have time for kissy-kissy with the FBI."

A flash of annoyance at the man's audacity caused me to speak more sharply to him than I ever had before. "That's all you have to say? No words of wisdom for your granddaughter? No apology?"

"Apologize? For what?"

"My mother. Your daughter."

I could have sworn I saw him flinch, but it might have just been a trick of the fading sunlight through the dappled trees. Edward Mandenauer cared for no one and nothing but the hunt.

"I had no choice," he said.

"You had a choice with me. You could have told me who I was. Given me some affection."

"No I couldn't." His bony shoulders slumped, and he turned toward the horizon. "I've lost too many women I love. Every time the monsters took another, a part of me was destroyed."

"He must have lost a lot of women," Jessie muttered.

I moved across the dry leaves until I stood right behind the man who was my grandfather.

"I didn't know what you would become," he said quietly, "if I might have to kill you someday. How could I bounce you on my knee and tell you everything would be all right? Wouldn't that have been a bigger lie than all the others?"

I wasn't sure, but I saw his dilemma. Besides, the idea of him bouncing a child on his knee was more frightening than some of the things that wandered the night.

"When I shifted, why didn't you kill me?"

"Every time I looked at you, I saw . . ."

"Who?"

"You have your grandmother's eyes." He took a deep breath and straightened his sloping shoulders. "I was right to keep you. You were the key to everything."

"Funny how that worked out."

"Life has a way of coming full circle if you give it enough time."

"You could have told me the truth after I came back from Stanford."

"By then it was too late. Too many lies. And I didn't want anyone to know."

"How mortifying to have a granddaughter who turns furry."

"Yes, it is."

He walked away without another word. Some things never changed.

"Well, that was . . . interesting." Jessie shifted her gun toward Jack, who was so confused he appeared in a near-catatonic state.

I stared at Edward, who had gotten as far away from us as he could without leaving the ravine.

"He'll come around." Nic touched my shoulders. "Somewhere inside his icy cold heart he loves you."

"I doubt that." I turned in his arms. "I'm always going to be the way I am, and he'll never be able to love what he hates."

I paused and considered the rest. I had to tell Nic the truth. There'd been too many lies for too long.

"I had a choice in the Land of Souls. I could have become human instead of . . ." I lifted my palm.

"And left the world to rot?" He shook his head. "I don't think so. You made the right choice, Elise."

Some of the tension slid out of me. "Thanks."

The sun inched below the horizon, and I shuddered as the silver glow of the moon threatened.

Moving out of Nic's embrace, I murmured, "Stand back."

The moon rose, spilling light into the shadow, spilling magic across us all. Jack didn't change, but I did.

Instantaneous and without pain I became a wolf. Wild and free, I ran through the night. My beast at one with myself, I felt a peace I'd never suspected could exist within me and a power beyond anything I'd imagined.

As dawn filled the sky, I returned to the cabin. All was quiet. Edward was gone, along with Jack. Will was back. I was certain Jessie had already called Leigh, and soon I'd be able to fix Damien. Life was good.

I slipped into the bathroom and turned on the shower, then I stared at the brand-new me in the mirror.

No makeup, hair tousled and cascading to my waist,

I appeared younger, probably because the lines of worry and stress had flown, along with the shadows.

I didn't think I'd ever wear a suit again, to hell with panty hose, but I'd have to get some new Italian shoes. I liked them too much to give up.

My days in the lab were over, which was lucky since there wasn't any lab. I had places to go, werewolves to find, and I knew just who I was going to take with me.

As if my thoughts had conjured him up, Nic slipped into the room. His arms slid around my waist. He kissed my neck, then glanced into the mirror.

"You okay?" he asked.

"Better than okay. What about you?"

"Same." He laid his cheek on top of my head. "Or at least I am now."

"We won. Most of the bad guys are dead. Everyone on our side still alive. Sometimes that doesn't happen."

I hesitated. Nic wanted me, that much I knew, but he'd never mentioned love. I still didn't want him to leave—ever.

"I have a proposition for you." Nic wiggled his eyebrows and I laughed. "Not that kind. A job."

"I've got one."

My hopes fell. It really *wasn't* fair to ask him to give up a career he was so good at.

"Edward hired me."

My head came up so fast I nearly clipped him in the nose.

"Hey! Take it easy."

I spun around. "Really?"

"He pointed out that I couldn't go back to the tame

old FBI now that I'd seen the true nature of the world. He's right."

"You're sure?"

Now that I knew he was going to become a J-S agent, I was scared. He could get killed a whole lot easier that way.

"I accepted the offer, although I think Edward was just trying to be nice—"

"He doesn't know how."

"There'll be a lot of legal issues to work out."

"Like?"

"Are cured werewolves responsible for the actions they committed while possessed?"

Huh. That was a toughie.

"I'm going to be . . . a liaison I guess you'd call it— between the *Jäger-Suchers* and the Feds." He shrugged. "Someone has to."

I breathed a secret sigh of relief. That sounded safer than blasting monsters with silver. Although I had a feeling Nic wasn't going to stay in the office 24/7.

"As long as that's what you want."

"After all these years my law degree is going to come in handy." Nic tilted his head. "I still think Edward is trying to make up for his mistakes."

Nic didn't know Edward. The man apologized never, admitted he was wrong . . . also never. Still—

I stared at the pentagram on my palm. Times changed.

Edward and I would have a talk—a long one—about my mother and grandmother, and my father, too. We'd need to discuss our pasts and the future.

"Whatever his reasons," Nic continued, "I agree with him. The FBI was just a job; the *Jäger-Suchers* are a lifestyle."

"If we ever need a recruiting poster, I'll be sure to use that."

"Ha-ha." He tugged on the ends of my hair. "Edward was right about one thing. This is just the beginning. There are a lot of werewolves to find, and someone has to hold them down while you heal them. If you don't mind a rookie on your team."

"I can't think of anyone I'd rather have next to me."

He went still. Everything that hadn't been said, and a lot that had, hung in the air between us.

"Elise, I—"

I caught my breath, uncertain of what he meant to say—fearing one thing, hoping for another, not really certain what would be the best for us both.

"I've been an ass," he blurted.

"Which time?"

His eyes narrowed. "Would you let me finish?"

"Sorry. Far be it from me to stop a man when he's admitting to being an ass."

"You're funny." He took a deep breath. "I was an ass when I said there was nothing between us but sex."

I no longer had any desire to make a joke.

"There's more than that?" I whispered.

"I love you. Always have."

"This wasn't something you thought I should know?"

"You left me, Elise, when everything was great. I had no idea why. I figured there was something wrong with me."

"Not quite."

"When I found out the truth— Well, it was a little hard to declare everlasting love while you were drooling."

"Now who's funny?" I muttered.

That he could joke was encouraging. Only if he was comfortable with what I was, would he be able to do that. The weight on my chest lifted just a little.

"All this secret J-S stuff, conspiracies, witches, silver bullets—I was afraid you might be killed. I didn't know if I could stand to lose you twice. I didn't handle the first time well at all."

"You didn't?"

"When you disappeared, I lost it. Spent months searching. Sometimes I think I went into the FBI subconsciously believing I could find you that way. But years went by, and you were just gone. I got over you."

"You did?"

"No. I told myself I had. Believed it, too. Until I walked into that office and saw you again. I thought my heart had stopped."

"Mine did."

"You've been a part of me from the day I first dropped that book on your foot. I don't ever want to be separated from you again."

"And I don't want you to be. Except—"

I took a deep breath. There were quite a few things that we had to discuss. I loved Nic, but I'd been given a job to do, and no one could stop me from doing it. Not even him.

"You need to know what you're getting into."

"A life with you. It's all I've ever wanted."

"Life with me means *no* life, Nic. Constant threats, too much work, the high probability of a bloody death."

"And that differs from my present life how?"

"Being an FBI agent is a far cry from being a *Jäger-Sucher.*"

"I know," he said. "I can hardly wait to start."

I shook my head. "There'll be no children."

"I don't recall saying I wanted some."

"You did. When we were at Stanford."

"When I was a kid myself. For me the world's a different place than it was last week. Bringing children into it . . . I'm not sure that's the best idea."

My thoughts kept coming out of his mouth. Eerie.

"You're all I need, Elise. My dream has always been you."

"I'm more like a nightmare."

"You're the same *you* I fell in love with, both then and now. Becoming a wolf under the moon doesn't change anything."

"Then you haven't been paying attention."

"I see who you are inside."

"Woof, woof," I mocked.

"That's only a small part."

"Shows what you know."

"I know the truth, and I don't give a damn. You're Elise Hanover. You collect toy crows and Italian shoes. You like rare cheeseburgers and white wine."

"Not together."

"You laugh at my jokes, when I used to make them. Now that I've found you, I might even learn to laugh again myself."

"Did you know I won't age? Ever."

My gaze wandered over the sparkle of gray in his hair, the lines the sun, the wind, time had put next to his eyes and his mouth.

"I'm always going to appear to be twenty-two, which is going to get harder and harder to explain."

"Who do we have to explain it to? The people who matter know the truth."

I'd never looked at the situation quite like that before. Still . . .

"You'll die," I murmured, eyes burning. "And I won't."

"Everyone dies, Elise."

"Not me. At least not from disease or old age."

"You'd rather not be together at all than worry about my expiring ahead of you? The way I see it, your days are a little more numbered than mine."

I frowned. He made excellent points.

Nic grabbed me around the waist and hauled me against him. "You can try and convince me to leave you for the rest of our lives, but the only thing that'll make me go is your telling me you don't love me."

I stared into his eyes. Was he hiding his doubts? I couldn't see any. All I saw was love.

When I continued to hesitate, he leaned in slowly, giving me time to protest, to escape, to lie and tell him I didn't want him, didn't need him, didn't love him.

I couldn't, so with a kiss, I surrendered.

He lifted me into his arms and carried me across the hall to the bedroom. Excitement prickled along my skin as he laid me on the bed.

As our lips touched, our bodies joined to the sound of gentle whispers and promises for a future that suddenly seemed so bright. There was nothing we couldn't accomplish.

"Together," Nic murmured.

Later, much later, when the sun was high in the sky, and we were still in bed, I contemplated the white wolf icon Nic had brought back from the forest. I should destroy the thing, but . . . you never knew when something like this might come in handy. Instead, I slipped the talisman around my neck, and it settled comfortably between my breasts.

The moon would always call to me, and that was okay. That was as it should be. Instead of dread I awaited the next month with anticipation. The monsters would change the rules again—they always did— and the *Jäger-Suchers* would have to adapt.

What would the future bring?

A phone rang somewhere in the house. Nic woke up and glanced my way, then took the hand marked by the pentagram and kissed me right on my tattoo.

"I love this," he whispered. "Very hot."

For Nic, I never had to be anything other than what I was. What a gift. What a guy.

There was a knock on the door.

"Get up," Jessie announced. "We've got work to do."

*Look for A SOLDIER'S QUEST, by Lori Handeland,
coming in August 2005 from Harlequin Superromance.*

Crescent Moon

Lori Handeland

Diana Malone's late husband was the famous cryptozoologist Simon Malone, who became obsessed with finding a werewolf. But Diana never believed him or in the paranormal. Now ridden with guilt for not believing her husband, she has vowed to clear his name by proving his theories were true. A cryptozoologist herself, Diana travels to New Orleans to investigate reports of a loupe garou, or a werewolf, in the Honey Island Swamp. But soon after she arrives in New Orleans, land of voodoo, ghosts, and magic, Diana realizes she is out of her element. Then she meets Adam Ruelle, a sexy Cajun with a mysterious past—a man the locals believe is dead. There is something about Adam that frightens yet fascinates her, and it isn't long before they begin an affair. But what secret is he hiding from her? And will unearthing it bring her closer to a danger for which there is no rescue?

"Fresh, fun and fabulous! Lori Handeland is an exciting new voice in paranormal suspense."

—Sherrilyn Kenyon, author of *Night Play*

ISBN: 0-312-93848-9

FROM ST. MARTIN'S PAPERBACKS

Visit www.lorihandeland.com